GRAVITY GIRL

A GRAVITY SHATTERED NOVEL

V. R. FRIESEN

DIMMARE
—PRESS—

Published by Dimmare Press, 2021

Cover design by Bukovero

Editing by Caroline Kaiser

ISBN: 978-1-7774062-1-9 (e-book)

ISBN: 978-1-7774062-2-6 (paperback)

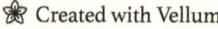 Created with Vellum

ALSO BY V.R. FRIESEN:

For Jen and Santiago

1

A DARE

Things that used to be safe:
Dogs
Children
The ground

~ Veronica Park (*Lists of the Apocalypse*)

Jasper Pine had been falling her whole life. Falling was inevitable in a city where gravity could just as easily pull you toward the horizon or up into the sky as down to the ground, and most people avoided it—the falling, as well as the broken gravity—but Jasper sought it out. She liked to say she never fell, that she just took unplanned jumps.

She wasn't afraid of falling. It was how she expected to die, after all, and what was that if not a giant dare from the earth itself? Jasper never turned down a dare, not from the earth, and definitely not from Merlot Park.

Call it a character flaw. Her brother, Ben, certainly did.

That was why she'd climbed the telephone pole in the first place. She even added a cartwheel along the pole's length to show her disdain for the easiness of the dare.

The pole groaned ominously under her weight, mocking her cockiness. Jasper froze in a crouch.

Dying would mean she'd failed the dare, and she wouldn't give Merlot the satisfaction.

The telephone pole stood upright, more or less, just as it was meant to, rooted in the earth and reaching for the sky, but thanks to a little gravitational event fifteen years ago called the Shattering, the pole now occupied a north-draw side-gee zone. So "climbed" wasn't exactly the right word. Jasper could walk along its southern side as if the pole were lying on the ground.

"When I said scout ahead for any sign of our copper thieves, I didn't mean climb a telephone pole where anyone could see you," Ben said from the sliver of down-gee across the street.

From his perspective she'd resemble a flag in a stiff wind being drawn up a flagpole, her feet on the pole and her body parallel to the ground.

"Really?" Jasper said. "Because that's definitely what I heard."

"In what universe would I tell you to do that?"

"It did seem unlike you."

From Jasper's perspective she could also be walking the plank of a pirate ship. Or balancing on a log in a river like an old-timey lumberjack. But if she fell, she wouldn't land harmlessly in water. Only open air would greet her on the northern side of the telephone pole. She'd fall horizontally to the earth until she crossed into another gravity zone or impacted with lethal force on one of the derelict townhouses that lined the street like crumpled aluminum cans.

Merlot Park, the third member of their gravving team on this trip, crouched in down-gee beside Ben. He spat out a sunflower seed shell. "Why are you even surprised, Ben? It's Jas. You have to specifically tell her not to do stupid things."

"You're the one who dared me," Jasper said.

"You're the one dumb enough to do it," Merlot retorted.

"Since when have I ever turned down a dare?"

Merlot jabbed a finger at her. "That's your problem, and always has been."

"Oh yeah—you're the expert on all my flaws, aren't you?"

"I can't figure out," Ben said, "why you two broke up. So weird. I guess it'll always be a mystery."

The soil around the base of the telephone pole already showed an ominous hump. Too much strain and the pole would snap off. She regretted now not attaching a rope to her climbing harness, but she wasn't about to admit that to her brother. Not in front of Merlot.

Ben's voice rose on cue. "You could've hooked up your rope at least! How you managed to survive to the age of twenty will never cease to amaze me. Look at my hair! It's grey, Jas. Grey! You know why?"

"Are you going to let me guess for once, or just tell me?"

Under his helmet Ben's shaggy, dark hair was indeed clouded with grey, but more due to drywall dust and cobwebs than worry over Jasper's poor decisions. He glared at her even as his mouth tightened, flushing into view what she called his worry dimples. She had the same black hair and brown eyes as Ben, the same sun-darkened white skin, but only the regular smiling dimples. When she worried, she didn't let him see. Worrying had been Ben's self-assigned, full-time job ever since the Shattering had killed their mother and left them orphaned.

Merlot popped another sunflower seed into his mouth. "If she falls, I get her share of the copper."

"Over my dead body," Jasper snapped.

"Yes, exactly. That's what I meant."

Merlot Park had eyes the colour of licorice and a personality to match; that was to say he wasn't to everyone's taste and revelled in it. He squatted at ease, like a crow, all angles and edges and lanky limbs, his long black hair tied back in a grudging concession to practicality. He flashed her a grin, hard enough to cut and sweet enough to render her speechless with irritation. There was no winning when it came to Merlot. Unless he choked on those sunflower seeds. That would make this whole week worth it.

"Nobody's getting any copper if we don't find the thieves who stole it," Ben said. "So if you must risk your dumbass neck, Jas, please be so kind as to tell us what the fuck you see up there."

Copper was the reason they were out here in the wild zones, and thieves the reason they weren't on their way home yet. They'd spent most of the week-long gravving trip carving out the innards of walls and smashing through drywall to find precious threads of copper wiring, the most common and easily salvaged source of income in the zones.

The survivors of the Shattering might be trapped in an ineffably broken city by the towering quarantine walls that the government had hastily built, but over fifteen years a trickle of trade had developed through the quarantine gates. Salvaged metals and other found valuables in one direction, and seeds, food staples, and medical supplies in the other.

They'd returned to their campsite a few hours ago only to find their stashed coils of copper wire missing, along with most of their food. That copper was too valuable and they'd worked too damn hard for it to abandon it, despite the danger of confronting the unknown thieves.

She balanced on the side of the telephone pole.

To her right, the vertical wall of the earth.

To her left, the dizzying depths of the sky.

Jasper scanned the ragged horizon for any sign of the thieves across the rubble and decay of a formerly prosperous suburb. The borders of gravity zones were invisible and irregular in size, but from long experience she could map and categorize zones at a glance according to the pattern of collapse and debris.

There, three houses leaned southward like three drunks who had staggered into each other and tipped back onto their heels in unison. A sedan had punched into one house's north-facing side, the vinyl siding caving inward beneath the ivy-smothered vehicle.

That was south-draw side-gee.

There, the remains of a house stood perfectly upright, but its roof floated a hundred metres above it like a levitating hat. That hovering roof marked the upper edge of the zone, the border where down-gee pressed the roof downward and up-gee pushed it back up until it came to a halt in mid-air. Other debris, flotsam of the skies, drifted around the roof. Tree branches, shingles, bicycles, an inflatable swimming pool, lawn chairs, baby strollers.

And, of course, bones. The whole city was a boneyard, even the sky.

That was up-gee.

The pole groaned and dipped a few inches. Knees bent, Jasper threw her arms wide to hold her balance, heart pounding. Gravitationally below her, empty air gaped northward. The next solid structure she'd encounter if she fell would be a townhouse a good hundred metres away—far enough to be a splat as opposed to a rib-cracker or a bruise-and-roll.

"Enough, Jas. Get back here," Ben said sharply.

Merlot spat out another shell and straightened, reaching for the coil of rope at his hip.

"Wait." She squinted. She'd seen movement several zones over. A feral cat or raccoon, or maybe even a coyote.

In the distance a small figure, down-gee oriented, ran over a roof and disappeared on the other side.

"Got 'em," she said.

Crack. The pole sagged as its base splintered.

Thrown off balance, Jasper twisted as she fell and lunged to grab on to the pole. She hooked an arm over the leaning pole as her legs dangled over oblivion. Splinters dug into her fingerless climbing gloves as she scrabbled for purchase on the rough wood. The pole was still attached to its base, but barely. It listed northward like a sailor leaning into the wind. She wrapped her arms and legs around it, heedless of splinters, but it drooped lower and lower.

"Hang on, Jas!" Ben called.

A quick glance across the street showed that Merlot already had the extra rope clipped to his chest harness with a carabiner. Ben looped it around his waist to anchor it more securely while Merlot swiftly tied the end into a loop and attached another carabiner. Ben whirled the loop above his head and threw it like a cowboy with a lasso.

It landed on the pole just out of arm's reach.

The rope slid off the pole and fell. Both of Jasper's arms were fully occupied anyway.

"Hold on!" Ben called, his voice tight and panicky. He and Merlot hauled the rope back hand over hand as fast as they could.

Jasper stared at the cracking base of the pole, several metres away. Strands of wood separated from each other almost in slow motion. She set her rubber soles against the wood and pushed herself up the slant of the pole, trying to get closer to the ground.

Her breath ached in her throat. Sweat trickled out from under her helmet. Her muscles were already quivering from a long day of hard labour and hunger. She hadn't eaten since lunch.

She didn't look down at the empty air below her. Her death had been waiting for her for a long time; it could wait a little longer.

A familiar voice in her head taunted her. *Just let go. Hell's lonely without you, pet.*

Shut up, Darius. You're dead. I'm not.

Not yet. What've you got left? A few months? What difference does it really make?

It made all the difference.

The pole leaned northward at a near forty-five-degree angle now. She drew up both legs, set her feet, and pushed herself upward, toward the base, toward the earth.

Ben threw the rope.

Crack. The pole snapped. She fell.

The rope sailed toward her. She let go of the pole and lunged for it. The rope brushed past her outstretched arm.

Gravity pulled her away from the earth, perverse and inexorable.

The earth had never wanted her anyway.

She flailed with her left hand and caught the rope. Then she grabbed on with her right hand too. Her weight stretched the rope taut, and gravity swung her like a pendulum toward the ground. Jasper slammed full length into the crumbling sidewalk. She bounced once, twice, and then dangled northward, parallel to the cliffside of the earth.

Far below her dangling feet, the pole crashed into the side of a townhouse and sank halfway through its living room.

The rope squeaked against her leather-clad palms and chafed her exposed fingers. Her arms screamed at the strain.

Her heartbeat chanted, a*live*, a*live*, a*live*.

For now, Darius reminded her. *I'll keep some flames warm for you.* He laughed soundlessly.

She growled against the adrenalin burn and the nausea in her throat. If it were possible to carve out memories from your mind and ghosts along with them, she'd have stabbed out half her brain long ago.

"We've got you," Ben said from above her. Safely in their sliver of down-gee, he and Merlot anchored the rope with their bodies, braced against her dangling weight.

"Feel free to start climbing anytime, though." Merlot's voice was strained with the effort.

She swivelled herself around and set her feet against the vertical ground. After a moment of scrabbling, she found purchase on a tough clump of grass. With traction under her feet, she hauled herself upward and then hung on with one hand long enough to snap the carabiner onto her harness.

"You want to use your ascender?" Ben asked.

Jasper assessed the climb above her. "Nah, I'll do it freehand." She reached for a crack in the pavement and pushed herself upward.

Merlot and Ben kept the slack out of the rope and let her climb.

Ben used the opportunity to begin his lecture. "All you had to do was keep the rope hooked to your harness before you stepped on that pole. It's the first thing Quick Rick taught us."

"Pretty sure the first thing he teaches all the grav-walking apprentices who've come after us is not to dump a bottle of whisky you've salvaged just because it tasted terrible when you tried it," Jasper said, reaching for another handhold.

Merlot must have smirked because Ben snapped, "This isn't funny, Merlot. She could've died."

Jasper didn't look up. She knew what the next words on Merlot's lips would be. *Yeah, exactly.* But the silence stretched.

Wonder of wonders, Merlot had detected the quivering line of distress beneath an otherwise familiar rant and restrained himself. For Ben's sake and *only* Ben's sake did such miracles happen.

She reached the curb, which gave her a tiny ledge to boost herself upward. She found handholds and toeholds in cracks in the pavement and the clumps of stubborn, low-growing shrubbery that grew out of those cracks, indifferent to the vagaries of gravity.

"Back in the day, I seem to recall you pulling some dumb stunts too, Ben," Merlot said.

She could hear Ben's deep inhalation all the way across the street and said slyly, "That was just when Charlie was watching."

"That's not—" Ben sputtered, derailed. "I never—that was a long time ago."

Longer even than the last time Merlot had joined them on a gravving trip. If their old friend Charlie were here, he'd already have Ben laughing. The most she and Merlot could manage was to distract him.

"What, did Charlie take your sense of adventure with him when he left?" Merlot drawled.

No, just Ben's heart.

"If by sense of adventure you mean general idiocy and dumbassery," Ben said, "I used to store those in my left foot, so .. . all gone." He pointedly tapped the toe of his prosthetic left foot on the ground.

"That must've been where you kept your sense of humour too," Merlot said.

"You mean the ability to delude myself into finding you two funny?"

"Yes, that," Jasper said with a sigh. "I miss that one the most."

Ben had his hands full coiling up the slack in the rope, so Merlot crouched to extend a hand across the border as Jasper drew close to him. The gesture surprised her enough that she paused to stare at him. The sleeves of his faded Batman sweatshirt were pushed up to his elbows, and sweat cut lines of bronze through the dust that coated his arms. His dark eyes, carved sharp by their epicanthal folds, held hers for a second too long, as if he'd forgotten that meeting each other's eyes was something they no longer did.

His eyes were Vron's eyes.

Even after all this time, loss could surge out of nowhere and punch the breath from her lungs.

She'd hesitated too long to take his hand. His lip curled. He withdrew his hand, straightened, and turned away. She had to drag herself over the border, which was visible only because on one side grass grew in a tall cheerful tangle, and a centimetre beyond, the grass sagged almost flat to grow northward. Jasper could feel the border, though. She was swept with its sharp static tingle as she rolled from side-gee into down-gee.

The world reoriented around her. She no longer clung to a perpendicular cliffside like a spider. She lay on flat ground under a vast but harmless sky.

She gave herself a few seconds to lie there and breathe before she clambered to her feet. This tiny down-gee zone was about the size of a minivan, which forced her to stand close enough to Merlot to smell the sharp tang of his sweat. She checked her hands for splinters to avoid looking up. A sudden overwhelming shakiness filled her. She struggled to draw air into her lungs smoothly enough that neither Ben nor Merlot would notice.

Merlot was actively trying to ignore her, which helped, and Ben was still furious. Furious because he'd been scared shitless. He re-coiled the rope with sharp and jerky movements.

"So," he said tightly, "have we gotten the stupidity out of the way for the day, or would you like to go explore some up-gee before we continue?"

"Dude, it's a good thing you didn't say that with *d-a-r-e* in front of it."

She was almost grateful for Merlot's snark, as her voice was currently unavailable for speech.

Ben turned away. "We only have an hour of light left, and the thieves are long gone. Let's go back to camp."

The copper. The stupid stolen copper. It would buy sugar and flour and salt and pain medication for Harmony's arthritis, and a new frictionless sock for Ben that wouldn't irritate the skin under the prosthetic. They needed the copper. Jasper had to provide for her family while she still could.

"We can't just give up yet," Merlot said. "The zones are too politically unstable these days to be doing as many trading trips as usual. Doing business with the Knowles community feels ickier and ickier, and now Sparrow's talking about sanctioning them for the way they use kids. Damascus doesn't feel too safe to visit either—they're worse as an army than they ever were as a cult. Quick Rick and I might have to put peddling on hold for a while, which'll cut into our income. I need this copper."

"What would you suggest?" Ben said after a pause. "We've lost their trail."

"No, we haven't," Jasper said. "I saw the thieves before I fell. I know where they are."

2

TO CATCH A THIEF

The croaking song of frogs on hot, damp summer nights
Dirt under your fingernails from gardening

~ Veronica Park (*Things I Will Miss/Reasons to Live*)

Sunset turned the sky the heady hue of spilled red wine. A vast flock of starlings soared above them, diving and turning like the broad twists and curves of an abstract painting. Late sun caught the iridescent glimmer of their feathers as they banked to fly upside down through up-gee.

Birds shouldn't have adjusted to broken gravity as fast as they had. It made no sense.

Perhaps humans shouldn't have either. It didn't have to make sense.

Like life, gravity was a disease infecting them all, with no hope of recovery.

When it came to gravving, Merlot fit seamlessly back into the team dynamics of long ago. Jasper led the way, taking the risks: the first leap across a gap, the first test of a rope or piton, or of the solidity of a foothold or handhold. She used more caution now in choosing what risks to take, and not only to prevent another lecture; whatever route she chose had to be one Ben could traverse. She'd risk her own neck happily enough, and Merlot's too, but not Ben's.

Ben followed her lead without complaining or second-guessing. In this, he trusted her. His powerful upper body muscles moved him across gaps and around obstacles where his prosthetic leg couldn't give him full mobility. Merlot brought up the rear in the anchor position, securing their safety lines.

In down-gee, reaching the spot where Jasper had seen the thief would've been a ten-minute walk, but with three different zones to cross, it took close to a full hour. The sun slanted warm red light across the broken city. Shadows clotted in hollow windows, crumpled walls, and dense shrubbery.

If the thieves turned out to be too much for them to handle, escape would be difficult. Gravving through unfamiliar zones in the dark was a good way to die or break a limb.

At last they reached the down-gee zone where Jasper had spotted somebody running across the roof. In the dimming light the zone appeared to encompass three or four houses and a good portion of the street. Roofs and fences sagged but remained intact, windows contained most of their glass, trees grew upright, and several rusting, ivy-covered vehicles remained parked at the curb on flat tires.

They crouched behind a sprawling rosebush, the heady sweetness of the roses filling their lungs. The first stars glittered above, like sleepy celestial eyes opening.

Ben signed, "Sentries?" The dim light was just sufficient to see the movement of his hands.

Both Merlot and Jasper shook their heads. They hadn't spotted anybody keeping watch. The wild zones were mostly uninhabited, as most survivors of the Shattering stayed clustered in the down-gee strip near the quarantine walls, but that didn't mean they were empty. The thieves were either being careless or believed no one could've followed them this far.

"Behind the house?" Merlot suggested with his hands.

A faint glow was coming from somewhere, along with the smell of woodsmoke, likely a campfire in a backyard. Jasper signed for Merlot to go around one side of the houses while she and Ben took the other side.

The glow grew stronger as she and Ben crept along the side of the house, stepping carefully over an ancient plastic toy car, a rusted bike, a deflated soccer ball, all barely visible in the tall shadow-choked grass. They had to force their way through the encroaching border hedge's snagging branches and hope their approach wasn't as hideously audible to others as it was to them.

The fire flickered in a stone-lined firepit on the concrete deck surrounding a swimming pool, which was empty but for dead leaves and an old tarp. The stolen pack of food and the two coils of copper wire sat beside the fire. Seated in a rickety lawn chair, poking at the fire with a stick, was a boy.

No one else was in the yard.

The hedge on their right would have towered over two adults, utterly impenetrable. The wire fence around the rest of yard showed another empty, overgrown yard next door and the alley at the back. Somebody might be hiding in the house, but a jumble of garbage cans, large toys, and barbeque equipment blocked the door so much that no one would be able to exit the house swiftly. A frayed and dirty backpack, a makeshift harness, a coil of rope, and a loop of carabiners sat beside the boy, and a single sleeping bag had been laid out.

Ben caught Jasper's arm, sensing her thoughts. "Kids are rarely alone," he signed.

"But if this one is, I can get the copper from him in five

minutes and get us back to camp before full darkness," she signed back.

"How? Are you going to tell him who you are?"

She didn't answer or wait for him to talk her out of it. She walked into the circle of firelight.

The boy looked up. His dark hair was greased into a spiky mohawk, and his fair skin darkened by dirt and a tan. He looked twelve, but he might have been as old as fifteen. He didn't move from his lawn chair or reach for the knife at his hip.

"You been finden something of mine," Jasper said without preamble, dropping naturally into packspeak, the patois the kids in the zones used. She jerked her chin at the coils of wire. "I'm wanten it back, see?"

He studied her through narrowed blue eyes. He didn't seem surprised at all. Which made her wonder, a little too late, how one scrawny boy had not only carried an extra pack and two coils of wire by himself, but also gravved with it.

"You can be keepen the food," she said. "But I'm taken the copper."

When he still didn't move or answer, she walked closer. She bent to grab the wire.

"No," the boy said. "Mine." He jumped to his feet, threw back his head, and howled.

The crumpled tarp at the bottom of the swimming pool came alive. Whoops and ululating yells filled the air as filthy little figures swarmed out of the pool and from under the hedge to surround the fire.

The kids' hair-raising screeches swam like nettles in Jasper's veins. She reached for the knife at her hip but didn't touch it as a familiar nausea rose in her throat. Outsmarted by a bunch of kids. She was definitely going to be getting another lecture from Ben.

The pack circled her now, grimacing and leering. They wore

a motley assortment of rags and badly cured animal pelts, and unlikely ornaments like lampshades, bicycle chains, and plastic tiaras, amulets strung around their necks. Each with a knife or a sharpened stick or a metal pipe or a slingshot, all aimed at Jasper. All sizes but uniformly skinny, their skin all colours from white to brown but uniformly smeared with dirt. With expressions ranging from giddy excitement to jittery anxiety. Awash in lurid firelight, triumphant in their successful ambush, they were the feral personification of the urban wilderness.

The boy watched her from the other side of the fire, arms folded across his skinny chest. She should have recognized him as an alpha from the first uncompromising stare of those hard blue eyes. He lifted a hand. The screams and whoops ceased.

"Impressive ambush," she began.

The boy's lip curled and he spat. "Biggies. Not talken with you."

Every child turned and spat as well. A poisonous murmur rippled through the group.

Jasper suppressed a shiver. Pack kids' entrenched hatred and mistrust of adults dated back to the early years of the Shattering and were not unjustified.

It all started with you, Darius pointed out.

And now she was on the wrong side of the divide. Becoming an adult had been another unplanned jump.

The alpha made a sign, and several kids peeled off from the group and ran to either side of the house. A spate of swearing broke out. Merlot and Ben came stumbling out of the shadows from opposite sides, herded by kids with pointy sticks and savage, gap-toothed grins.

"Oh, brilliant idea, Jasper, just brilliant," Merlot said angrily as he and Ben were shoved into the heart of the circle. "You really thought this one out, didn't you?"

"This is a misunderstanding," Jasper said to the alpha. "I

been thinken those're my copper wires, but I been wrong. Yours, obviously."

The alpha stalked up to her. He was scrawny but compact too, with sinewy muscle under his darkly tanned skin. A handful of amulets hung from thongs around his neck. "We been finden it. And you're tryen to steal it! You Damaskers?"

"You're the ones who stole it, you fucking ferals," Merlot cried, enraged.

A makeshift spear jabbed at his throat. Kids leaned in hungrily like dogs smelling blood. He shut up.

"You're a peddler, Mer," Jasper said. "I thought you and Quick Rick dealt with packs all the time. Does screaming at them usually work?"

He scowled at her.

"Obviously, Quick Rick does all the talking," Ben said.

"That's true," Jasper said. "Explains why they're still alive."

"Literally nothing explains why *you're* still alive," Merlot muttered.

That was also true.

"We're not Damaskers," Ben said to the alpha. He tapped his cheek. "See? No scars. This is a mistake. We're Yorky citizens. We have nothing to do with the Damaskers. We—"

The nearest kid whacked him over the face with the handle of a garden rake. He cried out and clutched his face.

Her rage was so quick and overwhelming that it wasn't until sharp metal pricked Jasper's throat that she realized she'd lunged at the alpha. He grinned, a chilling expression.

"Don't you dare fucking touch him," she said, ignoring the knife he held to her throat.

"Be doen what we're wanten, biggie. We're the Crows!"

On cue the kids threw back their heads and whooped and cawed.

"We're not Damaskers," Jasper said, staring hard into the

boy's eyes. "We're not caren about kids. Just wanten our copper and then we'll be gone."

"This is Crows' land," the alpha said. "Our territory." Each word was cleanly edged, hurled like a missile. None of that garbled, barely verbal slop that passed for speech among most of the feral kid packs.

Pack kids were usually small for their ages, but these ones didn't show the distended bellies of malnutrition. Somehow the alpha had kept a dozen kids fed, a demonstration of intelligence and resourcefulness. This one could think and strategize and harness the energies of a whole pack. The mood of the whole pack quivered taut as a bowstring, and he was the one bending the bow.

"Enough of this," said Ben, still holding his cheek. "Jas, tell them who you are."

She forced herself to exhale and edged back from the alpha's knife. "We're not knowen this is Crows' land. Be letten us go and we'll be goen. Never comen back. No problem."

"Never comen back. Yeah, if you're dead."

A frisson of electricity leaped through the circle. Small hands adjusted their grips on their weapons. Eyes reflected flickering flames. The alpha's mouth formed a narrow line as final as a razor blade, and somehow disturbingly familiar.

"I'm not understanden why you're wanten the copper." Maybe she could distract them from the dangerous mood they were in. "Azuros aren't traden with kids. It's useless to you. You trusten some biggie to be your middleman to trade it in?"

"Only trusten dead biggies," he said and chuckled. The kids laughed too, like wild dogs yipping in the night.

"Quit playing around, Jas," Merlot said. "Tell them!"

The entire pack hung on the alpha's every word. She had never seen this level of discipline and loyalty from a kid pack. Who was this kid?

The alpha waved his pack forward.

"Wait!" she cried. For an instant everyone paused. She couldn't breathe or speak. Some old instinct, never unlearned, turned her gaze to Merlot for help.

"Idiots," Merlot said softly, stepping forward. "*Idiots.* Who do you think you're dealing with here? Don't you know who this is? Your amulets can't protect you, not from her, not if you piss her off."

Jasper forced her lips into something like a smile as the kids stared. The alpha's lids flickered, showing uncertainty.

Merlot swung his arm wide toward her. "Look at her. That's the fucking Pinegirl."

3

THE PINEGIRL'S CHOICE

Manipulating gravity is not a new concept. Just because humans haven't figured it out yet doesn't mean it's impossible.
Of course, it would help if gravity could be properly explained in the first place.

~ Dr. Zenobia Allan (personal journals)

"Liar!" The alpha's face screwed up in rage. "Biggies are lyen."

The pack surged forward, snarling like starving dogs.

"Wait," said the girl standing at the alpha's left.

He hesitated but held up an open palm. The pack shifted and murmured and swarmed, caught between discipline and a mob's bloodthirstiness.

The girl's hair was separated into multiple tiny braids, and she wore oversized gardening gloves. A faint scar, pale against her brown skin, gave her mouth a whimsical twist, as if she were thinking about a secret.

"You da Pinegirl?" she asked.

"That's what they're callen me," Jasper said.

The girl's eyes, the colour of burnt sugar, searched her face. "You're a biggie."

"Even the Pinegirl's been growen up."

The alpha said, "Be showen us the scar."

Jasper hesitated and Merlot nudged her. Reluctantly, she pulled up a corner of her T-shirt to expose the right side of her abdomen. Cut into the hollow above her hip bone was one long vertical line bisected by several smaller lines curling away from it in half moons, forming a crude pine tree. She didn't need to see it to remember the bright scarlet agony of Darius's knife sinking into her flesh over and over again as he reopened the wounds day after day to ensure the ridged scars would form.

You should thank me for that, ungrateful pet, Darius whispered in her mind. *I might have just saved your life.*

"Da Pinegirl," the girl said in wonder, her eyes wide.

"Now you know," Merlot said. "So give us our copper and fuck off."

The alpha growled, but the girl looked pensive. Caught between the two reactions, the pack shifted and muttered. Some danced on the balls of their feet, itching for a fight. Others fingered their amulets and held up their palms, fingers half folded down, in warding gestures.

The girl turned to the alpha and murmured something Jasper couldn't catch. The alpha eyed Jasper with an edge of venom but also caution. He sighed and sheathed his knife.

At once the kids' stances loosened, as did their fists, and their knuckles unwhitened. Some kids looked disappointed. Others stared at Jasper with wide wary eyes.

Jasper clasped both her wrists in front of her. "Be callen me Jasper Pine," she said. "The Pinegirl. I'm callen you what?"

The girl imitated her gesture. "Be callen me Neverwhen."

"I swear to gravity, pack kid names get weirder and weirder," Merlot said.

Jasper jabbed him with her elbow. "This is Merlot and my brother, Ben. We're just wanten our copper, okay?"

"To be clear," Merlot said, dropping ominously into packspeak, "we're taken the copper and the food, and you're letten us go. And then maybe the Pinegirl won't be cursen you so your fingers and toes are fallen off and your eyes are turnen into tinyling eggs."

A restive murmur from the kids followed that, and a few flexed their fingers anxiously and rubbed at their eyes at the mention of tinylings, malicious, invisible demons who lived in dirt and had to be washed away or they'd make you sick.

Neverwhen chewed on her lower lip. "We're folldown the rules. Taken care of the pack."

"By robbing the Pinegirl?" Merlot said, in a tone of outrage.

"Robben *biggies*," Neverwhen retorted quickly. "Never trusten biggies. That's the rules."

"Who were you going to trade the wire to, though?" Ben wondered.

The alpha made a slashing motion with his hand. "We're letten you go," he said curtly. "So no cursen us. But we're keepen the copper. Finden it, see? Is fair."

"No, is *not* fair," Merlot snapped. "We worked our asses off for it."

"How about one coil of wire each?" Ben suggested.

Neverwhen cocked her head and glanced at the alpha. He considered, fingering the amulets strung around his neck—a jade ring, a mouse skull, a thimble, a pinecone. And something else.

Jasper lunged forward and grabbed his wrist. "Where did you get that?"

In an instant he jabbed his knife tip against the soft point just under her breastbone. He didn't try to pull away. The bones in his wrist felt thin and birdlike in her hand. His blue eyes blazed with alarm, then anger. But his grin was wild and fierce, a dare.

"Uh, Jas," said Merlot. Sharp-edged weapons pointed at his and Ben's throats and other soft, vulnerable parts. The kids' bared teeth and grimaces conveyed that, however much they feared the Pinegirl's curses, they would follow their alpha's lead to the death.

Jasper had eyes only for the small shape on the alpha's palm, strung around his neck on a cord. A small clay bird, twin to the one around her own neck. Catherine Pine had made three—one for Ben and one for Jasper and one for herself. Her mother had never taken hers off that Jasper had ever seen.

"Where did you get this?" she shouted into the alpha's face. "Tell me!"

His knife pressed harder, cutting the fabric of her T-shirt and stinging the skin. He could pierce her lung like this, but she already couldn't breathe. He hadn't killed her yet, though.

"Gift," he said, "from Up-gee Witch."

It was a bluff. She knew bluffs when she saw them.

"Bullshit," she said. "She's just a story. Tell me the truth. *Where?*"

"For gravity's sake, Jas," Ben said in a strangled tone. "What's going on?"

The sudden fear in the alpha's eyes was sharp and unnerving. "Can't be tellen you."

"Was she alive?" she shouted at him. "The woman you took this from, was she alive or dead?"

She and Ben had known for a long time that their mother

had probably died along with millions of others in the Shattering. But Jasper had never let go of the childish daydream that somewhere in the zones their mother had survived— possibly with amnesia or as a prisoner to some deranged villain like in Merlot's comic books; either would explain why she hadn't come to find her children. And now this amulet had appeared out of nowhere. It was a sign. It had to be.

But the boy shook his head, fear expanding across his face. "Curse is killen everyone."

A ripple of unease passed through the pack. The alpha pulled his arm away and held up his palm, pinky and ring finger folded down in warding. The defiant set of his mouth and the sharp angle of his eyebrows stirred a memory in Jasper.

"I'm callen you what?" she demanded.

The fear vanished, shuttered away behind the alpha mask. He bowed mockingly. "Be callen me Grammar, Pinegirl."

"Grammar," Merlot muttered. "Yeah, right. Now he's just fucking with us."

An owl hooted. Grammar's head went up as everyone froze.

A child appeared at the edge of the roof. "Damaskers!" she cried. Then she groaned and tumbled slowly forward and fell over the edge of the roof. She landed heavily in a pile of dead leaves.

A crossbow quarrel jutted from her shoulder.

Screams and shouts created a cacophony of panic. Grammar yelled commands. Kids grabbed the food and the wire and raced for the back fence. They scaled it with startling agility, bigger kids boosting smaller kids over. Grammar tried to shove Neverwhen after the others, but she ran to the child who'd been shot.

"We need to scramble," Merlot said.

Ben tried to hurry Jasper back the way they'd come. She pulled her arm away.

Neverwhen had thrown herself down beside the fallen child. Grammar ran to her other side, but the girl screamed in pain as they tried to hoist her up.

And then the raiders came.

They loomed out of the shadows around the house and the neighbouring yard, dressed in black and their faces painted in camouflage patterns. Triple rows of scars on their cheeks identified them as Damaskers. They carried crossbows and wore climbing harnesses.

Ben stopped abruptly as the narrow passage beside the house was blocked by a tall teenager with a crossbow aimed at them. He forced them back into the yard into the firelight.

Most of the kids had escaped, but the raiders rounded up a few of the stragglers. Damaskers tied up a struggling Grammar and Neverwhen. They ignored the girl with the crossbow bolt in her shoulder. She crumpled to her knees, whimpering in pain.

The leader nudged the injured child with his toe and scolded one of his men, "If you been shooten her proper, she wouldn't have been given them a warning."

"Be letten us go," Grammar cried as he was hauled to his feet. "We're given you copper."

"What, again?" The leader seemed amused. "You thinken that'll work twice? Where are you getten more copper?"

"Stealen it, of course," Grammar said. "Got two coils. Be letten us go."

So that was why kids were stealing copper wire! Bribes for kid hunters like the Damaskers. Clever, but risky.

The Damasker leader, a young white man with zigzag-braided blond hair, noticed Jasper, Ben, and Merlot for the first time. He grinned, a slash of white in his camouflage face paint. "Well, if it ain't da Pinegirl. Hey, baby."

She gritted her teeth. "If it isn't scum on two legs," she replied. "Hey, Dragon."

Crossbows were pointed at them from all directions. Many of the raiders were only a few years older than the pack kids; nearly all had once *been* pack kids. A few years of quasi-military training and a liberal sprinkling of indoctrination had only made them more dangerous. Kids could be distracted or overawed, but Damaskers were trained for and encouraged to violence. They were unlikely to be impressed by a grown-up Pinegirl.

"Hunting children again?" Jasper said. "I guess anything else would be too challenging for you."

"Is called recruitment," Dragon said. He gestured at Grammar and Neverwhen. "These two are plenty old enough to join a gang." He turned back to Jasper and leered. "Missen me, baby? You followen me around now? How romantic."

Jasper fought the urge to spit.

"You know what's romantic? Not shooting children," said Merlot. "I'm old-fashioned, though."

"We're Yorky citizens," Ben said loudly to cover the tremble in his voice. "You can't hold us. So we're going to leave now."

"Oh, really?" Dragon grinned.

"A whole lot of little eyes and ears saw us here," Merlot pointed out. "If we go missing, everyone will know who did it. I don't think your boss will be pleased to hear you killed a Yorky peddler and the Pines."

Dragon flapped his hand. "No need for getten dramatic, Merlot. If it's your wire the kids been stealen, that'd be satisfaction enough for me. And look, here it is."

A youngling now returned, lugging the coils of wire behind him. Damaskers weren't interested in kidnapping small children, so he was safe.

"It's there," Grammar said, lifting his tied hands to his captor. "So be letten us go."

Dragon scratched his chin and shrugged. He nodded and the

captured kids were released, except for Neverwhen and Grammar. Many were too young for the Damaskers anyway. Most of the kids ran immediately, but two dared to creep back and help the injured girl to her feet.

"Aw, how sweet," said Dragon. "I could've been putten her out of her misery and saven 'em the trouble. Right, Pinegirl?"

"You're a fucking psychopath," Merlot said.

Dragon just laughed. "One rat's same as another. Be killen one, a dozen more be appearen."

Grammar still had his arms raised, waiting for a Damasker to cut his ties.

One of them strode over to claim the coils of wire. The youngling who'd brought them hesitated, glancing at Neverwhen and Grammar. The raider made a threatening gesture with his crossbow, and the boy broke and ran.

"Us too," Grammar insisted. His rigid shoulders couldn't hide his growing fear.

"Price is goen up," Dragon said. "One of you I'm keepen."

"No!" Grammar cried in rage.

"It's two full coils of wire," Jasper snapped. "Just let them go, Dragon, for gravity's sake."

He wheeled to face her. "You da Pinegirl, so we're not killen you. But you ain't my fucking boss, bitch, so don't be given me orders. Copper's nice but we're needen recruits, needen soldiers."

"They're kids, not soldiers."

"We're all knowen what kids are capable of. Ain't that right, *Pinegirl*?"

The darkness around Jasper grew blank and bright as static, blocking out all sound and thought. She fought it back by focusing on her body. Splinters in her hands, exhausted trembling in her muscles. Sweat trickling from under her helmet. Her climbing harness and gravving pouches chafing her waist and thighs. The weight of the knife at her belt.

Dragon gave her an unpleasant grin. "Tellen you what. You be choosen which kid is stayen and which kid is goen. Go on. This is your game."

The blankness invaded her eyes and chest and made her ears ring.

"You're as bad as *him*," Ben whispered, as if the volume had been knocked from his voice.

"Fuck off to hell with your fucking games, you fucking Darius Dalca wannabe!" Merlot had no shortage of volume. "You're going to do whatever you fucking want anyway, so you can just—"

"The boy," Jasper said. Her vision sparkled with grey. Had they heard her, or had she spoken inside her head? "Keep the boy. The girl goes free."

A long pause. Dragon chuckled. "See? You're so good at that."

Neverwhen stared from Jasper to Grammar as a Damasker cut the rope around her hands and feet. "No!"

"Run, Nev," Grammar said, his voice soft and colourless. Like a knife sinking into the earth.

She ran, sobbing.

"Too bad. She's pretty," Dragon said. "But this one'll be maken a better fighter."

Grammar spat at him. Dragon backhanded him across the face. "Of course, gotta beat the alpha outta him first."

Crossbows swung around to point at Jasper. She'd taken a step forward without thinking.

"Kid's just another zone rat," Dragon said, a warning tone entering his voice. "Nothing to you, Pinegirl. Don't be stupid."

"The most ineffective three words in the English language," Merlot muttered.

Ben's hands on her arms held her still as the raiders scooped up the copper wire and melted back into the darkness. They must have been confident in their route if they were willing to grav in the dark. More likely they had a campsite nearby.

Dragon slung a trussed-up Grammar over his shoulder. Grammar twisted to look back the way Neverwhen and the kids had gone, and then at Jasper. In the dying firelight she couldn't read his expression, but she knew what his look meant. He was telling her she'd chosen right.

She already knew that. It didn't help.

It never had.

4

A GRAVITY SHIFT

Perfect unexpected coincidences
When a kid says they want to be just like you

~ Veronica Park (*Things I Will Miss/Reasons to Live*)

When they were sure the Damaskers had gone, they set up camp in one of the down-gee houses. The kids had already looted it of any useful goods small enough to carry, but enough large furniture remained to use for firewood. Ben built a small fire in a metal garbage can lid in the living room near the window, where the smoke could waft away while the curtains suppressed the light. Jasper and Merlot dragged out a couple of mattresses that didn't seem too mouldy or mouse infested. They turned out the contents of their pouches and came up with some jerky and a handful of seeds and nuts. It wouldn't be the first time they'd gone to bed hungry. They'd forage for some greens and berries in the morning.

"Before the Damaskers came," Ben said, "why were you

freaking out about the alpha's amulets?" He'd removed his prosthetic for the night and was rolling down the sock.

She'd almost forgotten. "He had this." She lifted her clay bird amulet.

Ben touched his own reflexively. "That's . . . that's impossible."

"Not impossible. Haven't we often wondered if we'd stumble across Mom's body one day? Obviously, he did."

He eyed her across the fire. "You asked him if she was dead or alive."

"Hey, there's always a chance," she said defensively.

"Best you assume she's dead," Merlot said harshly.

On this subject she had no intention of arguing with Merlot. His mother had lost custody of him and his sister Vron when Merlot was only a few years old. She'd been long out of the picture by the time of the Shattering. Then their father had disappeared in the early months after the Shattering. They'd never found out what happened to him or why he'd left. When it came to parents, Merlot held on to his hurts like a barnacle to rocks, then acted as if those rocks didn't exist. Anyone who tried to separate the two would only get shredded hands for their trouble.

Jasper took off her helmet and ran her hands through her short hair, limp with sweat after the day's exertions. "It would be nice to find her body, though."

Ben shot her a look. "We've got more important things to worry about."

She wouldn't argue with him with Merlot here. "Well, it's not like we can ask Grammar anymore anyway. Stupid Dragon."

The memory of Grammar, tied up and being carried away from his pack, snagged her from every direction, as if she was pushing through blackberry thickets.

"That damn cult is snatching up more kids than anyone else in the zones," Merlot said. "And now they've got my copper."

"They're not a cult anymore," Ben said. "They're an army."

"Same difference."

"Except an army is armed and disciplined."

"I think 'disciplined' is an overstatement when it comes to the Damaskers."

"Disciplined enough," said Jasper. "Especially with Nico Mavuto in charge. He used to be an actual soldier."

"Nico likes you," Merlot said. "As much as the old bastard likes anyone. Maybe you can ask him to talk to Grammar about finding your mom."

"He doesn't like me that much," Jasper said. "I spend too much time with the Azuros."

"He's not the only one to find that weird." Merlot exchanged a brief look with Ben.

The Azuros gang controlled all trade in and out of the zones. Perhaps this alone would have made them a target for resentment, even without the ugly role they'd played in the chaotic early years after the Shattering. But no one who had lived through those events would forget their grudges against the Azuros anytime soon. Nowadays they were tolerated but never accepted.

Jasper had more reason than most to want nothing to do with the Azuros. Which was why she couldn't explain, even to Ben, her continuing relationship with the diminished gang. She could hardly explain it to herself.

"You could at least ask Nico," Merlot said. "And tell him to give our copper back while you're at it."

"Mom's dead," Ben said curtly. "We've got other priorities."

Merlot narrowed his eyes at Ben. "Like what?"

"Just other things," Ben said, avoiding his stare.

Jasper jumped up from the mossy mattress and strode over

to the window, unable to sit still. Rotted fragments of a curtain still hung in front of the cracked glass, veiling the darkness outside. She could remember, just barely, how this city had once been a firefly carpet of warm yellow electric lights with orange streetlights in neat grids. Now in darkness and shadow, abandonment possessed it, the small god of Vron's stories spreading its fingers through the cracks and alleys and empty spaces left behind.

"Is this about your little gravity malfunction, Jas?" Merlot asked suddenly.

"Why would you think that?" She didn't turn around. Reflected in the glass, his eyes looked like dark holes.

"You said a long time ago that Zenobia was trying to find a cure for you. Hasn't she found one yet?"

"She's still working on it," she said as neutrally as she could manage. Zenobia Allan, ganglord of the Azuros, had been working on that cure for nearly thirteen years.

With a great deal of unnecessary jingling, Ben divested himself of his harness and ropes, ascenders, descenders, and strings of carabiners so that he could examine them for fraying and damage, a nightly ritual.

"It must be difficult being stuck here in the zones without equipment or electronics or a lab," Merlot said, probing. "If anyone can help you, it's Zenobia, I suppose. She is, as they say, a witch—"

"Scientist," Jasper said.

"Same difference." He took a breath to continue. He wouldn't stop unless she gave him something.

"It's starting to look like there will be no cure," Jasper said.

Ben's hands stilled. His shaggy, dark head stayed bent over his harness.

Merlot sat back against the cushion-less couch, satisfied he'd finally hit upon some truth. "That's too bad. But I mean, you've survived having the shifts for this long, right? What's really changed?"

If she hesitated, he'd only press harder. "Of course. Nothing's changed."

Merlot dug in one of his thigh pouches to pull out a joint and then his doodling notebook and a pencil. He held the joint to a smouldering chair leg to light it. "And Ben, you think there's still something you can do about it? How? Zenobia's the only person in the zones who knows anything about the graviteria."

As if in response to his words, a tingle jabbed, harsh and electric, in the pit of Jasper's stomach. She groaned and wrapped her arms around her middle as if she could hold gravity in place, keep the dragon from hatching. "Speak of the devil," she said.

"Oh, were we talking about Darius?" Merlot asked.

"Zenobia, actually," Ben said.

"Funny," Jasper said.

For once she almost welcomed the sensation, as it interrupted Merlot's questioning, but it was an unpleasant reminder of the secret she was keeping. The tingle itched in her internal organs, in her cells. A warning. The earth whispering, *Get your feet off my face, Jasper Pine.*

"Why, why, why does the earth hate me?" she complained.

"She's a classy lady, is the earth," Merlot said. "She has standards." He scribbled idly in his notebook, alternately chewing on his pencil and drawing on his joint and occasionally mixing up the two.

"The earth isn't sentient—it can't hate you," Ben said.

"She metaphorically hates me, and it's getting kind of offensive." Jasper moved to the middle of the room and dropped to a crouch, hands on the floor. "Why else do my shifts only happen after I've set foot in down-gee? Like she forgets about me until I set foot on her again."

"It's the graviteria making you shift, not the planet, and they're not sentient either," Ben said.

"You don't have to live with the little bastards," Jasper muttered. "Feels awfully personal sometimes."

The tingle expanded outward from her core and along her limbs, a zone being born inside her body.

What had she done to offend a planet? Was her presence so vile, so unbearable, that she alone must be shrugged off the earth violently, and for what? The crime of shuffling through humble dirt? For daring to claim the force no other living creature, plant, or rock had ever been denied?

But Ben was right. The graviteria, those bacteria-like alien invaders and co-inhabitants of her body, liked to flex their gravitational muscles at her expense. The planet was as much their victim as Jasper.

The tingle reached her fingertips and toes and crescendoed into a white burst in her brain.

Her gravity shifted and she fell. Just another unplanned jump in a lifetime full of them.

Today the graviteria threw her upward.

Gravity lurched her belly in the opposite direction. She pushed off the floor with her hands, reorienting her body to its new gravity so that she fell feet first. Jasper landed on the ceiling with a thump and a roll through cobwebs and dust, narrowly missing the ceiling light fixture. She sat up and promptly sneezed three times in a row.

Seeing she was unhurt, Ben returned his attention to the ropes in his lap. Merlot had barely glanced up from his sketching. From the ceiling she had a good view of the tops of their heads, Ben's shaggy, dark mane and Merlot's glossier black ponytail, as well as a glimpse of Merlot's sketch. With only a few lines he'd conveyed the essence of Grammar's scrawny, mohawked figure, taut with wariness and poise.

The end of the joint glowed, and Merlot's cheeks hollowed as he inhaled. He turned his head to exhale a pale streamer of smoke, his face in profile as precise as the space between heartbeats.

She'd been six when she first met him and he'd been seven, both of them flotsam of the Shattering chaos. His first glance at her had been a gossamer thread, as desperate and sticky as spider silk. Over the years that glance had grown into a braided rope as thick as her wrist, and even when they were apart, she'd feel the weight of it swinging between them, by turns a bridge, a burden, a lifeline. Though they'd cut that rope between them long ago—hacked it to bits and left it on Vron's grave—she felt the ghostly weight of it still sometimes, tugging at her heart.

She looked away hastily and got up. The ceiling creaked, as if surprised at her unexpected weight, but it held. She walked to the window, now upside down, and peered out. From her perspective, the broken silhouette of the city formed a ceiling to the world, and the sky, washed with moonlight, pooled in a reflection-less ocean below.

If she'd been outside when her gravity shifted, she'd be swimming in that ocean now, falling into that eternal night. Like her father had after the graviteria infecting him had Shattered gravity, destroying a city and killing millions.

Darius murmured, *See, wasn't I a better father? He killed far more people than I ever did.*

She pressed her fingertips to her temples. *You were never my father!*

Wasn't I? You never even met him. I raised you.

"Merlot," said Ben, "you mind taking a walk around the house? I don't think the Damaskers will come back, but just for peace of mind . . ."

Merlot frowned at him, annoyed, but then glanced up at Jasper. He sighed. Ben's detached limb, his prossie, lay beside him, and Jasper was exiled to the ceiling for the next ten to twenty minutes until her shift ran its course and she returned to zone-normal gravity. Merlot stubbed out his joint, took a burning chair leg as a makeshift torch, and left the house, slamming the door behind him.

"You're the one who invited him," Jasper said when Ben's silence grew loud.

"You're the one who's given up on Zenobia's cure," he said. "Maybe you two should bury the hatchet if you're so damn sure you're going to die."

The words snapped and sparked like the campfire and died into nothingness.

"Merlot would love to bury the hatchet. In my back."

Ben was silent.

"Is that why you invited him? So we could make peace or something? Gotta hand it to you for your optimism."

"There's still time, you know," he said without looking up.

She forced out a long slow breath against the wishes of her lungs. "If Zenobia hasn't made the cure work after all these years, what will a few extra months do?"

"She already *has* an antibac, remember? She just needs to . . . improve it."

In its current state Zenobia's best prototype still had more than a 50 percent failure rate. It might be capable of killing the graviteria in Jasper's system, but it was just as likely to kill her in the process, or leave her with so much brain damage that the difference was moot.

When every option was a bad one, the horizon became a cage.

Jasper had a very personal hatred of cages.

She paced across the ceiling, skirting the fire that spat sparks and smoke at her. Ceilings were flat and boring when the house was in down-gee. Everything worth poking through for salvage or just curiosity was anchored to the floor by gravity, mostly out of her reach. She paused, arrested by the sight of crayon drawings on the white-painted wall, spiky yellow suns and wobbly stick figures holding hands. A child had lived in this house, had maybe been scolded for this innocent vandalism.

And was probably dead now. Killed by Jasper's father and his alien infection.

Jasper touched her amulets and muttered Vron's ghost-away spell.

The child on the roof, falling, a crossbow bolt in her shoulder . . .

Her mind shied away in a flinch that carried her to the other side of the ceiling. The windows were open, but she couldn't breathe. Fire lit the room, but she couldn't see. The snap and crackle of flames, the clink and jingle of carabiners in Ben's hands. The smell of smoke and mould and dust, and a hint of roses. She rubbed her hands hard over her face, feeling every callus, scrape, nick, and splinter.

In one corner, just above the baseboards, drawn in ash, was a pine tree. Twin to the one carved on her belly. A small pile of pinecones in front of it, the stub of a candle.

A pack kid shrine to her.

The sour twist in her belly almost distracted her from the returning tingle. Hastily, she tipped over into a handstand on the ceiling. When the graviteria's tide washed through her, returning her gravity to zone-normal, she dropped lightly back to the floor.

The door opened and Merlot poked his head in. "Jas, are you —? Okay, good. I found something."

He stepped inside and opened the door wide. Neverwhen's small solemn face emerged slowly from the darkness. Firelight warmed her brown skin, but tear tracks shone pale on her cheeks. Instead of gardening gloves, she now wore black-and-purple Zombie Princess mittens, her hands clutched protectively to her chest.

"Seems to be alone," Merlot said. "Wants to talk to you, Jas."

Of course she did. Jasper braced herself, a dull, bubbling flip-flop in her stomach.

Neverwhen stepped warily up to the door, eyes darting from Merlot to Jasper. "Been given them copper once before, the Damaskers," she said. "Of course they'd be comen back. I been knowen they would. And now Grammar . . ." She swallowed a sob. "I been prayen to da Pinegirl and . . . and you're here."

Something dull and hot jabbed Jasper in the throat. "I don't answer *prayers*, for gravity's sake. Not even God does that. I came because you kids stole our copper."

"But you gotta help him," Neverwhen said earnestly. "Our pack, we can't be fighten an army. We're haven younglings, small ones. Grammar wouldn't be wanten me to put them in danger. And we're haven only slingshots and knives. The Damaskers, they're biggies, and they're haven guns and crossbows and walls and dogs." She advanced two steps into the house, then stopped and glanced back to ensure her avenue of escape remained clear. Amused, Merlot stepped away from the door.

"How old's Grammar?" Jasper asked. "Twelve? Thirteen? None of the gangs let teenagers roam the zones. I'm sorry, but it was going to happen eventually. Anyway, what the hell do you expect me to do against the entire Damasker army?"

"You da Pinegirl!"

"And that makes me magic?" It did; she could see it in Neverwhen's eyes. The Pinegirl was supposed to be a superhero, larger than life. She was supposed to blow down the gates of Damascus with the power of her breath, knock down an army with a sweep of her hand. It singed the edges of her heart, that sadly misguided hope in Neverwhen's eyes and the glossy fairy tale it was based on. None of it had anything to do with her, Jasper.

It had taken guts for Neverwhen to come here, to appeal to a biggie, but for Grammar's sake she'd done it. All for nothing, as it turned out.

"Welcome to disappointment," Jasper said bitterly. "I'm just another boring, useless biggie. I grew up and you need to grow up too. Grammar's gone."

"Jas," said Ben.

Merlot leaned a shoulder against the wall, arms folded over his chest. "You should never meet your heroes, kid. They do nothing but let you down."

Ben stood, one-footed, and Jasper moved automatically to his side in case he needed to put a hand on her for balance. "What Merlot and Jasper are *trying* to say is that we'd like to help, but there's nothing we can do. The Damaskers have him now, just like they have hundreds of other kids. They're an army, and we're not fighters. We don't have any special powers. Not even the Pinegirl."

Neverwhen's eyes shone a firelit cinnamon, liquid with growing desperation. "If you're not helpen, they'll be killen him when they're finden out . . ." She stopped and bit her lip.

"When they find out what?" Ben asked, but Neverwhen stared at the floor, shoulders hunched.

"Do you know where Grammar got that bird amulet?" Jasper asked.

"I'm not knowen. He been goen there alone."

"If you want my help, don't play games with me," Jasper said. "You must have some idea where he got it." The burning threatened to fill her whole chest. Everybody wanted a piece of the Pinegirl, but she wasn't the goddamn giving tree.

Neverwhen's gaze sharpened. "Is that what you're wanten? Then you better be helpen him." Faced with a recalcitrant, unpredictable hero apparently immune to a tearful appeal, she'd switched to bargaining. Quick on her feet, this one.

Merlot grinned, enjoying this far too much. "Kid's got pepper."

"You been choosen him," Neverwhen said, now cannily adding guilt as a weapon.

Jasper fixed her eyes on the ceiling and waited for the roaring in her ears to subside.

"Because Grammar will survive," Ben said. "A kid like him, he has a chance. What the Damaskers would do to you, though . . ." He shook his head. "I'm sorry, but Jas chose right."

Neverwhen continued glaring at Jasper. Watching her shiny gold hero fade to tarnished brass, then to gaudily painted plastic.

"Go take care of your pack," Jasper said. "And don't think that the next time the Damaskers come you'll be able to buy them off again."

"If you been choosen me, Grammar would be finden a way to save me," Neverwhen said. "But I'm not a fighter like him. I can't be plannen a raid. I can only be tryen to protect the pack. You been choosen him, and you been choosen *wrong*. That's maken this *your fault*."

"Jesus, kid," Merlot said, sounding less amused now.

"You not da Pinegirl," Neverwhen said flatly. "Da Pinegirl's a hero. You're just like all the other biggies."

She ran out the door, her footsteps fading fast.

"So stop praying to me!" Jasper shouted after her. "Nobody's saving you. Nobody's saving Grammar. Nobody fucking saved *me*, did they? That's just fucking life."

She kicked a toy truck and sent it crashing into the wall above the drawn pine tree. She stalked over to the shrine and stomped on the clump of pinecones until they were splinters under her foot.

Ben sighed.

"So dramatic," Merlot mocked, which was such a matter of the pot calling the kettle black that rage paralyzed Jasper's tongue. He took advantage of getting the last word in and strolled out the door, presumably to ensure Neverwhen had left and wasn't going to return with her pack to burn down the house.

Capricious, unhelpful, and quick to anger, Darius mused. *You make a perfect god, really. I only aspired, but you became. Well done, pet.*

"There's nothing you can do to help Grammar," Ben said firmly. "None of this is your fault."

There were a whole lot of things she could do nothing about, and each one was a porcupine rolling around in her chest.

Jasper tapped a toe behind her left foot. She ran at the wall, hurled herself upward. Touched a foot to the wall, launched herself into a backflip. Landed in a crouch, breathing heavily. Feeling that tiny bit less as if grasshoppers were swarming under her skin.

With a balance that put hers to shame, Ben lowered himself neatly to a cross-legged position. He picked up a carabiner and snapped it open and closed. "So let's find Mom," he said abruptly.

Jasper ran at the wall and threw herself into another backflip. "How? If Grammar's the only one who knows where he got the amulet."

"Kid like him, there have got to be stories floating around. Kids gossip like no one else. We'll check out the Kornelsens' soup kitchen and ask around."

She hopped, two-footed, onto the TV stand, and from there to the mantel over the decorative fireplace. It was barely wide enough for both feet, but she held her balance with one hand on the stone chimney. "I guess it'd be something to do." With her foot she nudged a dusty framed photo of a smiling family— mom and dad and two chubby, complacent children—and it crashed to the floor.

"While we wait for Zenobia to fix the cure," Ben said firmly.

The cure. Right. She perched on the narrow mantel between floor and ceiling and touched the clay bird amulet to her lips.

This is how the graviteria grew and progressed in your father in the final stages, Zenobia had said the last time she'd examined Jasper's blood under her microscope. Six months, she'd predicted. Probably. It was hardly an exact science when Jasper was only the second human ever to be infected and the first one to be born infected.

Six months to find out if Zenobia's antibac worked well enough to leave her alive and functional while killing the graviteria inside her. If it didn't work, the gravity-controlling alien organisms infecting her would explode into another Shattering large enough to wipe out half the country.

Neverwhen was right. She was no hero and never had been.

5

HOME

Things a brother is good for:
Eating your peas
Taking the blame for a fart
Remembering your memories for you

~ Veronica Park (*Lists of the Apocalypse*)

In her dreams she is trapped on the flamingo stand, balancing one-legged on this raised platform the size of a man's hand. The dogs prowl below, sniffing the mist of her sweat in great gulps. Their ribs twang against the flamingo's single leg and it sways. Sometimes the dogs have eight legs, sometimes two. They flick their tongues like lizards. Their growls scratch the concrete walls. They are always hungry.

"Just fall," Darius taunts, his pale face swimming out of the shadows. He likes it when she wins. He likes it better when she fails.

"I won't fall," she whispers. "I'd rather jump."

"That's exactly your problem," the dogs say in Merlot's voice.

Then she's alone and falling into a darkness that's always waiting in the borderlands between dreaming and waking. She's falling up, not down, up to her destiny, her death. Up to the waking world.

Jasper woke so slowly, it seemed she had never been asleep at all. She had been lying there for an eternity while the room shrank and the walls curved around her like a giant's hands, poised to catch and crush her in an instant. Her breath sawed raggedly in her throat. Her mouth was as dry as dust. Sweat trickled down her sides, pooled between her breasts. Her heart pounded from the dream, from the bloody, sticky memory of Darius's voice and the growl of the dogs still buzzing in her bones.

I'm home, I'm safe, I'm grown up, she chanted in her head. *I'm home, I'm safe, I'm grown up.*

In the moonlit darkness she could make out her bookshelves, crammed with books and comics that she'd never returned to Merlot after their breakup. Framed beside the bed was the cover of one of Merlot's original Peter and Jazztree comics, hand-drawn, laminated copies of which still circulated around the zones.

She threw off her bedding. Her faded and threadbare Zombie Princess doll fell off the bed with the movement. She set the doll gently back against her pillow. It was the only thing she'd taken with her when she and Ben had left their childhood home for the last time.

Her discarded clothes and gravving equipment created a map of shadows across the floor, and she had to step carefully to not make a racket. A pile of used helmets loomed in a corner, each with a dent, gouge, or scrape that had ended its usefulness. Vron had scribbled on each helmet the story of the gravving accident or fallen debris it had saved Jasper from. Sometimes

Jasper would read her helmets one by one, just to see Vron's handwriting again.

She opened the window. Air flowed cool against her burning cheeks, easing briefly the sensation of suffocating. The moon hung among the dissipating clouds, a flat silver disc of light.

She climbed out of the window and pulled herself onto the roof. The shingles were damp and scratchy under her bare feet. Near the peak of the roof, she lay down and, muscle by muscle, forced herself to relax. There she was enclosed by only air and stars. She took a deep breath. There her lungs could expand wide enough to take in the whole night—the pungent smell of goat and chicken manure; the rich, damp, earthy aroma of growing things; the sharp tang of woodsmoke. The smell of Yorky, the smell of home.

She stared up at the stars with eyes that wouldn't shut. Exhaustion rumbled in her bones like a distant thunderstorm. Who needed sleep anyway? It was just practice for dying. Every night people surrendered to the dark unknown in the faith that they would open their eyes and find themselves unchanged on the other side of oblivion. But there was no guarantee, was there?

In the year after Harmony had adopted her and Ben, Jasper would wake up every morning and stand naked in front of the bathroom mirror and check that no part of her had gone missing in the night. She'd count the freckles on the pale skin of her wrists, the scars on her legs, and the lines in the palms of her hands. She'd stare into her own eyes from inches away to ensure that her irises remained the exact shade of autumn acorns and that no one but a tiny reflected Jasper looked back at her from the darkness of her pupils.

Then she'd run into Ben's room and verify that he hadn't changed either. Two arms, one and a half legs, an unruly storm cloud of black hair. Finally, she'd jab her fingers in his cheeks to locate his dimples. The half-awake grumbly sounds he made during this examination were further reassurance, like a cat's purr, that he was still wholly her Ben.

In the east, dawn soaked into the indigo sky like cream diluting blueberry juice.

A window slid open. Ben's hair, sticking up in six different directions, appeared over the edge of the roof first and the rest of him followed, crawling three-limbed to join her, as he hadn't yet attached his prossie.

"How long have you been up here? Do you ever sleep?" he asked, yawning.

"I'll sleep when I'm dead." A prospect she was rather looking forward to.

"In your own bed, I meant." His eyes opened and he came awake. "You don't have a single rope on you. Jesus, what if you'd shifted?"

"I'd have enough time to climb back in the window."

"Not if you were asleep."

From inside, Harmony shouted, "Breakfast!"

Startled awake, the rooster crowed hastily and the hens clucked. The goats baaed to be milked.

"Don't tell her I was up here without a rope," Jasper said.

"What's that? Sounds like you just offered to do my chores for me." Grinning, Ben dodged her swat, then slithered over the edge of the roof and back through the window.

When Jasper came into the kitchen carrying the basket of eggs and bucket of milk, Harmony was packing lunch for them: jerky and hard-boiled eggs, pickles and kimchi, cheese and dried fruit, and bottles of sweetened tea. A tiny Korean woman with silver hair, she was a compact engine of colour and energy in a flowery purple shirt and loose plaid pants and pink slippers.

Taking in the amount of food spread out over the counter,

Jasper said, "We're just visiting the Azuros for a morning, not going on another gravving trip."

Harmony shook a finger at her, her gnarled hands dripping with bright red kimchi juice. "You told me you've been living off wild strawberries and dandelion greens for three days. You need to be fattened up."

"To make up for it, I won't stop eating for the next three days," Jasper promised. She bent and smushed her lips against Harmony's soft, wrinkled cheek and then kissed the other cheek too, the stiff, plasticky one. One side of Harmony's face showed the high cheekbones and fine, papery skin from her once beautiful youth. The other side had been melted into a lumpy, waxen horror mask. She smelled of baking bread and basil and damp soil.

"Who taught you to kiss, a golden retriever? Eat your eggs, Jaspa, before they get cold." Harmony shooed her to the table.

Through a full mouth, Ben said, "I ate your toast."

"I hope you choke on it." She shovelled a forkful of cheesy eggs into her mouth.

"If you don't have any copper to trade, why do you need to see Zenobia?" Harmony stepped over a cat to stir the strawberry jam thickening in a pot on the wood stove. "I could use some help with the Zones Day prep. The schoolchildren made banners that need to be hung in the community centre. Also chairs need to be carried over from the school." She impatiently nudged aside the cat, who remained stubbornly underfoot.

"Ben can help," Jasper said.

Ben shot her a look, but it was edged in relief. After all this time, he still found it hard to walk among the Azuros, to look Zenobia in the eye and speak to her civilly. He'd never said so, but she knew he didn't understand how Jasper could.

"The Kornelsen girls will be at the community centre,"

Harmony said. "I thought you'd want to ask them about the kids who stole your wire."

"I'll do it," Ben said.

Jasper dumped her plate and fork into the basin of water in the sink. She stopped in front of the memento board, a corkboard with notes and to-do lists and the week's work schedule tacked onto it, along with one precious photo. Ben had snatched the family photo from their fridge when they finally made the decision to leave their house, weeks after the Shattering. Other than the clay bird necklaces their mother had made for them, this photo was the last tangible reminder of her.

In the photo they were in a park, sunlight filtering through the leaves above them. Catherine Pine sat with her arms wrapped tightly around four-year-old Jasper in her lap, and nine-year-old Ben leaned against her shoulder, all of them grinning at the camera, a trifecta of dimples. It had been taken four years after the Tower staff told Catherine Pine that her husband had died in an unfortunate workplace accident.

In fact, he'd been accidentally infected by the alien organisms he'd been studying, the first human so afflicted. His colleague, Dr. Zenobia Allan, claimed that Andrew had voluntarily quarantined himself in the Tower to be studied, and that he'd agreed to be declared dead early because at the time the only cure was death, so it was only a matter of time anyway.

Jasper had her doubts about her father's disappearance being voluntary, but then, she'd made it a habit not to fully trust anything Zenobia told her. In any case, five years after his reported death, he'd died for real when the graviteria inside him matured and Shattered. He never even knew Jasper existed. Because Jasper had been conceived in that small window of time after Andrew was infected but before he realized he was infected, and because Catherine didn't know she was pregnant until after Andrew had been quarantined and declared dead,

Jasper's very existence, let alone her infected status, had gone under the radar. If anyone at the Tower had found out about Jasper, would they have "quarantined" her in the Tower too?

Zenobia always dismissed this question. The past was past. They lived in a post-Shattering world now, and everything had changed.

A knock sounded at the door.

"It's open," Jasper yelled.

"Is that Jasper I hear?" a woman called back as the door opened. "I thought I smelled trouble."

Sparrow Abebe strode into the kitchen, at once seeming to fill the entire space. The Yorky ganglord grinned at Jasper and Ben, her teeth white against the rich dark brown of her skin.

"Ippy," she said, turning to her wife behind her, "Did I not tell you I smelled trouble? Here she is." She engulfed Jasper in a giant hug. "What have you done now?"

"What?" Jasper's indignation was muffled against the pillowy depths of Sparrow's ample chest. "We literally got home last night. I haven't had time to do anything."

Sparrow's hugs were restorative the way hot baths were, grounding and refreshing. Jasper disentangled herself with reluctance.

Ibtisam Hamid emerged from behind her wife's imposing figure, carrying her medical bag in her good hand while using her forearm, which ended in a hook-like device, to wipe perspiration from her forehead. Her round cheeks were as rosy as her pink hijab.

"Sweetie, the trouble you're smelling is the rumour that Jasper was seen arriving at the gates with Merlot," she said.

"I guess I was just invisible, was I?" Ben said.

"Oho!" said Sparrow. "You gravved together? And nobody's eyes were gouged out? No hair pulled? Did you guys finally make up? I want details."

"Unfortunately, I'm on my way out the door," Jasper said hastily.

"Hi, Ben, how are you? And how did you handle the very awkward position of being between two exes who hate each other and who happen to be your sister and your former best friend? However did you survive without killing either of them, Ben?" Ben grumbled, buttering another slice of toast.

"We assume you handled it with your usual grace and patience," Ibtisam said with a smile. "Jas and Merlot, though—you just never know."

"The disrespect!" Jasper said huffily. "In my own home!"

Harmony asked Ibtisam, "Did you come to see about Mira? She's been looking poorly for two days now."

"Absolutely. I know how important those goats are to you." Ibtisam winked at Jasper. She'd been a veterinarian prior to the Shattering. As Yorky's only remaining medical professional, her patients were mostly human nowadays, but she'd still examine ill or injured animals when she could.

"Help yourself to breakfast, Sparrow," Harmony called as she led Ibtisam out the back door.

"And try sitting down for five minutes, sweetie," Ibtisam added. To the others she said, "She's been going non-stop since before dawn."

"Are you here about Zones Day stuff?" Ben asked Sparrow as she plunked herself at the table opposite him and helped herself to some toast.

"It's a never-ending list. Food, the talent show, the kids' activities, the songs list for the band, alcohol. I have to sort out the shifts for the gangers who'll be on duty. Everyone wants to be off in the evening, but I want my more level heads on shift. If we're going to have Azuros and Damaskers in the same space . . ." She grimaced. "I'd love to have a Zones Day where I can actually relax and drink, but no, I have to be sober to break up the inevitable half dozen fights."

"Oh, you love it, Madam Ganglord." Jasper dropped a peck on Sparrow's cheek. "Okay, I'm gone. Behave, all." She waved to Ben and left.

She closed the front door behind her just as a young woman with bright blond hair pinned up under a black *duak* turned onto their front walk. Like most Mennonite women, Esther Kornelsen wore a hand-sewn, calf-length dress with socks and sneakers in addition to the black kerchief over her hair. She held a toddler by the hand, which slowed her pace to a shuffle.

"*Gu'n dag*, Esther," Jasper said in the Mennonites' Low German dialect.

"Oh, hello." Esther scooped up the toddler and propped him on one hip. The boy stuck a dirty thumb in his mouth and stared solemnly at Jasper with eyes the colour of overripe blueberries. He'd be a nephew, son of one of Esther's two older sisters. Or else a cousin, cousin's child, or just a random Mennonite youngling. Most Mennonites shared a certain look that made them hard to tell apart, a lot of blond hair and blue eyes and old Germanic features. Their families were so large and intertwined that resemblances were pervasive.

"Are you here about Zones Day stuff too?" Jasper asked. "Sparrow and Ibtisam just arrived, so it's a regular party in there."

"Oh, I—yes, I'll certainly go in and say hello." She shifted the boy to her other hip. "I'd heard you and Ben were back."

"Did you also hear Merlot was with us? Because that gossip's sure to be everywhere by evening," Jasper said, rolling her eyes.

Esther hesitated, surprise and something more complicated flitting across her face. "No, I hadn't heard that. How did that . . . ?" She focused on detaching the child's fingers from her *duak*.

Esther had the rosy, scrubbed face and bright blue eyes of

someone who hopped out of bed at dawn, sang while she did the chores, and said her prayers every night on her knees with her hands clasped. Probably birds and woodland animals ate out of her hands. Jasper didn't resent her for that, though. Not very often anyway. Only once or twice per interaction. How could you not be annoyed by someone so sweet and righteous who still had two living parents and sisters galore?

Suffering wasn't a competition, Quick Rick liked to tell Jasper.

If it were, Jasper would clearly win, so she didn't argue the point.

The first summer after the Shattering, as the quarantine walls rose inexorably around the city and the military continued to refuse to let survivors leave, a group of Mennonite families had settled on a large park and begun plowing the land. Their experience as farmers, sensible practicality, and willingness to share had kept many people from starvation the following winter. A community had grown around them, the core of what would become Yorky.

When Darius Dalca and his ex-convict thugs had taken over, he'd had enough sense to see that without the food the Mennonites grew his little empire would quickly crumble. He put more time and energy into controlling the output of those farms than he did into controlling the Mennonites themselves. Declared pacifists, they sought to help those they could but refused to lift a hand in violence against Darius and his men. While not exempt from his games, they had suffered the least at his hands, and for this reason undercurrents of resentment still existed against them.

The boy on Esther's hip was a child raised in civilization, such as it was. A child who, small god willing, would never know a cage.

What a fat little snack he'd be for the dogs, eh, pet? Darius said.

The memory of powerful jaws crunching on tender young bones rippled down Jasper's spine and blinded her for an instant. She blinked rapidly and stared at the street, keeping her face rigidly still so Esther wouldn't notice anything was wrong. The boy struggled and whined to be set on his feet again, and by the time Esther straightened, Jasper had her face under control.

"We ran into a kid pack in the zones," Jasper said. "Alpha's named Grammar, and his second is a girl named Neverwhen. They ever come into your soup kitchen?"

"Neverwhen, yes," Esther said promptly. "The Crows. Their territory is deeper in the zones, so I only see them every few weeks. They say please and thank you and are rarely the ones to start a fight. Although," she added with a wince, "they sure can finish one."

"Do you know their alpha?"

"He hasn't come in the last year or so, probably because he's getting older."

Gangs saw children as a useless resource drain, but teenagers left to run wild caused trouble, so the zones' various gangs aimed to recruit pack kids at the cusp of puberty, often forcibly. Grammar would have stayed away from biggies to avoid this unwilling recruitment.

"Their pack stole our copper and then got snatched up by Damaskers."

Esther hissed between her teeth, brow knitting. "The children are all afraid of those Damasker raiding parties. They're scared of the workhouses in Knowles too, but they don't hunt kids there in the same way. They just buy them." She frowned. "I've often told Sparrow that if we just welcomed all the children as citizens and took care of them, this wouldn't be a problem. Jesus told us to suffer the little children to come to him, and we should do no less. If we just—"

"The kids would refuse," Jasper cut her off, her annoyance rising. "They don't trust adults, and for good reason."

"Are you saying they shouldn't trust Sparrow?" Esther said, perfectly aware of Jasper's friendship with the Yorky ganglord.

Jasper could understand Sparrow's side of the recruitment debate, that it was necessary to maintain security in a lawless land and that Yorky's relative prosperity made its inhabitants a tempting target. She also understood that while feral children roaming the zones was bad enough, feral teenagers were out of the question, with the corresponding increase in violence and youth pregnancies.

Despite this logic, Jasper's sympathies lay firmly on the side of the kids' continued freedom. If they wanted more permanent homes with adults, Esther and her sisters usually found ways to foster them out. Some kids did choose this option. Most didn't. They visited the community centre for the free food, especially in the winter, and then they vanished back into the zones.

Esther changed the subject. "I had a question for you, actually. Have you seen Grace?" Grace was her sixteen-year-old sister.

"The Graceling? No. We only got back last night."

"I know. That's why I was—" Esther stopped. "Okay. Never mind. Thank you."

"Maybe ask Merlot. He talks to Grace more often than we do, so he might have an idea."

"He may talk to Grace, but he doesn't much like talking to me," Esther said, lips tight.

Hardly a surprise. Jasper restrained herself from commenting. "Well, I better go."

"Jasper," Esther called after her, and she turned. "It may be nothing. Kids brag and tell tall tales all the time. You have to discount nearly half of what they say. But I've heard . . ." She hesitated.

"What?" Jasper asked impatiently.

"The boy, Grammar. I've heard other kids calling him the Devilman's son."

Something cold shot down Jasper's spine. Those blue eyes, that contemptuous mouth . . . "Impossible. That's—no."

"It's just a story, I'm sure," Esther said hastily. "Kids will say anything to make themselves seem tough and invincible."

"Just a story. Right." Jasper walked away without a wave or a word of farewell.

Devilman's son. It shouldn't be possible. But a large solid chunk of her already believed it because *of course*. Why was she even surprised? Lies and secrets, secrets and lies: they were Zenobia Allan's stock-in-trade.

6

THE AZUROS

How can bacteria manipulate or affect gravity?
Are the so-called graviteria actually even bacteria?
Even after years of study, we still don't understand what they
* are or how they do what they do. The universe is much*
* stranger and more marvellous than we ever suspected.*

~ Dr. Zenobia Allan (personal journals)

J asper had to walk an hour from Yorky to reach the Azuros'
trading post.

It was conveniently located near the only set of gates in
the towering wall that surrounded the entirety of the zones. The
wall had started out fifteen years ago as a barbed wire fence
supplemented by a cordon of soldiers, all to ensure that
Shattering survivors stayed put within it and no mysterious alien
infection escaped. Fear of the inexplicable and unfixable zones
had led to building the wall in record time. The military had

withdrawn behind it, and zoners had been abandoned to their own devices.

No zoner had ever escaped quarantine and lived to tell the tale.

Meanwhile, outside the walls, in what the zoners called downieland, that strange place where gravity still obeyed the laws of physics, people had electric lights and governments and takeout pizza and internet and laws and airplanes. They could swim in the ocean, eat foods grown a thousand miles away, and call their parents on the other side of the world. With the truth of the Shattering suppressed and kept top secret, their world had gone on as if nothing had happened, as if the gravity zones didn't even exist. As if the survivors were merely ghosts going through the motions of lives that had ended years ago.

Which some days didn't feel far from the truth.

That didn't mean they were completely isolated. Zenobia Allan had an influential contact outside the walls who kept a trickle of trade flowing past the quarantine walls. The gates opened once a month to allow Zenobia and her gang of Azuros to deliver the copper and other salvaged metals and miscellaneous valuables that grav-walkers traded to them. In return they received goods they'd ordered the previous month— food staples, seeds, medicine, vitamins, hygiene products, tools, cigarettes.

If Jasper turned away from the walls and looked into the heart of the zones, she could see the Tower, a soaring silver needle stitching together heaven and earth. Defiantly untouched by the destruction that surrounded it, the Tower was the centre and source of the chaos. That's where the gravity experiments had been conducted. That's where everything had gone wrong.

Of all the natural laws, gravity was the one least noticed, the bedrock upon which every drama of life and death was staged, a fact as unquestionable as the arrival of dawn each morning. A force born of the dizzying spin of a planet, an anxious mother holding on to the careless feet of children who wished only to dabble in the sky. The Shattering caused a fractal flowering of gravity, a mutating, cancerous bloom that violated the most basic precepts of what was up and what was down. With gravity in disarray, what was to prevent anyone from falling off the skin of the planet into the vastness of the universe?

The zones of warped gravity covered the land area of this one city and no more, and yet the Shattering destroyed people's conviction of safety and security and, above all, their confidence in their ability to understand the world around them. Most Shattering survivors lived in the buffer zone of down-gee between the quarantine walls and the wild zones. Only kid packs and grav-walkers and peddlers entered the wild zones regularly. And raiding parties.

Everyone else preferred to pretend the zones didn't exist. Sky above and earth below was the natural order of things. Everything else was a mad perversion of reality.

Jasper had been five years old at the time of the Shattering. She still remembered the roar of a city uprooted, of houses crackling and crunching as if being punched by invisible giants. Whole buildings broke off under the strain of gravity that capriciously pulled sideways or upward. Ungainly chunks flew in every direction, upward and sideways and down, smashing into each other and caroming away in a city-sized game of pinball. Scintillating clouds of falling, floating debris filled the air in odd patterns, as if drawn by invisible magnets.

Some fragments of debris had arms and legs that still moved.

In a single hour of horrible chaos, anything or anyone not secured to the earth itself had fallen. Fallen until they entered another zone, fallen until they were pressed flat between two opposing zones, or until they impacted some immovable object.

Jasper and Ben's babysitter had gone outside to see what was going on and unwittingly took one step too many across an invisible border. She fell across the street and smacked with a meaty crunch into the house opposite theirs, flattened full length against the door like a grotesque Halloween decoration.

Mercifully, their apartment building had remained in a pocket of down-gee, though without electricity. Jasper and Ben huddled in the dark for a week, eating unheated canned soup and soggy thawed waffles with chocolate sauce, waiting for their mom to come home, waiting for the world to make sense again, waiting for someone to clean up their babysitter's corpse before the crows and starving neighbourhood cats ate her down to the bones.

Their mother never came. Neither did anyone else.

Eventually, they had to leave to look for food and help. Jasper's memories of that first year post-Shattering were vague and cluttered. She and Ben had to figure out how gravity formed irregular zones of every conceivable shape and size and draw, marked only by the electric static sensation they would feel as they neared the zone borders. They had to learn how to manoeuvre from zone to zone without falling, without dying. How to pick locks and break windows to scavenge kitchens and restaurants and grocery stores for food. How to fight off starving dogs and not vomit at putrefying human corpses.

They wandered, from house to house, zone to zone, out of the suburbs and into downtown and back into the suburbs again. Where had they come from? Where were they going? The city had become a trackless wasteland, a tortuous maze of pitfalls, a Dali painting come to life. Their journey chased its own tail, endless and circular.

Sometimes Jasper felt that journey had never ended.

Here she was, returning again and again to Zenobia and the Azuros, even after they had burned the childhood right out of her. Circles and traps. Crossing and recrossing her own path, the footprints from her past. A dog pacing a cage.

God, she hated cages.

Jasper walked past an encampment of Damaskers come to trade. She tensed at the sight, but it was unlikely they were the same gangers who had attacked Grammar's pack. Dragon's raiding party would have returned to the Damascus community with their new recruit.

Half a dozen gangers stood around watching two of their number spar. They all wore knife-strapped black and carried themselves with the air of feral, barely tamed dogs, amiable for now but a hair-trigger away from biting on instinct. Triple ridged scars slashed their cheekbones. They'd originally belonged to the Saints of Damascus cult, but their leader had died of pneumonia, and a few years ago Sparrow's brother-in-law, Nico Mavuto, had co-opted them and trained them into his personal army. For the safety of the zones, he claimed.

Jasper didn't feel particularly safe, especially when she saw they were all armed, and not only with guns. More and more Damaskers were carrying the new bows and crossbows Knowles was producing. The supply of usable ammunition in the zones was running low, and Zenobia refused to trade for weapons through the quarantine gates, so Knowles would soon have a thriving trade in those bows and crossbows.

The young Damaskers—they were all male—turned to watch Jasper walk by. Some of them whistled and hooted. She gritted her teeth and forced herself to maintain her relaxed pace. There on neutral ground they'd behave. Probably. Or else risk losing their trading privileges. If they even cared about those.

"Hey, Pinegirl!" yelled one of the young men who had been sparring. "Why're you just walken by? Too good to be greeten us?" He had flaming red hair and a sunburned face dotted with freckles.

Before she could think of something cutting to say, his sparring partner bopped him in the face with his fist. It wasn't a hard blow, but it got his attention. "Hey!"

"I thought we were sparring," the other man said. He had brown skin and a riotous spill of locs over his shoulders. He wasn't speaking packspeak, meaning that, unlike most Damaskers, he'd been raised by adults.

His next blow landed hard in Red Hair's belly. Red Hair grunted, doubling over. From that position he lunged forward to tackle the other man at the waist. The rush bore Locs to the ground, where the momentum rolled him backwards, and then he used his legs expertly to launch Red Hair over his head. In an instant Locs sprang to his feet. He dragged Red Hair upright and delivered two efficient punches to his face.

Just like that, the fight was over.

And he didn't even have to use a knife, Darius said.

"That, gentlemen, is how you use a man's momentum against him," Locs lectured the open-mouthed group. Red Hair slumped to the ground at his feet, clutching his face and groaning. Locs assumed a fighting stance. "Okay, who's next?"

Nobody was in a hurry to be next.

Locs glanced over at Jasper. He didn't smile, but he tapped two fingers to his forehead in a kind of salute. His bearing was atypical for a Damasker, relaxed where the others were coiled for violence. They swaggered to prove how badass they were. He didn't have to.

She didn't respond to his look or his gesture—she wanted nothing to do with Damaskers, even the more chivalrous ones— and continued on.

The Azuros' trading post came into sight, a rambling brick structure swarmed with ivy. It had once been a police station and was divided into two parts—the main hall where trading took place, and the network of hallways and offices where Zenobia and her men lived. The trading hall was open for business, and a few people wandered in and out, each person checked for weapons by the Azuro on duty before being allowed in.

A whicker and a snort caught Jasper's attention, stopping her short.

Three horses were tethered away from the trading post entrance, an unusual sight. A man and woman stood on guard nearby. The man had a crossbow and the woman had a bow slung over her shoulder. The guards watched her with interest.

"You guys are ReGeneration," Jasper exclaimed.

Fifteen years ago, a conference for Youths of the Future had been held in the city. Teenage delegates from all over the country, along with their parental chaperones, had attended. They were stranded by the Shattering and the chaos that followed. Disillusioned by Darius Dalca's rule, they broke away from Yorky and formed their own gang with a home base deep in the zones that no outsiders had ever seen.

Under their mysterious leader, known only as the Guardian, they'd also developed a passion for the environmental rejuvenation of the broken city. They called themselves the ReGeneration, the generation who would restore the land.

"Don't see you folks around here often," Jasper called. "Found something good to trade?"

She'd sometimes see ReGeneration members from a distance while gravving, but they'd always melt away before she could get close. They came to the trading hall at odd times and slipped away again before anyone could register their presence.

They also owned the only horses in the zones and guarded them like gold, one reason for their elusiveness.

The man was older, with brown skin and gentle lines to his

face. Manifestly not Ben's ex-boyfriend, Charlie Grey. She hadn't seen Charlie in years, ever since he abandoned his friends to join the ReGeneration. Well, let him stay away. She'd have a few choice things to say to him about breaking her brother's heart if she ever saw him again.

"You're Jasper Pine," the young woman said and then flushed. She was white and wore a sleeveless shirt that displayed impressive arm muscles.

"We're not here to trade," the man said.

"We?" Jasper looked at the third horse. "Why are you here, then?"

"She wanted to talk to you, actually," the woman blurted. "But Zenobia said—"

The man quelled her with a glance. "It's not really for us to say."

"Who wants to talk to me?" Jasper asked with a flare of curiosity.

The ReGeneration knew how to get into the Tower. They were the ones who had fixed a collapsed subway tunnel to make it possible, and they kept it guarded and hidden. Jasper was one of the few people who even knew such an entrance existed, and only because Zenobia had told her.

The man shifted uncomfortably. "Perhaps you better talk to Zenobia."

As if talking to Zenobia had ever done her any good.

"Oy!" Socrates, Zenobia's second-in-command, stormed over to them from the trading hall entrance. "Get away from them, Pine. Boss said no one was allowed to bother them, and she was very fucking specific that *you* weren't supposed to go near them."

Jasper planted her hands on her hips. "Excuse me? Zenobia can't tell me who I can or can't talk to."

Socrates was looking very irritated that he'd had to leave his comfortable lawn chair by the entrance. His pale, gaunt face was covered in crudely inked crosses and tears, Bible verses, and naked women, and the blue scarf of the Azuros hung loose and grimy around his scrawny neck. He'd been in prison for four counts of murder, gang-related, when the Shattering smashed the prison complex open, allowing its inhabitants to escape.

"Just get moving, Pine."

"Or what?" But when she glanced over her shoulder, the ReGeneration guards were leading their horses away from her, the woman grimacing in apology over her shoulder.

"See?" said Socrates. "They don't want to be bothered."

"Fine," said Jasper. "But I want a word with Zen right now."

"Am I her secretary? She's in a meeting. Come back later." Then he glanced past her and said, "Jesus Christ, it's that kind of morning."

She looked too and saw Locs ambling alone down the road toward them. But for a knife he was unarmed, hands in his pockets. He had no scars on his face, unlike most Damaskers.

"Okay, fine, I'll tell the boss you're here. Maybe she'll see you." Socrates actually took her arm in his urgency to hustle her toward the trading hall.

She went with him. There were easier ways of getting information than digging in her heels and picking a fight with Socrates. "You know that Damasker?"

Socrates snorted. "Ryan? He's not a Damasker."

"Who is he then? I don't recognize him."

"Do I look like fucking Google?"

Jasper had no idea what Google looked like or what exactly it was, but she understood his question to mean that he knew the answer but didn't want to share.

Socrates hesitated inside the trading post, but seeing Ryan Not-a-Damasker approaching the entrance, he hustled Jasper away from the trading hall and down the hallway leading to

Zenobia's office. Jasper shook him off. Muttering under his breath, he left her there.

Zenobia's unofficial bodyguard, a tall white man named Tom Jitters, approached her with a frown. "Zenobia can't see you right now."

"I'll wait."

Tom nodded and continued to block the hallway with his heavily muscled frame, burly arms crossed over his chest. Jasper flipped over to do a handstand.

"You could wait in the trading hall," Tom suggested after she'd walked several figure eights in the hallway on her hands.

"Don't you want the gossip?" She backflipped to her feet. "Bunch of pack kids stole our copper and then Damaskers stole their alpha and we had to grav home without food."

"How exciting," Tom said.

"Don't believe anyone who says that Merlot and I have made up just because he went with us."

"I won't."

"The alpha they took, he had my mother's amulet. We think he knows where her body is."

Silence. Tom unfolded his arms. "Your mother?"

"Yeah, isn't that crazy? Why, what's wrong?"

"Nothing." Tom's expression flattened back to its usual reserve, but under his blond beard his face seemed paler than usual. "Go wait in the trading hall. I'll find you when Zenobia's finished."

She went. Tom didn't give orders very often. She glanced back over her shoulder to see him quietly knock and poke his head into Zenobia's office.

In the trading hall she nodded at a few familiar faces. The man with the locs—Ryan—was chatting with the Azuros by the weighing station. He spotted her across the room and lifted his chin in acknowledgement but returned to his conversation.

She slipped back out the door. "I'm going for a walk until Zen's available," she told Socrates when he started to get up. He grunted suspiciously but sank back into his seat.

She walked around the building, keeping close to the wall so no one would see her from the windows—specifically, Zenobia's office window. She rounded another corner to be sure she was out of sight of the entrance and scanned the face of the trading post. The bottom floor windows and doors were boarded up and reinforced, but the upper windows weren't. The old building had plenty of nooks and corners and edges. A playground for a grav-walker.

Jasper tapped the toe of her right shoe behind her left and gave herself a running start at the wall. Her momentum and two toe kicks let her wedge herself between a drainpipe and a jutting corner. Using the ivy and digging her fingers into tiny cracks and ledges, she climbed the crumbling brick wall.

She paused at the second floor to wipe the sweat from her forehead, fingers wedged into mossy brick. She tilted her head back to gauge how far she had to go.

With a scraping sound, a third-floor window opened above her. Leaning out of it, his elbows braced on the sill, was Ryan. He studied her with inquisitive eyebrows.

She nearly lost her grip and scrabbled for balance. "How'd you get up there?"

"Stairs. Ever heard of 'em?"

He was in the Azuros' living quarters. Only Azuros were allowed there.

He leaned out the window to examine the wall she'd been climbing. He whistled. "Okay, colour me curious. Why's the Zombie Princess climbing a building when she could just walk in the front door? No, wait, let me guess. You're here to rescue some damsel in distress. Oh, please tell me it's Crane."

"Crane? You have a twisted imagination." Was he going to rat her out? Why would he, when he was trespassing himself? "How do you know Crane?"

"She's Zenobia's little shadow, isn't she? So that's how we met. She tried to stab me one time, so I threw her into a table. She agreed to guide me through the zones, then left me to die when I fell. She changed her mind but ended up breaking her leg. I'm a nice guy so I pulled her out. We're best friends now."

"Oh, you're *that* guy." She'd heard a version of this story a few months ago, but only after it had passed through a long grapevine. Crane hadn't wanted to talk about it, but then, even in the best of circumstances, Zenobia's knife-obsessed protege would rather stab than talk. "You were trying to get to the Tower or something? It's completely inaccessible. Where are you from that you don't know that?"

And why hadn't Zenobia warned him off? Anybody could have told him the Tower wasn't accessible, and everyone who knew it was would lie to him.

"I'd tell you, but you're giving me vertigo hanging on to the wall like that, princess. Also, Socrates is going to make a circuit of the building in about three minutes."

"How do you know that?"

He shrugged and watched her with interest.

"Wait, did you call me the Zombie Princess?"

"You've got that look of undying rage, like you might bite someone if they pissed you off. All you need is a machete and dead, rotting skin and a crown. But of course, if you tell me your name, I'll call you that instead." His grin was cocky and distracting, almost hiding the look of cool evaluation in his eyes.

She remembered belatedly that she was wearing a purple T-shirt with a graphic of the Zombie Princess on it. She liked his explanation for the nickname better. And the fact that he didn't know her name, apparently, or her face.

"No, I'll answer to Zombie Princess," she said.

She leaped across a gap and landed on a two-inch ledge, gripping brick with her fingertips, the toes of her sneakers scuffing against the tiny sill. She had the satisfaction of hearing his indrawn breath.

"So if you're not launching a dramatic rescue, what then?" he said. "Window washer? Pigeon enthusiast? Cobweb collector?"

"None of your business."

"Is that what you're going to tell Socrates when he comes around the corner in, oh, about thirty seconds or so?"

He couldn't know that, but she glanced at the corner of the building involuntarily. If both Socrates and Tom were as concerned with keeping her away from Zenobia's meeting as they seemed to be, then Socrates might very well follow her to see what she was up to. He knew her habits as well as anyone.

She was drawing close to the window, but Ryan still had his forearms braced on the sill, blocking the opening.

"I need to talk to Zenobia and don't feel like waiting," she said. "Also, I wanted to eavesdrop on her current meeting."

"Oh, so you're not just trying to impress me with your ninja skills? Because it was working, but I'll hold off on the swooning if it won't get me anywhere."

She reached the window and hauled herself upright by her forearms on the sill. He didn't move out of the way, even though their faces were within inches of each other. A bruise darkened on his cheekbone, a remnant of his sparring match with the red-headed Damasker. When he grinned, his teeth were straight and white, as if he'd grown up with actual dental care or with someone as fanatical as Harmony about maintaining oral hygiene.

"Well?" she demanded. "Are you going to let me in or what?"

"So you're a spy."

"Got a problem with that?"

His eyes were a deep river brown with sharp flecks of green.

Not that it mattered, but she could hardly help noticing when they were inches away.

"Not at all. I've been frustrated by Zenobia's habit of keeping secrets too. I support your mission."

He stepped back and politely held out his hand to help her in. She ignored it, but in dragging herself over the sill and ducking under the window, her feet got tangled up and her hip pouch caught the sill and sent her sprawling face first onto the floor.

Well, that could have gone better.

"I'll give you two seconds to wipe the grin off your face," she said to the floor.

When she sat up, he was pressing his lips together hard. He rubbed a hand over his mouth for good measure.

"Your Highness," he said, and his lips curled upward as soon as he gave them freedom, "I think you just fell for me."

"And yet as soon as you opened your mouth, it was all over."

This time she took his hand, and he pulled her effortlessly to her feet. Long fingers, dry and sinewy against her palm, cords of lean muscle in his arm. A row of tattooed blue dots, dark against the warm brown of his skin, traced an enigmatic pause from wrist to elbow on both arms.

He reversed his grip on her hand and shook it vigorously. "I'm Ryan Latrans. Nice to meet you. You've always been my favourite movie princess."

She bit down on a smile. Cocky son of a bitch, sure, but charming.

A thought occurred to her and she stepped back to the window. Moments later, Socrates walked around the corner of the building, idly thwacking the tall grass with a stick and glancing around as if looking for someone.

She stepped out of sight and eyed Ryan more carefully. He carried himself as if he'd been bigger once, until a scouring wind had whittled away every scrap of excess, down to the raw braided wire at his core. There were sharp, wary edges to the bones of his face, but with barely hidden pockets of softness where smiles might bloom when he allowed it.

His clothes were an ordinary zoner mishmash of salvaged items, patched and faded. A military-style knife was sheathed at his hip. His boots, though, barely had a scuff mark on them and had thick clear treads, and those rows of tattooed blue dots on his forearms were sharp and crisp, similar in quality to the tattoos she saw on older generation zoners.

He stared right back at her with an interest that made her wary. The most she could say for her appearance was that she was clean for the first time in two weeks, though her walk had warmed her up enough that her hair was already sticking up in short sweaty spikes.

She was tall for someone who'd lived through years of hunger as a kid, and it was unusual to meet someone her age who topped her height, much less by a good five inches. No one would ever call her scrawny now; Harmony made sure she had meat on her bones, but thanks to the physically gruelling demands of gravving, it was mostly muscle. She had shed the harness, ropes, carabiners and helmet of a grav-walker and wore only a minimal three pouches strapped to her thighs, and a knife. She looked like a grav-walker on her day off. What else was there for him to see?

Most people looked at her and saw only the Pinegirl. She didn't know what he'd see if not that. She wasn't sure she wanted to know.

She stepped past him. He was a mystery to solve later. Right now, she had a conversation to eavesdrop on.

SECRETS AND STRANGERS

The roar of intense rain on the roof
Being the first one awake in the morning

~ Veronica Park (*Things I Will Miss/Reasons to Live*)

"Distract Tom," she told Ryan.

"Excuse me?" he said politely while his eyebrows added expletives.

"That was two words. Which one didn't you understand?"

They'd descended two flights of stairs without seeing anyone, but of course Tom Jitters would be standing directly outside Zenobia's office.

Ryan gave her a hard stare. He opened the stairwell door and stepped into the hall. She could hear Tom informing him sternly that this hallway was currently off limits.

"Sure, right, of course, but I just saw this chick with short hair and a bad attitude literally climbing the wall outside like a damn spider. Maybe someone should check that out."

Okay, maybe she deserved that.

It worked; Tom's footsteps moved swiftly away. "Show me where," he snapped, and Ryan's footsteps joined his. Jasper poked her head out to see them disappear around the corner. A step behind Tom, Ryan grimaced at her, the adult version of a blown raspberry. How mature.

She ducked into the adjoining room to Zenobia's office and put her ear to the wall.

". . . appreciate it if you'd stick with guarding the Tower and leave the cure to me." Zenobia's calm voice held a slight impatience, as if she wanted to wrap this conversation up. "This is no time to be introducing uncertainty and experimentation. Time is running out, and we have to stick with what we know will work."

The answering voice was female but hoarse and gravelly. "A cure that kills is not a cure at all."

"Only seven percent of the mice—"

"Even if I accept your interpretation of the data, that's still thirty-eight percent that suffer catastrophic physical and cognitive disabilities. Even your best prototype, according to you, only has a fifty-five percent chance of her emerging alive and reasonably whole. And you're presenting it as her only choice."

"And I've been waiting for you to offer something better, and all I'm hearing is new age-y, pseudo-scientific quackery. We're both scientists. You have to give me more to go on than speculative what-ifs. What you're suggesting isn't exactly the sort of thing you can test on mice."

"Of course it's theoretical. All of this is a new experience for humanity. It's been twenty-five years since we first discovered the graviteria on that asteroid, and we still have no idea how this alien micro-organism can possibly manipulate gravity. But we do have a very long history with terrestrial bacteria and other micro-organisms. My ideas may be unorthodox, but they're based on valid scientific theory and they fit the facts we have. This is my field, remember, or as close to it as humanity currently has. And my way gives her actual hope—"

"False hope," Zenobia snapped. "The risks go beyond simple death or disability. We don't know what they *want*, what their purpose is. Even if your suggestion worked, we have no idea if the end result would still be . . . Jasper."

"We hardly know that now."

A moment of silence. Jasper's jaw hurt. She forced herself to unclench her teeth. What was that comment supposed to mean? And aside from another Shattering, what risks could be worse than Jasper's death or disability?

"We'll do what we planned," Zenobia said. "This is no time to experiment. We tried that once and look what happened. Never again, do you hear me?"

"And yet she's not the only person who—"

"Enough. We've been over this. I don't want you speaking to her about this. It'll only muddy the waters."

Another pause. "If she asks, I won't lie, Zenobia."

"Why would she ask? She doesn't even know who you are. And you'll keep it that way. We agreed. What happened last time was my responsibility, so I have the right to decide this. I'm the lead on this project."

"The graviteria are a future-changer. You're concerned with saving one person's life, with keeping the status quo. My vision is a little broader than that."

"Is the Shattering broad enough for you? Because I won't risk it again. You're an expert in your field, but I know the graviteria better than anyone alive."

"That's certainly true," the stranger drawled, then paused. "What Tom said about Jasper finding a clue to her mother's body . . . Aren't you afraid she'll actually find it?"

"It's a needle in a haystack, and there's not a lot of time remaining."

"But if there's a kid out there who knows where her mother is, it might not take that long."

Jasper held her breath, head whirling. Why in the small god's name would Zenobia and her visitor care whether Jasper found her mother's bones or not?

The stranger continued, "If Catherine really did steal what she said she did and Jasper finds it—"

"Catherine had nothing," Zenobia said curtly. "She was upset and making threats."

"You've said Jasper barely trusts you as it is."

"Let me worry about Jasper." Zenobia's voice crackled with finality. Jasper heard the rumble of her wheeled office chair being pushed back. "Can I offer you any more tea before you go?"

The meeting was over.

Jasper crouched, frozen in place, trying to absorb what she'd heard. First, this unknown scientist speaking to Zenobia knew about Jasper's condition. She had to be the mysterious Guardian, leader of the ReGeneration, who had helped engineer the opening of the subway tunnel to the Tower so Zenobia could work on Jasper's cure.

And apparently, she had an alternative solution to the antibac that Zenobia was trying to produce, an antibac that could easily cripple or kill Jasper while eliminating the graviteria from her system. Why wouldn't Zenobia want Jasper to know about other options? It was her body and mind that were on the line here.

If she Shattered, half the continent and millions of lives would be at risk. The priority of any proposed solution had to be to prevent a Shattering. Jasper's well-being came a distant second.

Still, if there were other options, she wanted to know about them.

Second, what had Catherine Pine stolen from the Tower that Zenobia didn't want Jasper to find? What was Zenobia keeping from her? That was an unanswerable question; keeping secrets was Zenobia's default setting.

Jasper had told Tom about the amulet Grammar had found, not realizing it would have any significance for Zenobia. Now she knew that Zenobia wouldn't want her finding her mother, but Zenobia didn't know Jasper had been eavesdropping. Jasper had to act as if her interest in finding her mother was purely sentimental or else Zenobia would find some way to stop her.

She also wanted to see the Guardian. The ReGeneration's strange, elusive leader had so many contradictory, improbable stories attached to her that Jasper had almost doubted her existence.

She didn't want to stick her head into the hallway, in case Zenobia saw her. Instead she climbed out of the window, crawled up the wall to the roof, and ran to the front of the building.

The visitor emerged, not from the main entrance but from a side door. The Guardian was an older white woman with a long silver braid. Despite her apparent age, her stride was long and loose, her shoulders square under a voluminous patchwork cloak. She walked briskly across the street in the same direction the two ReGeneration guards had gone with the horses.

As if sensing Jasper's gaze, the Guardian turned and glanced up at the roof. With a cocked head, she considered Jasper for a moment. Then she pulled her cloak around herself and spun in a circle, stamping her feet in a staccato rhythm, like a danced incantation. She threw her head back in a silent laugh, waved at Jasper, and disappeared between two buildings.

The minor encounter left Jasper more unsettled than

seemed reasonable. Who was this woman, and what did she know about Jasper? Why had Zenobia never let Jasper meet her?

"Jasper!" Tom shouted. He and Ryan were standing on the ground below, looking up at her. Tom demanded, "What are you doing up there?"

"I got bored waiting for Zenobia," she called back.

She didn't wait for him to scold her, just crossed back to the other side of the roof and climbed down the wall until she came to Zenobia's office window. She knocked on the glass.

"Jasper, what on earth?" Zenobia peered out at her. She pushed the window open. "What do you have against doors?"

"Elitist. They keep people out."

She scrambled into the office as Zenobia moved out of the way. The ganglord's dark eyebrows arched in question, stark against her pale skin, her perfectly curved lips puckering slightly. She was neat and slight in slim jeans and a long-sleeved black shirt, a blue scarf around her neck. Her smooth chestnut hair was tightly braided and coiled into a knot on her head. She braced her slender, blue-nailed hands over the top of her cane.

"I thought you weren't supposed to be back from gravving for another week," Zenobia said with only a hint of alarm in her voice. She'd probably scheduled this meeting with the Guardian of the ReGeneration to coincide with Jasper's absence. Typical secretive bullshit. Jasper wanted to call her on it, but she also didn't want Zenobia taking further steps to prevent her from finding the ReGeneration members and talking to them herself.

"Pack kids stole our copper."

"Tom mentioned it. Why are you here if you have no copper to trade?"

"Maybe I just missed you."

Zenobia tilted an eyebrow, not appreciating the flippancy. "If that's all, then I'm going to see my dogs. Walk with me if you like."

Jasper would rather eat glass than visit Zenobia's dogs, and Zenobia knew that perfectly well.

"I might have a way of finding my mother," Jasper said casually.

Zenobia's face remained a smooth, blank mask, cool and pale as ice, marred only by the tiny lines that over the years had gathered at the corners of her eyes and mouth.

Fursa, a big black shepherd mix, had been lying quietly on a blanket in a corner. Now he pulled himself heavily to his feet and trotted stiffly to Zenobia's side. She touched his greying muzzle and he licked her hand. Old scars covered his body, bite marks, burn marks, knife slices, silvering hairless patches telling a story of cruelty and a savage youth.

Jasper gave the dog a look, he gave her a look back, and then they ignored each other.

"Your mother?" Zenobia's voice betrayed nothing beyond mild interest.

Just then, the door opened, and Crane wandered in. "You been finishen your dumb meeting now?"

Attracted by the movement, a tiny black cat raced out from under a chair to attack Crane's shoelaces. Crane hopped up on a table like a frog, all elbows and knees and long skinny legs in heavy boots. Her frizzy hair formed an explosion around her small brown face. She pulled a slingshot out and aimed it at the cat, who crouched in front of the table, tail swishing.

"Zen, be callen off this hell creature."

"Marvel won't hurt you if you leave her alone," Zenobia said distractedly. "Get your boots off my table."

Crane ignored the command. She screwed up her face in concentration and released the missile in the slingshot. The cat meowed and chased after it, an acorn.

Zenobia wheeled around. "Crane, you'd better not be shooting at my cat."

Crane sat back on her bum and let her long legs dangle off the table, one of them still encased in a heavy knee brace to support the newly healed bone. She'd broken it during her adventure with Ryan in the zones. "I'm missen," she said. "On purpose."

Zenobia frowned. "Let's review. What is our cardinal rule?"

Crane scowled and rolled her eyes. "No killen."

"And?"

"No hurten the cats and dogs."

"And how about humans?"

Crane swung her legs restlessly. Yellow patches had been sewn over the knees of her favourite red jeans. "Only if you're tellen me. Or if they're threatenen you. Or me."

"And do insults count as threats?"

This apparently was a point of contention because it took a long pointed stare from Zenobia before Crane mumbled a reluctant "No."

"That's right. Now, didn't I send you to get some tea?"

Crane kicked her heels, brown eyes falling on Jasper. She said slyly, "But I'm your bodyguard. Shouldn't be leaven you alone with the Pinegirl."

"I'll take my chances," Zenobia said with no apparent irony.

"I'd like to see you try and stop me anyway," Jasper said. The Pinegirl comment had rankled.

Crane's heavy boots hit the floor, and a long wickedly sharp knife appeared in one skinny hand. "I'll be wearen your face one day."

"It'd be an improvement on your actual face," Jasper retorted.

"Yours too," Crane said, grinning sharply. The knife spun on her palm.

"Girls," Zenobia said. "Tom just fixed the table from your last squabble in here. Start another fight and you'll both be cleaning out the dog cages. Crane, the tea, please."

Crane flicked the knife back into its sheath. As she clomped out of the room, she flashed a rude sign at Jasper. Jasper crossed her eyes in return and stuck out her tongue.

The door slammed behind Crane. They were alone.

"Must you provoke her?" Zenobia said. "You know how she is."

Jasper certainly did. Crane had once been part of Jasper's kid pack long ago. They'd run free and wild together. Then they'd walked side by side through the valley of hell. They'd crouched in adjacent cages. They'd survived Darius's games. But in the younger girl, Darius had broken that shiny, sharp glass thing, that barometer of right and wrong that most people had and Crane no longer did. Crane could be frankly fucking scary. But no scarier than the inside of Jasper's head on any given day.

"It's entertaining," Jasper said flippantly. "Makes me feel alive."

Zenobia shook her head. "You're two of a kind, I swear."

For an instant she hated Zenobia intensely. She and Crane were not the same. Crane didn't feel guilt or question why she was the way she was. She didn't even realize how broken she was.

Says the broken pot to the broken kettle, Darius said.

"Tell me," said Zenobia. Nothing in her voice or face suggested she was less than eager to hear Jasper's news.

"One of the kids who stole our copper was wearing Mom's amulet." Jasper pulled out her own. "We—she, me, and Ben—made them together before the Shattering. She never took hers off, so he must have gotten it from her body."

"And did the child agree to take you to your mother?"

"He was in the process of robbing us, so no, he didn't agree to do us any favours. But right afterwards he was captured by Damaskers."

"Ah. That makes things difficult." If Zenobia was relieved, she didn't show it.

Difficult for whom? Jasper felt a stab of alarm. If Zenobia didn't want Jasper to find her mother, what would she do to the one person who knew where to find Catherine Pine? Had Jasper just put Grammar in danger? But he wasn't exactly safe as it was; he was trapped in the heart of Damascus. At least Zenobia had no influence there.

A knock on the door. Tom poked his head in and frowned at the sight of Jasper. "Young lady—"

Jasper stuck her tongue out at him just as Ryan squeezed past him to enter the room uninvited. "Sorry about that," Ryan said cheerfully. "I guess we're all friends here after all. I got concerned—I mean she could've been an assassin for all I knew."

Tom snorted, an involuntary sound of either amusement or disapproval.

"Is that a joke?" Jasper demanded, caught between wanting to laugh and suspicion of this stranger who seemed to know both too much and too little.

"All right, a bad joke, I'll admit," Ryan said, eyebrows lifting. "Assassin's a bit of a stretch—"

Zenobia laughed. It was so unexpected and strange that Jasper stared at her. Zenobia swallowed her mirth almost instantly and put a hand to her mouth. "Sorry."

Jasper glared at her and pointed at Ryan. "Okay, what's going on with this guy?"

"With me?" Ryan looked confused but also wary. "What do you mean?"

But Zenobia understood what Jasper meant. "He's from the other side of the city."

Scattered communities, families, and individuals lived all around the circumference of the city in the down-gee buffer zone inside the quarantine walls. Quick Rick and Merlot and other peddlers visited these people regularly. All of them would have heard of the Pinegirl.

However, a large portion of the city remained unexplored, even by grav-walkers and pack kids, because it was riddled with impenetrable swaths of foam zones. Foam zones were conglomerations of tiny gravity zones packed densely together, as fragile and insubstantial as dish soap foam. They were filled with a floating honeycomb of debris and nearly impossible to navigate safely.

Reasonably sized down-gee pockets could conceivably lie hidden within those foam zones, and if so, people might have managed to survive there for fifteen years, so cut off from the rest of the city that they'd never heard of Darius Dalca or the Pinegirl. So theoretically, Ryan could have found a way through the foam zones. But if so, he'd be the first person in fifteen years to do so.

Tom's face was nothing but an impassive, watchful mask, so Jasper studied Zenobia, marvelling again at what an accomplished liar the Azuro ganglord was. "No, he's not," Jasper finally said.

Zenobia's eyes cooled into Arctic darkness. "No?"

"Look at his shoes."

Ryan looked down. "What's wrong with—?"

"Nothing. That's the problem. They're brand new. Not just well-preserved—the design and material are new. Then there's the teeth. And the tattoos." *And the fact that he doesn't know who I am.*

Zenobia and Tom exchanged a glance. Tom's face said, *I told you so.* Zenobia's face said, *Shut up.*

"Ryan's not a zoner," Jasper said. "He's a downie."

8

THICKER THAN BLOOD

That warm, golden summer dusk, potent as wine
Tea and a good book when it's storming out

~ Veronica Park (*Things I Will Miss/Reasons to Live*)

"I feel like I've been insulted," said Ryan. "What's a downie?"

"The fact that you don't know is proof that you are one," said Jasper.

Zenobia sighed in annoyance and turned to Ryan. "I thought I told you to go talk to the Damaskers."

He shrugged, still eyeing Jasper. "I did. We talked, we fought, I left. They really hate you, Zenobia. They think you're the devil's whore. That's a direct quote."

"I was hoping for new and useful information, but thank you —you can go."

Before Ryan could protest, Tom hustled him out of the room, shutting the door behind them.

84 | V. R. FRIESEN

"So I'm right. He's an outsider. He came through the quarantine gates," Jasper said. "He's not a zoner at all."

Zenobia moved slowly over to her leather chair and lowered herself into it, leaning her cane on the table beside it. Fursa lay down at her feet. "Yes. It's an unfortunate consequence of the messages I've been exchanging with my colleagues on the outside, concerning materials for the antibac."

"How so?"

Though a narrow stream of trade could pass through the quarantine gates, information was strictly controlled. Nobody but Zenobia had ever received communications from the outside world, which had been told that the Shattering had left no survivors—and the powers that be wanted to keep it that way. It was less messy and required fewer explanations for things that defied explanation and could cause panic. Zenobia had some influential contacts, however, and she'd been using them to obtain the tools and materials and research data she needed to develop Jasper's cure.

"All our messages are encrypted, of course, and I relay as little information as possible about the situation, about you. That still leaves enough breadcrumbs for someone to draw conclusions. Fortunately for us, they're mostly the wrong conclusions."

"What does Ryan know?" Jasper perched on the table.

"Whoever sent him thinks there's still graviteria samples in the Tower, and he doesn't believe me when I say there's no way into the Tower. Needless to say, Ryan can't know about you."

He couldn't know because Jasper was a walking graviteria sample, the only living human host to an alien. She was a Shattering waiting to happen. If anyone learned of her existence, she'd either be worth more than the economic output of some countries, or she wouldn't be worth the dust on her shoes. They'd either find some way to exploit and monetize her unique condition, or they'd kill her instantly to remove the possibility of another Shattering.

"Why would they send only one guy?"

"After what happened to the last few expeditions, they must have decided a small undercover operation would be more effective. One man can blend in, pretend he's a zoner and enlist the help of locals."

The first downie expedition had entered the zones only a few months after the quarantine wall went up. The human element in the zones at the time had been chaotic, desperate and violent, and the zones themselves were terrifying, possessed by an inexplicable sorcery understood by no one. Gravity had been broken by magic or aliens or time travellers or lightning bolts from a petty god throwing a tantrum for reasons as trivial and arbitrary as any toddler's— such as people daring to love the wrong people or to cross imaginary lines on the ground in search of safety and better futures. Nothing made sense. No one knew what to expect, what supernatural entity to propitiate and how, what sins to mend, and what sinners to sacrifice.

No one from the first expedition survived.

Jasper had heard a pack kid chanting a song that listed the deaths. Not the most reliable source, but it claimed that three had died of falls, stumbling into zones they hadn't been expecting or looking for. Two had died in a gas fire explosion. One had been killed by a starving grizzly bear escaped from the zoo. One had died when a lawn mower blew out of an up-gee zone and fell on her head. The remaining two had gotten into an altercation with some desperate Shattering survivors and ended up bludgeoned to death.

The second expedition had been better equipped and prepared, and they had arrived three years post-Shattering. They had initially been greeted with open arms by zoners hungry for contact with the outside world and desperate to be released from quarantine. It quickly became clear, however, that they had no plan to rescue survivors and that quarantine would remain in place indefinitely. Anger and resentment flared hot and ugly, violence erupted, and soon half the expedition were killed and a dozen zoners as well. The remainder of the downies were stripped of their gear and supplies and deposited unceremoniously at the gate, with the message that until the Shattering survivors were released and quarantine lowered, no one else would be permitted to enter the city.

"We're zoners now," Sparrow had said afterwards. "If they won't let us out, we won't let them in. If they won't help us, then we owe them nothing. This is our city now, our zones, our land."

The outside world had other problems to deal with, more pressing, comprehensible, and solvable ones than one violent and rebellious, scientifically impossible, potentially infectious, electronics-killing city.

At her most cynical and bitter, Sparrow would mutter about how the majority of the people unable to escape the crumbling city in the hours after the Shattering had been the ones without vehicles; the ones who didn't live in fancy suburbs in the city's outskirts but in cramped inner-city apartments; the ones with no homes at all; the ones who didn't understand enough English to read or hear the evacuation directions; and the ones lacking the influence, connections, or money to wheedle their way out of quarantine in the early days when the fence was still porous.

Many of those people happened to have skin on the browner end of the spectrum. Apparently, the outside world had no problem forgetting their existence and leaving them to rot. So what else was new? At this point in Sparrow's diatribe, Ibtisam would send her to go hit a punching bag until she could breathe again.

No more expeditions into the zones had been authorized.

"Ryan's a soldier," Zenobia said. "Don't underestimate him,

and don't be charmed by that smile of his. In fact, just stay away from him."

"So why are you letting him hang around? And don't say anything about the kindness of your heart. I'm trying to have a serious conversation here." Jasper leaned forward. "Hey, did you tell Crane to kill him in the zones, or was that her own idea?"

"I thought if he saw the foam zones around the Tower with his own eyes it might satisfy him that there's no way in and then he'd leave. And for heaven's sake, I did *not* tell Crane to kill him, Jasper. I love how you still insist on thinking the absolute worst of me."

You've earned it, Jasper thought. "But did you tell her specifically not to? I mean, it's Crane."

"Very funny. They never actually got to the Tower, so he's not ready to give up. I thought it best for him to stay here where I can keep an eye on him. He wants to try again once Crane's leg is fully mended, which it essentially is now." She frowned at Jasper. "I was hoping he'd never meet you at all."

Jasper kicked off her sneakers and stood up on the table, balancing on the balls of her feet. She stretched her arms up to the lofty, vaulted ceiling. "Hey, if the Damaskers are camped outside, does that mean Nico's here?"

"He's in the trading hall. Why?"

"Because his gangers stole our copper and I want it back."

Also she might be able to negotiate a chance to speak to Grammar. Zenobia didn't need to know that, but judging from the narrowing of her eyes she'd guessed.

"Be careful with him," Zenobia said. "Nico might have a soft spot for you, but the Damaskers don't exactly worship you. Your association with me dilutes your legend."

"Worth a shot, though."

Jasper leaped from the table to the low bookshelf and from there hopped onto the taller bookshelf, which wobbled under her weight but held. From there she could almost touch the ceiling.

Zenobia sighed. "Thank you for taking off your shoes, I guess."

"One problem." Jasper sat on top of the bookshelf and kicked idly. "One little detail about this kid. Maybe it's nothing, but I'm sure you can tell me if it's true or not."

Zenobia propped her head on her hand. "Jasper, spit it out. Contrary to appearances, I've got more going on in my life than your problems."

"So it would seem. This kid calls himself Grammar, and he's known as the Devilman's son."

Zenobia opened her eyes wide and sat very still.

"He looks like he could be twelve or thirteen."

"Hmm," said Zenobia after a while.

"Is that all you've got to say?"

Zenobia levered herself to her feet with her cane and walked over to a cupboard to pull out a syringe. She pointed to a chair. "Get down from there. May as well check your blood while you're here."

Jasper obliged without taking her eyes off Zenobia.

"Grammar," Zenobia said, her voice steady. She swabbed Jasper's arm. "What an interesting name."

Blood rose in an ochre column, filling the syringe. Zenobia carried the sample to the microscope kept on a shelf by the window. Jasper glanced at the door. Crane hadn't returned yet; neither had Tom Jitters.

"That son you had twelve years ago," Jasper said. "Is it possible he's not quite as dead as you told people he was?"

Zenobia kept her back turned. She placed a drop of blood on a glass slide. "What a thing to say, Jasper. I think I can tell the difference between a living child in my arms and a dead one."

Yeah, I'll bet.

"Anyway, it's the sort of thing a pack kid would claim to seem badass. It means nothing."

"Sure," said Jasper. "Except I was face to face with him, and trust me, I won't be the only one to see the resemblance—like Nico when he hears about this Devilman's son his gangers have captured. I'm sure he'll be ecstatic to know he has your son in custody."

Zenobia stiffened. Jasper waited, fascinated. Trying to elicit reactions from the ganglord was an unrewarding game at the best of times, and Jasper hungered to land a good jab, to force out a genuine sliver of emotion. She might even get an answer to the age-old question: Did Zenobia Allan have an actual heart, or just a clever machine built of copper and steel that pumped ice water and secrets through her veins?

More to the point, Zenobia wouldn't hurt her own son, even if he held a secret she didn't want Jasper to know. Or would she?

"Fine, Jasper." Zenobia turned. Her face was as blank and pale as Jasper had ever seen it. "Yes, Grammar is my son. And I'll trust you with that knowledge, because you of all people should understand how people will never see *him*. They'll just see his parents. And they'll hate him for it. They can't touch Darius and there are consequences for touching me, so they'll heap the punishments we deserve on him instead."

Except for the expressionless face, she was almost convincing as a human being who cared about the well-being of a child. An outsider like Ryan might even believe her words to be those of a loving mother rather than those of a calculating manipulator.

"More importantly, people would try to use him against you," Jasper said. "Like Nico and the Damaskers. Endangering everything you've built. The kid makes you vulnerable. He could be your downfall. You can't have that, can you? He's an inconvenience, a weakness you can't afford."

And he was the only person who knew where Catherine Pine's body was, along with whatever she'd stolen from the Tower.

Zenobia compressed her lips but she didn't respond.

"What was your plan anyway?" Jasper asked. "He's close enough to puberty. It was only a matter of time before he got caught up in a raid and joined a gang. What were you going to do then?"

Zenobia stood still, calculation passing through her eyes. "You have to break him out," she said at last.

"Excuse me?" Jasper was thrown off balance, but only for a moment. It was obvious Zenobia thought she was choosing the lesser of two dangers. Her son in Nico Mavuto's hands posed far too much risk to herself and her Azuros and to the hard-won acceptance and prosperity she'd built for them. Zenobia couldn't reach him while he was in Damasker custody, but if he was freed, she'd have access to him. Jasper conceded that Zenobia probably wouldn't kill her own son, but she was perfectly capable of abducting him herself and extracting the necessary information. Then she would send someone to grab whatever Catherine had stolen before Jasper could find it.

"How am I supposed to break into the Damasker compound? They're a fanatical army."

"You're the Pinegirl. You'll figure something out."

"Don't you fucking call me that."

They stared at each other across the room. Zenobia looked away first, shoulders softening. "I'm sorry, Jasper."

"And don't pretend you're sorry!" Anger exploded in her chest and clawed at her throat. "Sometimes I can't even stand the sight of your face, you know that?"

Zenobia stared at the wall and waited. Her patient "Yes, I know I deserve this, but can we get on with it?" face. Jasper wanted to scratch her icy eyeballs out.

Fursa sat up and watched Jasper under twitching eyebrows. She hissed and kicked in his direction. He didn't move. He was missing a chunk of his left ear. She'd bitten a dog's ear off once. That had been a Rottweiler, though, and he'd eaten a chunk out of her leg, so fair play.

Zenobia lifted the glass slide with Jasper's blood on it. "Can we talk about your blood now?"

Jasper took a breath and forced it out until her lungs ached with emptiness. "You said last time I had six months."

"As the graviteria mature, they're replicating faster. I'd say three months now is more realistic."

Three months. Not even long enough to see the leaves change colour.

Sunlight filled her eyes, blinding her. It was too much to absorb. Even if she had an ordinary lifespan, she'd never be able to contain this much light. It would spill out of her eyes and glide down her skin and leave her as dark inside as before.

"How's that cure coming?" Her voice came out flat.

"It's promising. There's a very good chance you'll come through unscathed."

And an equally good chance she'd end up so impaired she'd never walk or form coherent sentences again. But at least there'd be no second Shattering, right?

A trio of crows flew across the face of the rising sun, like a flutter of scars on the eye.

"About the boy . . ." Zenobia hesitated. "It's not his fault who his parents are."

"It sure isn't, poor little bastard." She narrowed her eyes at Zenobia. "If I do this insane thing and break him out, it won't be for you. I'm not taking him to see his mom for tea and cookies."

"I doubt he'd want to see me anyway." It was impossible to tell if she was bothered by this or not.

Zenobia wouldn't get her own hands dirty, even if her body

were physically strong enough to do so. If not Jasper, she'd send somebody else for Grammar—Crane maybe, or even Tom. Or pay a stranger.

Jasper leaned forward, studying Zenobia's controlled expression. "But you do care for him, right? Like, he's your son. If you didn't love him, you wouldn't care if Nico got his hands on him, and you'd let him die without blinking an eye. Isn't that right?"

Zenobia returned her stare long enough to make it clear she had no intention of answering. Was she capable of love? Jasper wouldn't have bet a lot of copper on it. Some, but not a lot.

A sharp knock at the door turned them both around.

Tom Jitters poked his head in. "Crane and Nico are arguing in the trading hall," he said tersely. "Doesn't look good."

Zenobia muttered something under her breath that sounded like a curse. She grabbed her cane and stalked out of the room with Fursa trotting at her heels. Jasper hastily pulled on her shoes and followed.

9

FATHERS AND DAUGHTERS

A set of dumb nicknames with somebody that no one else is
   allowed to call you by
The dip and swoop of swinging on a swing set

~ Veronica Park (*Things I Will Miss/Reasons to Live*)

I n the middle of the trading hall, Crane, a narrow furious figure in skinny red jeans and with a dramatic shock of hair, faced off with her father. Knives sheathed at her hips, across her back, strapped to her ankles, hidden under her clothes. The air itself edged warily past her, shredded by her sharp points and angles and scissory eyes.

Nico Mavuto, commander of the Damasker army, was as thick and broad as his daughter was thin and rangy. Despite his size, he moved lightly, deliberately, as if ensuring the ground would hold him before setting his weight down. Lines of self-inflicted scars formed geometric patterns across his flat cheekbones, a map of grim pain carved into his dark brown skin.

"I'm tellen you not to talk to me, old man."

"I was just saying hello, Freeya. The least you could do is say hello back."

"*Crane!* My name's Crane!"

Nico's face fell into familiar lines of anger and annoyance, his fists forming belligerent punctuation to his words. "I'm your father, and I'll call you by the name your mother and I gave you if I goddamn like. If she could see you now . . ."

Crane's lips curled back from her teeth. "You ain't my papa."

"No matter how many times you say it, missy, it doesn't change the fact. Christ, you have your mother's stubbornness."

Crane stilled. "Got no mama."

Nico scraped a hand across the wiry, greying hair he kept shaved close to his skull. He shook his head in frustration. "Not anymore, but you did. With my own eyes I watched you come out of your mother all smeared in blood and screaming your head off. Martha Abebe was your mother, and she loved you a damn sight more than she loved anything else on this earth— including me. And I know Darius Dalca, that fucking monster, brainwashed you but—"

"Don't be talken about him!" Crane screamed, her voice as high and thin as a child's.

"I'll talk about him if I damn well please," Nico shouted back. "The man's fucking dead, and good riddance. And one of these days, you've got to realize that his bitch over here is just as bad as—"

Crane lunged at him, pummelling him with her small knobby fists.

"Crane, stop right now!" Zenobia's voice cut through the scuffle and the voices of the bystanders.

But Jasper knew that Crane was in another place now, a place where rage became so pure, it flattened reality into one dimension. There was no alternate side to the story, no morals for balance, no voice of greater authority, no concept of future consequences.

Jasper felt the thrum of that rage keening behind her eyes and lifting the hairs on her arms. This was old, old anger between Crane and her father, anger with the metallic aftertaste of a child's uncomprehending pain. Jasper knew that unique taste, that flavour of an open wound immune to the passage of time.

The Azuros watched and muttered wagers to each other, but they made no move to interfere. Crane was a fellow Azuro now, but even they were wary of her, this creature Darius had created. Zenobia shouted again, to no avail. Fursa barked furiously, as if reminded of his violent youth.

Nico was a brawler and a former soldier, easily twice his daughter's weight. Even as Crane struck wildly at him with her hands and feet and knees, he held his fists up to protect his face and crowded her until he could lunge close and wrap her in a bear hug that pinned her arms to her sides. She bucked and fought and cried out in frustration.

Then somehow, even with her arms pinioned, a small blade appeared in her hand. A flick of her wrist and a rip appeared in Nico's shirt across his ribs. He cried out in pain and Crane tore free.

A man threw himself between Crane and Nico. It was the downie soldier, Ryan Latrans. Crane aimed a savage thrust at Ryan's rib cage.

He slammed her knife hand between both of his, jarring the knife loose. Then a shift of weight, a jerk and a twist of her arm, a kick to the back of her knees, and he had her kneeling with her arm twisted up and back at a painful angle. Crane screeched with pain and rage but couldn't move.

Nico started forward with a growl, his bloodshot eyes focused on Ryan's back. He was spoiling for a fight even after Ryan had saved his life.

Jasper darted in front of Nico and planted a hand on his chest. "It's over, Nico. It's done."

Meaningless words. So many things were over and done and left in the past, yet their ghosts remained in the present, taking up space so solidly, they left bruises.

"Stay out of it, Jasper." But Nico stopped, swaying forward as if only her hand held him up. She caught the whiff of alcohol on his breath, but it was only a hint compared to the miasma he'd carried with him for years after Darius Dalca's death. Too bad he'd cured his drinking by creating an army of feral teenagers. An army fuelled by hatred of Zenobia and her Azuros, and by deeds committed so long ago that few Damaskers were old enough to remember them.

Not that memory of a thing was a prerequisite for it being able to fuck you up. A case in point: Crane.

"Had enough?" Ryan asked Crane.

She snarled in response, and he twitched her arm up. A stream of curses and then an annoyed "Okay, yeah, downie, enough!"

Ryan grinned over his shoulder at Jasper. "Oh, hey, princess. Thanks for the assist."

"I have a soft spot for idiots." Jasper eyed Nico so he'd know she wasn't just referring to Ryan.

"You need to mind your own business, Latrans," Nico said. Belatedly, he reached down to touch the rip in his shirt and the line of red across his ribs.

"It *is* my business if I'm the newbie around here who has to do all the shit jobs like cleaning up blood," Ryan said.

Nico studied him. "You move like someone who served."

Ryan's smile faltered for barely a second. He said smoothly, "I was trained by a soldier."

Nico gave him another evaluative look, then grunted and turned away, seeming to accept the cover story.

Zenobia strode forward, leaning on her cane. "Crane, how many times have we gone over the rules about fighting?"

Crane's rage had switched off cold. Despite the uncomfortable position Ryan was holding her in, she looked up at Zenobia. "Not been tryen to kill Ryan. I been knowen he'd stop me." Her grin sliced narrowly across her face. "Just testen him."

Zenobia sighed. "And your father? What did I tell you would happen if you started another fight with him?"

"Consequences," Crane answered, sullen now. Under her breath, quietly enough to be ignored, she added, "He *ain't* my papa."

Zenobia nodded at Ryan and he released Crane. She picked up her knife and unfolded her body and got to her feet, swivelling her arm gently. The circle of bystanders backed away several steps. Ryan stood his ground, but his relaxed stance was deceptive. When Crane set her feet and faced him squarely, he smiled. Spectators leaned forward, braced for the show of a lifetime.

Crane smiled back at Ryan, toothy as a crocodile. "Little wildcat downie."

"Knifey little hedgehog," he responded easily.

"Should've left you in the zones."

"Same."

Crane laughed, a less than reassuring sound, but sheathed her knife. Everyone breathed easier.

Zenobia rapped her cane on the ground sharply. "Show's over, folks. Back to work."

The Azuros returned to their posts, and the few zoners who had arrived early to trade drifted away, discussing the fight in pairs and clumps.

Zenobia turned to Nico. "You have permission to be here only on the condition you cause no trouble."

Nico's eyes flared with hatred. "Listen, I didn't start anything. All I did was greet my daughter. You're the bitch who stole her from me in the first place and turned her against me."

"Trade or leave, Nico. There is no room for violence or verbal abuse in my station."

"Oh, *your* station, is it?" His laugh was vicious. "You shouldn't even be breathing the same air as the rest of us."

Zenobia didn't flinch. "Say what you like about me, but this is my house, my rules. Feel free to take your business somewhere else, to all the other gates in quarantine."

Of course there were no other gates. Zenobia had a monopoly on trade with the outside.

Nico laughed mirthlessly. This close, Jasper could see every ridged scar on his face. She'd watched him inflict some of them. They seemed less disturbing than the puffy hollows under his bloodshot eyes and his raw, chapped lips. He'd held his grudge for over a decade, and he seemed willing to hold on to it for a little longer. He hacked up some saliva, and Jasper moved aside just in time before he spat it on the ground between himself and Zenobia.

He shook himself free of Jasper, gave her a bitter look, and walked away. He didn't hate Jasper, not yet. He was a man who held on to gratitude as stubbornly as grudges, and he continued to honour Jasper for the deed that had earned her name. But every time she stepped up to defend or support Zenobia, his respect for her eroded a little more. His goodwill wouldn't last forever, and when it was gone, very little would remain to protect her from his feral followers.

Zenobia turned to speak to Socrates, who had been relieved from his post at the entrance. As he spoke, he kept a jaundiced eye on Nico's progress around the hall.

Crane chewed on a fingernail. Slouched and graceless as any sullen teen, she seemed unfazed by the fight just past. She had carelessly wiped her knife on her red jeans, leaving a smear of darker red.

Tom Jitters approached Crane quietly and held out his hand. She worked her tongue around her mouth and then spat between his boots. He didn't move. She pulled out her belt knife and slapped the hilt into his hand, followed by the two sheathed across her back. He waited. Crane pulled two more blades from her boots, another from under her shirt, and a tiny dagger cunningly hidden in the buckle of her belt. Tom looked at the blades in his hands, as if counting them, and then back at Crane. She scowled but shoved her hand down the waistband of her jeans and pulled out one last taped-up razorblade. Tom nodded and gave a jerk of his chin. Crane stalked past him, and people scurried to get out of her way.

Ryan also watched Crane leave. Absently, he cracked his knuckles. The line of tattooed blue dots on his forearms flexed with the movement.

"I'm no expert on healthy father-daughter relationships," he said. "But what's the deal with those two?"

So many ways to answer that question. Jasper's eye fell on Fursa, seated at Zenobia's side. His jaw gaped, tongue lolling between rows of worn fangs. Jasper shuddered. "Trust me, it's not a story you want to know."

Now he scrutinized her instead. "Did he hit her? Fiddle with her?"

His bluntness surprised her into answering honestly. "No. Not that I ever knew of anyway. If he fights her nowadays, it's because it's the only way he can make Crane even look at him. It wasn't Nico who did anything to Crane—it was Darius. He made Crane . . . he made her . . ." She ran out of words and she had to blink for a while to see anything but silent, screaming white.

When she could see again, Ryan was standing much closer to her. She still couldn't speak, so she shrugged. The language to explain what Darius had done hadn't been invented yet.

"I've heard people mention Darius," Ryan said. "Some psychotic white dude, wasn't he, who got broken out of prison by the Shattering? He and his buddies took control of the refugee camps, but apparently he was fifty shades of crazy and got himself killed, and people splintered into the separate gangs that exist today. Did I get that right?"

Jasper rubbed her fingers over her mouth, not sure if she was smoothing away a hysterical laugh or the urge to spit. Was that how the history books—if any were ever written about the zones —would sum up over two years of violence and suffering?

'Fifty shades of crazy'? Darius chuckled. That's . . . I think that's the nicest thing anyone's ever said about me.

"I take it there's more to the story than that," he said, watching her face.

She shook her head. No, leave it at that, a nice, dry, bloodless paragraph unadorned by a single scream or nightmare or severed appendage.

Raised voices got their attention, turning them around. A skinny white woman with a haggard face was carrying a small wrapped-up bundle and arguing with Socrates, who was preventing her from approaching Zenobia.

"Lady, I've told you a hundred times that we can't help the brat," Socrates said impatiently. "The downies don't let any zoner through the gates. Not once in fifteen years. You know that. Everyone fucking knows that. So bug off already."

"But if you told them he was going to die . . ." the woman

pleaded. "On the outside they could fix him so easily. They can send him back after. I'm not asking for him to be let out forever. I just don't want him to die."

"You think we haven't tried that?" Socrates was losing patience. "There've been sick and dying babies before, and not one has been allowed through. Now quit bothering the boss with this. There's nothing we can do."

A few feet away Zenobia listened, wrapped in silence, cool and remote. Nearly impossible to believe, looking at her, that she'd been a mother herself once. But she'd faked her child's death and given him away, and he'd ended up running feral in the zones. Hardly a role model for parenthood.

The distraught woman wheeled around, looking for support, and her untethered gaze fell on Jasper. "You have to help me. She'll listen to you." She thrust the bundle at Jasper.

Jasper caught a glimpse of a feeble, pale arm, translucent eyelids in a tiny thin face, and recoiled. Layered over the whiff of feces and illness, the smell of desperation and need hit her like a slap in the face.

Without waiting for an answer, the woman turned back to Zenobia. "Where's your compassion? Are you made of stone?"

"Time for you to leave." Socrates grabbed her arm to propel her toward the door.

"Wait." Zenobia's voice stopped them. She handed Socrates her cane, approached the mother, and held out her hands. "There is one thing I can do for you."

Trembling and pale with unwilling hope, the woman let Zenobia take her infant. The ganglord cradled the child expertly in the crook of one arm. She adjusted the baby's wrappings, taking one end of the blanket and winding it more firmly around his neck. And then again, tightening the cord of cloth. The child coughed and gasped, its tiny face turning red.

"What are you doing?" the mother whispered. Her voice rose to a shriek. "What are you doing? You *monster!*"

She lurched forward, but Socrates kicked her behind the knees, sending her sprawling.

"You wanted my help," Zenobia said. "A quick and merciful death is all I have to offer."

10

DROP OF RED

It's all fun and games
Till someone trips over the illusion of free will
And gets hurt.

~ Veronica Park (*Story of a Monster*)

The mother screamed, and Ryan moved. He leaped past her and Socrates.

Then skidded to a halt, facing the barrel of Zenobia's revolver. Because she was no longer using that hand to strangle the child, he stopped and stared her down. His hands were raised and flexed, ready to wrap around her throat. His locs crackled with barely restrained motion.

"Thank you, Ryan." Zenobia deposited the child neatly into his arms. Her revolver disappeared back under her shirt. She reclaimed her cane from Socrates.

Jasper sucked in a breath, feeling as if she'd been the one being strangled for the last few seconds.

Ryan turned away from Zenobia. As if mesmerized, he stared down at the wailing infant before surrendering him into his sobbing mother's arms.

"You'll not be permitted inside the trading hall again until your child has died," Zenobia said. "My condolences in advance."

Clutching her child to her chest, the woman's wild-eyed gaze fell not on Zenobia but on Jasper. "Why'd you let her live, Pinegirl? She was always the real evil one, a witch, the devil's own whore. You should've killed her when you had the chance!"

Something shook loose, dislodged in Jasper's chest and exploded out of her mouth. "Why didn't *you*? Why didn't anyone else? Why did it have to be me?"

Socrates had the woman's arm and was dragging her away, but she said angrily over her shoulder, "She's your responsibility now."

She and Socrates disappeared toward the exit. Jasper whirled and kicked a nearby folding chair and sent it flying into a table. Anger rattled against her ribs like broken teeth.

"What the hell was that, Zenobia?" Ryan asked coldly.

Jasper let her anger fall where it belonged, into the decaying graveyard of old dead things that didn't matter anymore. She turned.

"Do you have an opinion to share, Ryan?" Zenobia asked in a tone only somewhat warmer than frostbite.

"Were you really going to kill a child?" he demanded, his voice tight.

When Zenobia simply returned his stare, Ryan glanced at Jasper. The expression on his face gave her the same sickening roiling in her stomach as the first time Darius had made her choose somebody else's fate. She fought the urge to shout at him to run, to escape now before anyone said another word.

"What a naive question, young man." Nico had returned to

watch the altercation and grinned humourlessly, as if pleased that all his worst suspicions had been confirmed. "Zenobia Allan has never made an empty threat. It's almost as if you're not from around here."

Ryan's stance was now tinged with caution, but his expression didn't waver. "I haven't been on this side of the zones before, so yeah, I'm new here."

Nico raised his eyebrows incredulously. "There's a part of the zones that hasn't heard the stories of Zenobia and Darius? Take me to this magical land of innocence."

"Move along, Mavuto," Socrates said.

Nico shrugged. "Sure, sure, but it seems you've neglected this young man's education. I'd be happy to fill in the gaps for him, but I'm giving you a chance to tell your version first. Isn't that generous of me?"

Socrates glanced at Zenobia for direction. She didn't move for a long time. Then she glanced at Jasper with a wordless question, an apology in advance.

"Maybe someone can enlighten me on whatever I'm missing here," Ryan said, "since everyone else already seems privy to it."

Nico clapped him on the shoulder. "You seem like a good man, the kind who believes the best of others, like this nice lady here who just happens to be running one of the zones' most powerful gangs. What you just saw was a glimpse of Zenobia's true nature."

Ryan's frown deepened as he considered Zenobia. She looked back impassively.

Nico continued remorselessly, "Son, have you ever seen dozens of children kept in cages half starved and covered in their own filth? Have you ever heard the sounds a human makes when they're thrown into a pit of vicious, starving dogs? Have you ever played a poker game where the stakes weren't money but your limbs, your fingers and toes and arms and legs? Well, have you?"

Jasper closed her eyes. When she'd been eleven or twelve and Harmony was still attempting to give her an education, they'd done a simple experiment in diffusion. They introduced a drop of red food colouring into a glass of clear water. Just one tiny drop. But it could not, would not, maintain its discrete shape and identity. It refused to amiably coexist with the clean, innocent water. That one tiny drop unfurled, defying the laws of space and time with the payload of contamination it delivered. The process didn't end until every particle of clear water had been coloured red.

"This was . . ." Ryan cleared his throat and started again. "This was under Darius Dalca?"

"Let Jasper tell him, Nico," Zenobia said.

Jasper opened her eyes in shock at this betrayal.

"Of course," Nico said agreeably. "The Pinegirl is the hero of the story, after all."

She shook her head in denial. Ryan was the first clean glass of water she'd encountered in a long time, and only now did she realize how thirsty she'd been. Zenobia had told her to stay away from Ryan so he couldn't figure out that she harboured an alien inside her, but there were worse truths than his knowing that.

Every person in the zones had a different version of this story. Some days she could feel those versions battering her skin as if she was wading through an ice-choked river.

Ryan's brow was furrowed, dark, as if he already anticipated what he'd hear.

It didn't matter which story he heard. He could never truly understand.

She scrabbled around to find the words she needed, like searching for a handful of carabiners at the bottom of a stuffed backpack, and then tossed them out, fast and flat, "Darius Dalca was a monster, and the Azuros were the convicts who escaped from jail with him. In the beginning they kept people safe and made sure everything was divided fairly in the refugee camps. Pretty soon they had all the guns, control over all the supplies, and all the power. The Azuros carried out Darius's orders and organized his games. They put children in cages to keep people obedient. They held people down as Nico's wife cut off their limbs as punishment for stealing or hoarding, or eventually, just at Darius's whim. Nico was an Azuro too in those days." Jasper glared at Nico. He had made her do this. Nico glared back at her, but he was enjoying watching Ryan realize what kind of people he'd befriended.

"Zenobia was Darius's girlfriend, his second-in-command. She helped him play his games. She gave him ideas. Trust me, that baby wouldn't have been the first kid she or the Azuros killed."

"Let's stay perfectly accurate, Jasper," Zenobia said. "I never killed a child myself. Neither did any of my current Azuros."

"Fair enough," said Jasper. "But you watched it done over and over and didn't stop it."

Ryan had stilled, sinking deep into his skin, the expression in his eyes so far away, they appeared empty.

"Don't you want to get righteous with me, Ryan?" Zenobia said. "Go on. Let's hear it."

Ryan smiled bitterly at her. "Righteousness gets people killed just as easily as evil. Isn't that right, *Dr. Allan*?"

This time, for some reason, Zenobia flinched.

Ryan turned to Jasper. "And why are you the hero of this story? Wouldn't you have been just a kid back then? What did he call you? The Pinegirl?"

"*Hero.*" Jasper spat the taste of that word from her mouth. "I'm not a hero."

"Depends who's telling the story," Zenobia said. "Jasper killed Darius. She was seven at the time."

Blank white behind her eyes. She fought to remain present, to keep her weakness locked away. Eight. She'd been eight. Vron would have called that eight hundred in trauma years.

"Darius was giving her a piggyback ride," Zenobia said. "He trusted no one else, not even me—especially not me—but he adored her, for whatever that's worth, and I daresay it's very little. He never saw it coming when she pulled out a knife and stabbed him."

Improbably, Ryan was staring straight at Jasper with a blank expression, as if he'd already guessed the story, as if it had been written on her skin all along, on the angles of her elbows and the freckles at her throat. *Murderer.*

The silence was asymmetrical, awkwardly sized and shaped, its angles and edges pressing into her chest.

"A hero," Nico said, satisfied. "The only thing she didn't do was finish off Zenobia while she was at it."

"Almost sounds like something the adults should've been able to handle rather than a child," Ryan said pleasantly.

"Oh, we were going to, believe you me. We had them all lined up for execution. They'd earned it ten times over. But Jasper spoke up in their defence. How could we deny her anything, our bloody little child saint? If she could forgive those monsters, then surely we could do no less. Or so *Sparrow* would insist." His lip curled as he mentioned his sister-in-law.

Jasper nearly lost the ability to speak again. "You don't know fucking *shit*, Nico. I haven't forgiven *anyone* for *anything*."

She remembered the arguing after Darius's death, biggies yelling and shaking fists. Jasper had wandered into the midst of this furor. People never stopped her from doing anything in those days. She half believed she was a ghost because anywhere she went people pretended not to see her. But Sparrow saw her and cut through the noise with an authority that silenced people even then. She asked Jasper what they should do. Jasper thought she was being included with Zenobia and the Azuros. After all, she'd been Darius's privileged pet. *We deserve to be punished*, she said. Because her hands stayed bloody no matter how hard she scrubbed them.

Those were the last words she spoke for over a year.

The room grew dead quiet as if her voice had sucked in every vibration in the air. Her words should have supported what Nico and the others wanted, the execution of everyone who had collaborated with Darius. Instead they stared at her and were quiet.

Pastor Tim spoke up. She remembered the raw softness of his voice and the way he'd clawed back the anger in the room like a ragged quilt and forced them to face the hollow pit below their feet. He asked them if they wanted justice or vengeance, reconciliation or festering grudges. He reminded them that they were cut off from downieland and all they had was each other. What kind of community did they want to build in the wake of atrocity?

In the end every single person turned and walked away, leaving the Azuros alive and unharmed, with Nico the last to leave, trailing the scent of burned almonds.

The core group of Azuros, the worst ones, were banished from Yorky. In the following year, many of them ended up dead anyway, from an inability to survive the wilds alone or from injuries of the accidental and less accidental kind. No one investigated their deaths and no one mourned. A few of those Azuros survived to establish the community of Knowles, deep in the zones. The remainder banded together under Zenobia's leadership and, through her downieland trade connections, managed to win some grudging acceptance.

"Let's not forget you were an Azuro too for a while, Nico," Zenobia now said coolly.

"The bastard had my daughter, as you know very well. I had no choice." A vein throbbed in his temple, but he remained in control. "You might as well call my wife an Azuro."

"Yes, why not? She was his butcher." Zenobia said to Ryan, "Every amputated limb you see in the zones was likely the work of Nico's late wife, Dr. Martha Abebe."

"She had no choice, and you know it." Nico's big fists clenched. "Darius was chopping limbs off left, right, and centre with the same rusty old axe. People bled out or died from infection. She dared argue with him about it, and he told her, 'You do it or I do it.' She did it to save lives, and it destroyed her."

"That's my point, Nico," Zenobia said tiredly.

Jasper only remembered Martha after she'd been transformed from a doctor into a butcher, the king's executioner, a chopper-off of healthy limbs. Her surgical skills meant that people like Ben and Pastor Tim and Sparrow's wife, Ibtisam, survived their amputations, but Jasper knew a thousand saved lives could feel light as air while one destroyed life carried the weight of a black hole. Saved lives didn't provide any counterbalance, only the ability to continue breathing.

Just like the actual devil, Darius had framed every step down the road to hell as a choice, turning the blame game into a matter of degree. Martha's choices had eaten her from the inside out and dissolved her relationship with Nico into ash.

"Martha didn't have any more choice than I did," Nico said. "You and Darius had our daughter."

"That's true," said Zenobia. "So if you do horrendous things because someone you love is threatened, that absolves you? And is that kind of absolution reserved for you alone, or are the rest of us entitled to that too? You think you were the only one who helped him under some kind of coercion? Self-righteous bastard."

Jasper blinked, unable to get her balance. Was that real anger in Zenobia's voice? Was she actually defending herself? What was going on?

Fingers gripped her elbow, steadying her. The fingers belonged to Ryan, of all people. She met his eyes before remembering that she might find disgust in them or horror or discomfort or wariness or, worst of all, pity. Instead his eyes were as clear and cold as water over smooth stone, and she didn't know what that meant.

Her skin itched all over, and spiders crawled the inside of her skull. She needed to break something; she needed to jump off a building. She needed to turn herself inside out so her bones plated her outside like armour.

Zenobia was speaking to Nico, and there were splinters of ice in her voice, but Jasper couldn't hear the words; they ricocheted like aimless pebbles carried along by a river. The tingle started in her gut, a nauseating spiky twist, the earth echoing her own revulsion.

She fled.

11

BROOM CLOSET

Foot rubs and back rubs
A story told around a campfire

~ Veronica Park (*Things I Will Miss/Reasons to Live*)

T he broom closet was pitch-black and close, with only the faintest daylight entering the crack at the bottom of the door, but Jasper already knew its contents and dimensions from previous gravity shifts at the trading post. The cramped space was filled with a large set of shelves and some brooms, mops, a sink, and a mop bucket. The Azuros had cleared out the ancient bottles of cleaning chemicals, but the shelves still held mouldy scrub brushes and rags and a ratty feather duster.

Her tingle arced through her arms and legs, and then she was falling into the shelves.

She knocked over only one broom, although it took some painful clambering over the shelves before she could reach the cobwebby space between the shelves and the ceiling where she could sit comfortably on the wall. She deliberately positioned herself so that her back was flat against the top shelf. This way, if someone walked in, it looked as if she were lying on her back on the top shelf with her legs propped up against the wall.

She fiddled with her amulets to distract herself from how close the walls were, how cramped the space, how surely the air was leaking from the crack under the door. A spider, disturbed by her turbulent arrival, marched grumpily down her arm. She inhaled deeply and deposited it back into its web.

Footsteps sounded down the hall. She tried to ease the harsh urgency of her breath. The footsteps slowed and stopped outside the closet. The door opened, letting in a wash of light.

"There you are," said Zenobia.

She stepped inside and pulled the door closed. The glow of the candle she held softened and warmed her pale skin and emphasized the neat harmony between her mouth and her nose and between her nose and her eyes, capped by feathery black eyebrows. She was two decades older than Jasper but she would never look old. Perhaps that was why she controlled her expressions so strictly, to give away nothing more of herself than she had to. When your outer shell remained so unmarred by your ugly deeds, it could only seem like witchcraft, and people already had enough reason to hate her.

"I don't want to talk to you," said Jasper. "We are not friends."

"Yes, I know." Zenobia braced her back against the door and slid carefully to the floor and set the candle and her cane in front of her. She closed her eyes and leaned her head back against the closet door.

"I hope you're not under the delusion I've forgiven anyone, especially you," Jasper said.

"I'm not."

"You put me on the spot. You made me talk about Darius."

"Sometimes it helps."

"Nothing *helps*. You made me tell Ryan the worst thing about myself."

Zenobia cracked one eye open. "Why would you care what Ryan thinks, hmm? You're going to stay away from him, right? He's not just a handsome stranger. He's on a mission, skilled in undercover work, skilled in making people like him. He's not from our world. He comes from the outside."

Jasper fell silent. Fifteen years' worth of mould and decay filled her nostrils.

Zenobia's voice drifted to her ears, faint as dust and candlelight. "One deed doesn't define you, Jasper. You were just a child."

"Just a child," Jasper repeated. "Yeah. And how about that baby you nearly strangled?"

Zenobia lifted her gaze to Jasper, her eyes boggy with darkness. "Despite the dramatics, the child is still alive, isn't he? To die slowly and agonizingly as nature intended."

The scene in the trading hall replayed in Jasper's mind, outlined in a different light now. "You confirmed once again for Nico and everyone else that you're cold—so cold you'd kill an infant. So cold it might be useless to try to use your son against you."

A satisfied twitch of her mouth was Zenobia's only answer to that.

"But if Ryan hadn't stopped you, would you still have killed him?"

"Can't not follow through on a threat if you want to stay a ganglord."

"You knew the whole time Ryan would stop you."

"Thank you for giving me the benefit of that doubt."

"Anyone who's known Ryan for five minutes would know that," Jasper said dismissively. But Zenobia's words rankled, a thorn stuck at the back of her throat. "You'd have done it if he hadn't been there."

Zenobia exhaled. "You believe what you need to."

Jasper stared at the cobwebby ceiling rather than Zenobia's face. "Who raised Grammar? Who'd you trust enough to give him to when he was still a baby?"

"Ask him whatever you like about his life. He has no reason to keep secrets from you."

"And you do?"

A little tartly, she replied, "Secrets are for friends. Which you informed me we're not."

Zenobia knew the secret of Jasper's gravity shifts. She might be helping Jasper find a cure out of sheer self-interest—nobody in their right mind wanted another Shattering—but she wasn't obligated to hide that she knew the cause of the Shattering. At any time in the last decade and a half, Zenobia could have revealed to the zoners and even to the downies outside the wall that the person responsible for the deaths of their loved ones and the destruction of their homes was Jasper's father.

Zenobia possessed the patience to hoard a secret like that as currency for a future need. There was no reason to believe she kept it quiet out of kindness.

"You ever see Grammar after you gave him away?" Jasper asked.

"When he was younger, yes. Not since he joined the packs, though. I lost track of him."

Footsteps echoed in the hall outside. Zenobia sat up and blew out the candle. Jasper held her breath. She was still shifted side-gee.

The footsteps paused. The door jerked open, and daylight soaked away the shadows. In the doorway Ryan looked from Zenobia and her extinguished candle up to Jasper. From his perspective it would appear she was lying on her back on top of a shelving unit with her butt and legs pressed up against the wall. A silly and unexpected pose but, even based on the little he knew of her, not out of character either.

"Am I interrupting?" he asked dryly.

"You could have knocked," Zenobia said.

"On a broom closet?"

"People go into a broom closet for two reasons," Zenobia said. "For a broom or for privacy."

He was still staring up at Jasper. "And which were you looking for?"

"A broom, of course," Jasper said, talking fast to distract him. "The cobwebs up here were ridiculous."

"It looks much better now," Zenobia said. "Thanks, Jasper."

"Yeah, now they're all in her hair instead," Ryan said.

His expression made her uneasy. Was he looking at her hair? Though she kept it short, it could still give away her gravitational orientation by the direction it fell. Surely he couldn't notice that in the dim light. Even if he did, people saw what they wanted to see, what they expected to see. This kind of selective blindness had saved Jasper's secret more than once.

"Something I can help you with?" Zenobia asked frostily, drawing his attention away.

"Yeah, I want a word with you," Ryan said.

"Of course you do." Zenobia levered herself to her feet with the help of her cane, ignoring Ryan's offered hand, and walked out of the broom closet, forcing him backwards. "Come to my office." She headed down the hallway, but he lingered by the closet door.

"What do you want?" Jasper asked, deliberately harsh. She was shifted side-gee right in front of his eyes, proving herself to be the graviteria sample he was looking for. All he had to do was really see her. And she couldn't allow that.

"Need a hand down from there, ZP?"

"What do you think?"

His mouth twitched. He stepped back to give her space to jump down.

"Nah, I'm comfy here," she said. "What's that you're calling me now?"

"ZP for Zombie Princess." He looked her over in silence for a moment, his face unreadable. "Did Darius ever fiddle with you? Was that his deal?"

She almost laughed, but not from amusement. "He didn't get off on simple shit like that."

He tilted his head back and looked at the ceiling. She saw his lips move, repeating her words to himself. *Simple shit like that.*

"How about you?" she said, infuriated suddenly by his willingness to demand answers he wasn't entitled to. "Somebody ever fiddle with you when you were a kid?" *Since we're sharing traumas.*

"Tried to." He didn't blink or move.

Ah. She studied the spider in its delicate, trembling web. Remembering the feel of a knife hilt in her hand, she had to consciously unclench her fist.

"My brother cut the brake lines of the guy's car. He's a paraplegic now," he said.

Yes, that was what you did when your brother was in danger. Whatever it took.

"Darius would make me choose who would get hurt and how," she found herself saying. "Made me choose if they'd lose an arm or a leg. Or between the dog pit, the flamingo, the acid, or the cages."

He nodded slowly up and slowly down.

"Sometimes I could change his mind. Sometimes I could save them with a wager."

"What kind of wager?"

"'If I can balance on the flamingo for a full fifteen minutes, let this man keep his leg,' for example. He'd always make it harder, of course. 'Make it half an hour,' he'd say."

And for an instant she was there again, trapped in a scene cast in lurid firelight, flickering and unreliable. Darius looming over her small child self. His scalding blue eyes in a bone-white face, his shining, careless, burning bleach smile that could make you jump off a cliff if on a whim he wanted you to.

"I don't understand," Ryan said, "why the flamingo didn't just fly away if people were constantly trying to stand on it."

It took a second for the laugh to shake loose and burst out of her mouth, but once she started, she couldn't stop. The image of Darius wavered like smoke in her mind and wafted away.

"Sorry," Ryan said, though his mouth twitched. "I wasn't trying to make light."

"Make light all you want," Jasper said, choking off the laughter before it turned into something else and rose up to drown her. "I've had enough of the dark."

The tingle gathered in her belly and spread through her limbs like static fire, and her gravity shifted back to down-gee.

She sat up quickly so Ryan wouldn't have time to notice her weight settling differently or her hair changing direction. She pushed herself off the shelf and leaped down to the floor.

His hand was still braced against the door frame, and he stared at it as if questioning its existence. Across the fine bones of his hand was a shiny, puckered scar in the shape of a comet.

"Some people need killing." He said it remotely, as if he were proposing a mathematic proof.

"It's not that simple."

"I know." This time he met her eyes and it sent a tiny shock through her like a fingertip touching the pulse at her throat.

She was eye level with his mouth, wide mobile lips surrounded by the wiry, dark scruff that came from several days of not shaving. His mouth looked like one where smiles belonged even when his eyes stayed distant, veiled. Guarded. She looked away quickly, at his arm extended across the doorway, the line of mysterious dots marching from wrist to elbow, dark blue against brown, an ellipsis to an unfinished thought.

"Ryan," Zenobia called from down the hall. "Leave her alone already. I thought you wanted to talk to me."

"Hey, ZP." He stepped close. "Don't freak out."

She froze as his hand brushed past her cheek and into her hair.

He stepped back and held his hand palm up to reveal a spider. "It was in your hair."

"I wouldn't have freaked out." Her heart was racketing around like a Ping-Pong ball. But not because of the spider. Spiders she could handle.

She brushed the spider from his palm onto her own. Perhaps it was the same fellow as before. "I am not your home," she told it and nudged it back into its web in the closet.

12

CHURCH OF DARIUS

Job's life was a game piece
And his family the stakes.
God offered a bet; the devil said yes,
Let's do whatever it takes.

God wanted to brag,
The devil wanted some fun.
So who has the moral high ground
When Job's suffering is done?

A bet, a gamble, a game . . .
Why does
This song
Sound so
Familiar?

~ Veronica Park (*Story of a Monster*)

Darius Dalca had set up his kingdom in a church and put his throne in place of the altar. Limbs were chopped off in the glorious light from stained glass windows, and screams echoed like arias under the soaring ceiling. The blind eyes of saints looked down on pits full of snarling dogs and cages full of children.

Desecrated and defiled, the church now stood ostensibly abandoned, empty of inhabitants both corporeal and divine. But empty spaces didn't stay empty, and holes were all too easy to fall into.

Jasper sometimes thought the Shattering had been the manifestation of a death. The death of hope, of an era, of the beginning of the end for mankind, perhaps even the death of a deity. But dead or not, Jasper figured a deity who'd allowed kids to die in cages didn't deserve a cardboard box to live in, much less a big beautiful house with stained glass windows. In any case, he hadn't expressed an opinion on the matter, though plenty of people considered themselves entitled to one on his behalf.

Jasper paused before the entrance and glanced up at the steeple, empty of bells and of hope. Why hadn't they burned it down upon Darius's death? Why would anyone set foot again in a place so soaked in fear and suffering?

The pews had been removed from the sanctuary long ago and replaced with poker tables. In place of the altar, a long bar had been installed from which Liam and Ahmed dispensed drinks. In the centre of the room was the cage, empty this early in the evening and dark with old stains.

Jasper draped herself over a barstool and waved to Liam, who was unpacking bottles.

"Babe, I heard you went gravving with Merlot," he said by way of greeting. "I want the details this instant."

"Jesus Christ."

"That was my reaction too." Liam flashed her his supermodel smile, all cheekbones and white teeth. There was still a billboard with his face on it on Highway 9.

Jasper stared pointedly at the bottle in his hand until he laughed and poured her a glass. "Here are the details," she said after a healthy gulp. "We didn't kill each other."

"I hear you got robbed of your copper." Liam's partner, Ahmed, set down a box with a clank. He used the hook at the end of his right arm to tear it open. "How were you planning to pay for your drinks tonight?"

"Oh, hush, sweetie, it's our girl," Liam said. "She's good for it."

"And what about all the free drinks you slip her when you think I'm not looking? Not to mention all the nights she's passed out here. We should charge her rent."

Jasper leaned forward. "How about this? I'll trade you gossip for a stake. Exclusive juicy details about Merlot and me that will keep your patrons talking and drinking for hours. Some of them might even be true. I'll pay you back that stake by the end of the night."

"And if not?" Ahmed asked.

"Then I'll flamingo."

"Bullshit," said Ahmed. "You'll spill blood by the end of the night."

"You seem very sure of yourself," Jasper said. "Care to make that a wager?"

Liam laughed and Ahmed sighed. Liam poured her a drink and then wrote her a chit for copper, Ahmed watching over his shoulder. Jasper then provided them with several mostly fictional anecdotes about Merlot on the gravving trip. Liam took notes. Ahmed rolled his eyes and said Liam should start a tabloid of zones gossip. Jasper mimed vomiting and excused herself.

She parked herself at a table and in an hour doubled Liam's loan, which she paid back immediately—she despised debts. Debts lost you limbs and dignity and bought you betrayal. She let herself drink in earnest as she continued playing. The players came and went, many faces she knew and some she didn't. Her pile of chips rose and fell.

Pastor Tim had said to her once that gambling was a way to avoid responsibility for a decision. The ugly games of the Dalca era had shifted blame to the fickle entity of luck, the gods, random chance. A bet resulted in brutal consequences for the loser and moral freedom for the winner and superstition in everyone. A coping mechanism, he'd suggested, and not one conducive to healing from the abuse they'd all suffered.

If Ben could use a crutch to move around without his prosthetic, Jasper didn't see why anyone else should be denied their crutches—whatever kept them upright and functioning in the face of the void. Some people gambled. Some people drank. Some people pounded their fists into other bodies or carved their own inner wounds onto their skin. They'd all lost something, broken something inside. Ben's leg wasn't going to grow back; neither would psychic wounds magically heal. Nothing could ever be exactly the way it was before.

They all needed their prosthetics of the soul.

She knew how Pastor Tim would respond to that. He'd look at her so gently, she'd start to cry. She hated when he did that. So she'd kept that particular opinion to herself.

Noise in the church rocketed upward as more people arrived. Eventually, two men stepped into the cage, and the door slammed shut behind them. A crowd formed, voices calling bets, and then she heard the thud and smack and grunt and groan and the excited roar of the spectators, the spatter of fresh blood on iron bars.

Jasper kept her back to the cage and played on, betting and bluffing and reading her opponents like her life depended on it, like her limbs were on the line. The more she drank, the looser and wobblier she felt inside. As if her limbs would fall off at the slightest provocation and her ghost would pop free of her flesh.

She was ready to lose, ready to pay, but she kept winning.

Darius had never taught her how to cheat. He'd taught her how to bluff and read a bluff, when to bet and when to fold and when to ignore the rules and go with her gut, but never how to cheat. A game wasn't worth playing if the rules were ignored. A bet was worthless if there were no consequences for the loser or benefits for the winner. Darius Dalca loved the rules, needed them to give meaning to his entertainment.

Of course, he was the one who had made the rules and set the stakes.

The room spun around her as skin was torn and blood was shed and fists slammed into flesh. People cheered and shouted, and someone vomited behind her. The taste of alcohol burned her throat. Inside her, Darius chuckled drunkenly to himself and then was quiet, a sour, yeasty stillness.

She looked blearily over the cards in her hands to see Merlot across from her. He was slouched back in his seat as if he'd been there for hours, two empty glasses on the table beside him. His black hair, shaved on one side of his head, fell over his shoulder like a flag of war, the antithesis of a flag of truce. His eyes, heavy lidded, glittered in the dim light. With a languid flick of his wrist, he scattered chips into the centre of the table.

"Call."

"Hel-lo, Mer-lot," Jasper crooned in a singsong. She peered at her cards but they blurred coyly. She tossed a handful of chips a little too hard, and one skipped and fell in Merlot's lap. "I say, sir, there's a chip in your lap, a hip in your chap, a lip in your flap."

Merlot ignored her giggles, watching intently as the dealer turned over the last card.

Jasper slapped down her cards. "I lose!"

Everyone at the table regarded the overturned hands. Nico Mavuto, who was carefully nursing a drink and a small pile of chips, leaned forward to examine Jasper's cards.

"Actually, you win," he said. "Again."

"I do?" She fumbled to pick up the cards and held them in front of her eyes until they deigned to swim into focus. "Ah, fuck. Wouldja look at that."

"She's faking," said Socrates. "What's she been drinking all night? Water?" He grabbed her glass and sniffed. The tattoo of a saucy Virgin Mary shimmied on his cheek when he screwed up his face. "Never mind. Jesus."

"He's on her shoulder tonight," Nico said, rubbing a finger back and forth over the raised scars on his face. He realized he was doing it, clenched his hand into a fist, and downed his drink.

"Who? Jesus?" Socrates was none too sober himself. Being drunk was the only way he and Nico tolerated each other's presence.

"No, he means Darius," Jasper said. She dragged the armful of chips toward her. "Li'l Dalca on my shoulder. My lucky charm. Fucky harm."

"Listen to her, she's channelling Vron's ghost." Quick Rick's voice emerged from the faceless crowd that had gathered around their table.

Merlot's face hardened at the comment, and he threw back his drink.

"Quickity-Rickety!" Jasper called. She tilted her head backwards, and his face swam out of the shadows.

Her old grav-walking master was a scrawny stick of a Black man with a wry grin and a faded Jays cap jammed over long greying locs. With his faded, holey band tees, cargo shorts he wore in all weather, and scuffed skateboarding shoes covered in Jasper's doodles, he looked the part of an aging skater boy who'd grown grey but never grown up.

"Chickie." He patted her head. "It's a nice streak of luck you've got here, but whatever deal you made with the devil, it's not worth it."

"You're wrong." Jasper pointed in his general direction, still looking at him upside down. "It's always worth it when the devil shuts up."

"If only you'd follow his example, then," Merlot said.

"Don't say that," Socrates said, crossing himself sloppily. "This girl already needs Jesus."

Beyond Quick Rick's shoulder loomed a familiar figure, crowned in twisted coils—an unexpected hallucination of a halo in hell. Ryan?

"Who ordered a frowny downie?" Jasper asked.

"Probably a drunky monkey like yourself," Quick Rick said.

"The next person who goddamn rhymes is going to regret it," Merlot said.

Jasper rocked forward in her chair, slamming her forearms onto the table. "Fuck a duck, you slutty waffle truck."

For a delirious, delusional moment, she thought Merlot might actually smile. His mouth twitched. He took a deep breath through his nose.

"Oh, no," Jasper whispered. "You mad? You gonna spank me?"

His nostrils flared. "If you want to act out your daddy issues, I think you'll find plenty of volunteers to play Darius."

"I volunteer." Socrates leered. "I'll play any game you like."

"Why don't you play dead," Nico said to him. "You're fucking disgusting."

Jasper laboriously erected her middle finger and waved it at Merlot. "Why dontcha just meet me in the cage."

Merlot sneered. "I'm not feeding your hard-on for getting punished just because you still feel guilty for killing your psychopathic father figure."

Jasper rolled her head back and looked up at Quick Rick standing behind her chair. The hallucination of Ryan beside him was blurry but holding steady. "Aw, he thinks I have daddy issues," she said. "But, I mean, none of my father figures abandoned *me*, so . . ."

Merlot's face whitened, and his fingers clenched convulsively around his glass.

Bullseye, Darius crowed, breaking his woozy silence.

"Oh, shit," said Socrates.

"Jasper!" said Quick Rick.

Not only had Merlot and Vron's father left them shortly after the Shattering and never come back, but Merlot had also been later abandoned by his sister in the worst way possible. And then Jasper had broken up with him. With a single remark, she'd thoughtlessly aimed what she thought was a handgun but had pulled the trigger on a grenade launcher.

Kind of your style, pet, Darius roused himself to point out.

"And somehow," Merlot said, "*I've* never abandoned or killed anyone." *Unlike you.*

Quick Rick sighed. "Christ, what's gotten into you two?"

"Relax, it's how they flirt," said Socrates, reaching for his glass and missing twice before he grasped it.

"Give it up, Socrates. They are never, ever, ever getting back together," Nico said. "Sometimes when two people say they hate each other, they actually *do* hate each other. You know, like you and me."

"You need to apologize right now, both of you," said Quick Rick, splitting a disappointed frown evenly between Jasper and Merlot. "What would Vron say if she could see you now?"

"Probably nothing," said Jasper. "I mean, she didn't exactly care enough to stick around, did she?" Sour word vomit scoured her tongue, compulsive and unstoppable.

Merlot lurched to his feet, knocking drinks from the table in a tinkle of splintering glass. "Fuck you."

Quick Rick's fingers dug into her shoulder. "Jasper! How can you say that? That's not true."

"Isn't it?" Jasper slammed her fist into the table, making the chips jump. "I was her best friend. You'd think that'd count for something. Oh, but apparently not. Dying was better than hanging out with me."

"Can't say I disagree with her there." Merlot picked up a chip and threw it at her. "Here. Buy another drink on me. Maybe you'll finally get your wish and drown."

He stalked away, disappearing into the raucous crowd surrounding the cage.

Jasper dropped her forehead onto the tabletop, sticky with spilled drinks and other fluids. Somehow it always came back to Vron. That and the uncanny ability she and Merlot had to stab each other where it hurt the most. Across the table she caught Nico's eye. He rubbed a finger over his facial scars and nodded with a sigh.

She snatched up handfuls of the chips she'd just won and threw them at the other players. "Drinks for everyone," she said gaily.

As fast as she shoved away her chips, Quick Rick gathered them up again, glaring at anyone who sought to take her up on her offer. "I'm going to give these to Liam and Ahmed for safekeeping, chickie. Okay?"

Jasper jumped up from the table or tried to. She tangled her feet up in her chair, overbalanced, and fell against Ryan, who caught her. He felt unusually solid for a hallucination.

"Still falling for me, ZP?"

"You're not really here," she said into his chest. Denial. Yes, denial would work nicely.

"If I wasn't, you'd be flat on your face on the floor right now."

"You sound like the real Ryan," she said. "Snarky. Judgy. And um, like cinnamon tea."

His laugh rumbled in his chest. "What the heck is cinnamon tea?"

"A crime against nature, according to my brother."

Maybe gravity had gone a bit wonky even in down-gee, because the earth seemed to tilt her against his chest as if she belonged there, and since she didn't trust gravity for a second, she stayed put.

"You shouldn't be here," she said. "This isn't a good place for people like you."

"What kind of people is that?"

"Ghosts." She patted his chest experimentally. It remained firm.

"You may be the princess of the dead, ZP, but I'm definitely alive."

"That's exactly what a ghost would say."

"I think I'd notice if someone had killed me," he said dryly.

"It's amazing how few ghosts do."

Sometimes she bumped into people to prove she wasn't a ghost herself. Crashed into them with her eyes, her body, her words, demanding a response to prove she was alive. But maybe, as Vron had once suggested, the zones trapped ghosts with their lines of inexplicable energy, and she was even now surrounded by the dead, her fellow unhappy ghosts.

"You see ghosts often?" he asked.

"Sure. Don't you?"

He opened his mouth to answer and then checked himself. His smile disappeared.

"See?" said Jasper. "You've got 'em too. You know what you need? Amulets. Vron made the best ones with all her small god juju, but y'know, she's dead now, and ghosts can't do nothin' useful. Not that hard to make an amulet, though. Could make you one myself."

"If I'm a ghost, then your amulets aren't working too well."

"Too much Darius around here, you know. It's not the amulets' fault. He brings all the ghosts to the yard."

The church had acquired a genteel tilt that most people were gracefully accommodating, but it made Jasper stumble, and Ryan or his ghost seized her arms and restored her balance.

"I think it's time to call a cab," Ryan said, "so to speak."

Quick Rick reappeared beside them. "That's a good idea. I'll take you home, chickie."

"Wait, wait, wait," Jasper said. "Lemme consult the small god on this." She held up a finger and cocked her head. "Mmm, small god says nah."

"You've already drunk yourself blind, won big at poker, and picked a fight with Merlot," said Quick Rick. "I think you're done."

"And talked to a ghost." She patted Ryan's chest again. Still solid. Very pleasantly so.

"This is Ryan and he's not a ghost," Quick Rick said patiently.

Jasper stared at Quick Rick. He seemed to be swaying back and forth like a demented parrot, making it difficult to focus on his face. "Would you hold still," she said. "Oh, shit."

She turned and vomited. Ryan moved his feet swiftly out of the way but didn't let go of her until she'd finished retching up sour strings of bile onto the filthy church floor.

With her stomach emptied, she felt less like the world was

a glass and she was the liquid sloshing against it. Her head still felt stuffed with hot wool and her limbs were floppy as a doll's, but she could see again. She could see Ryan's face and he was here and of course he wasn't a ghost. Denial was bullshit and had never gotten her anywhere, though that never made it any less attractive. But not being a ghost meant he'd seen her at the poker table and heard what she and Merlot had said to each other and, oh God, she'd made a sickening mess of herself.

She grabbed Quick Rick's arm. "Why the *fuck* did you bring him here?"

"He asked about the nightlife," said Quick Rick. He was trying to steer her toward the door.

"He doesn't belong here." She twisted in his grip and pointed at Ryan. "You shouldn't be in here. You're not one of us. You wouldn't understand. You sh-shouldn't see this."

"Don't cry, honey. We're going home now," Quick Rick said.

"No." She tore free and faced Ryan. "You need to leave. This place isn't for you. I mean it. Go away!"

Quick Rick was talking, but Ryan just nodded and walked past them and disappeared in the crush of bodies.

Jasper snatched a drink from the hand of a passing patron and downed it.

"Take me to the flamingo!" she shouted.

"Flamingo, flamingo!" The crowd took up the chant, distracted from the bleeding combatants in the cage.

"No, chickie, you're too—" Quick Rick's voice was lost in the din.

She let herself be swept to the pit where the flamingo stood. Voices clamoured in her ear, placing bets and arguing about whether she was faking her level of intoxication.

The flamingo was a reedy iron stem with a platform the size of her hand at the top. Unlike in Darius's time, there were no iron spikes or starving dogs beneath it, but a fall from five feet onto concrete would still be dangerous if she didn't land right.

She climbed the two-step ladder beside it and placed her right foot on the tiny platform.

"Last bets!" Liam sang out, waving his clipboard above the bar while Ahmed took people's money.

"Countdown!" Ahmed roared a minute later. "Five, four . . ."

The crowd joined in the count. Jasper shifted her weight from her left foot on the ladder to her right foot on the flamingo platform. At "one" the ladder was pulled away.

The noise fell away like autumn leaves. Only the stark line of balance remained, running from her right foot up her leg, coiling in her hips and shooting up her spine, diffusing into silence in her skull. Her muscles were loose and intractable, her bones rubbery, her head a staticky, stuffy fire hazard. But her balance was an alien tree, rooted into some other dimension.

The earth didn't want her. She belonged here, elevated, almost suspended, drawn thin between floor and sky. All the dogs of her nightmares could prowl beneath her, the distant floor promising rent flesh and broken bones, but up here she was safe.

In the distance she heard Ahmed's voice counting, steady as a metronome. With each sixty count, people groaned as the time markers they'd bet on passed by and she remained unmoved.

Balance for her life, for her limbs, for the lives of others. Balance for the mastery over her body, the fear, the challenge, and the triumph. Balance for the pride in Darius's grin.

Balance through a murky muddle of memory, the bilious taste of a dark nostalgia, as nourishing as the regurgitated meal a dog returns to and eats again. Balance as if this time she wouldn't fall, and this time no one would die.

As if this time she'd figure out what it meant to win.

From the back of the crowd, Ryan's gaze shot through her, a tiny precise punch in the gut, impossible to recover from.

She fell.

Arms caught her, many of them, easing her to the ground. Hands clapped her on the back, squeezed her shoulders, tousled her hair. Their voices were a wall of sound, impenetrable, but she had no substance, and so she moved through the crush of people without resistance.

She washed up against a familiar body. In the anonymous darkness, she let her forehead drop against his shoulder as if she still belonged there.

"Idiot," Merlot said into her ear. "*Babo*. What's wrong with you?" His voice, drifting to her from the other side of her closed lids, could have been a voice from the past, an artifact of an all-too-brief period of happiness in her life, back when the future stretched like an endless horizon, when the monster was dead and wounds were healing and scars were a badge of survival. When love was a thing to believe in and old age was a possibility to strive for. "You didn't even try to fall right. You could've cracked your thick fucking skull—"

"Didn't know you still cared."

"I *don't*. But fuck me if I have to tell Ben—"

She was washed away again by the waves of bodies. Or maybe she ran, stumbled, crawled away, losing herself before she could grab on to him.

13

COUNTING SCARS

"How old are you?"
"A hundred."
"Looking good for your age."
"Not years. Traumatic events."

~ Merlot Park (*Peter and Jazztree*, Edition 48)

The church basement had once been used for after-service socializing, potluck meals and other church events. Later it had been filled with rows of cages, crusted in filth and soaked in the misery of their small inhabitants. It was empty now, a wide expanse of stained flooring and discoloured, graffiti-covered walls. The glass had been smashed out of the windows long ago, and the illusion of open air was the only reason Jasper could set foot in this space at all.

Nico sat at a table, slowly, methodically cleaning a scalpel of Jasper's blood. In front of him on the table was a candle and a flask of alcohol. The light rippled over the neat lines of scars on his face but left the heavy pouches under his eyes in shadow.

Jasper sat in a chair opposite him, jeans pushed down to her knees. She held a patch of gauze against the small new wound on her thigh, the size and shape of a penny. The price of forgetting.

Flesh was made to be cut, my pet. If it wasn't, why would it heal? A memory in Darius's voice that she'd never forget, no matter how hard she tried.

To forget Darius she'd have to strip off her skin entirely. The best she could manage were bite-sized snippets of memory, a few seconds' worth of emotion, a time-frozen image of a single moment.

Dozens of half-inch scars already created a whorled pattern around her thigh, her own map of the past, leading nowhere. Sometimes she used a pen to connect the dots, creating designs out of the deliberate damage—a seashell, a crane, a tower. Sometimes in the dark she'd let her fingers drift over the raised bumps, a message she'd written to herself in Braille and still couldn't read.

She waited for that burning square of pain on her thigh to carve its territory into her consciousness and sear away just a few brain cells' worth of memory. Just a few seconds' relief.

If only that was how it worked.

"There's a kid," she said. In the empty, stained basement her words sounded hollow, far away. "Your Damaskers caught him recently."

"What about him?" Nico asked.

"He knows where to find my mother's body."

Nico set the scalpel down. "You want to ask him a question? I don't usually allow fresh recruits contact with anyone outside the army for a few months."

"Oh, because of the brainwashing, right?"

Unruffled, Nico shrugged.

"I can't wait a few months. Besides I was hoping to borrow him. You know it's nearly impossible to give directions in the zones. He'll have to show me."

"I'm not going to lend you a recruit either now or later. They're flight risks, these kids, until they're fully trained, and it takes time and effort to train them. I'll let you ask him about your mom in a few months, and I promise he'll answer politely and thoroughly. How's that?"

"I can't wait months." But she couldn't explain to him why. She lifted the gauze from the raw wound on her thigh, and immediately blood welled up in a neat square. She pressed the cloth down again. She'd forgotten to bring a longer length of cloth to tie the gauze in place.

"Well," Nico said slowly, "maybe if I allow it as a favour, there's something you might do for me in the future."

"Like what?"

He didn't answer right away, instead staring down at the scalpel in his hands, a tiny precise instrument in his large soldier's hands. It had belonged to his ex-wife, Martha Abebe. "I don't even remember Darius's face anymore. Just another dead, faceless white man now who thought he could own my life, the lives of my wife and daughter. If there was any justice, his memory would have been wiped out when he died. But he'll never be dead, not truly, not as long as we remember him. And how can we forget?" He glanced at her with bloodshot eyes. "Your brother won't forget, will he?"

Jasper stiffened and clenched her jaw against the urge to speak. She flexed her strong hands, curled her toes, her flesh-and-blood toes, in her shoes. She and Nico had both survived physically intact when so many others hadn't. Oh, the spaces inside their skulls, the fractured landscapes inside their chests told a different story, but their bodies remained jarringly, undeservedly *whole*.

There was no rhyme or reason to who had survived and in what condition. No reason but Darius's whims.

"I wonder sometimes if Darius chose amputations for that reason," Nico said. "So his victims would never, ever forget him. Memories can be buried or forgotten or avoided. Even deaths eventually fade, and people remarry and have more children. But you'll never grow back a hand or a leg." He curled his hands into fists till his knuckles whitened.

Jasper found her jaw aching and forced herself to unclench it. She pressed the gauze down harder so the sting pierced the bloated darkness expanding behind her eyes.

When Nico spoke again, his voice was calm. "The Azuros may have kept their noses clean since you killed Darius, but people won't forget what they've done. How can they when they or their loved ones are missing limbs? Eventually the Azuros will show their true colours again. Or else people will decide they don't like Zenobia's monopoly on all outside trade. Or they'll find out something about her they can't tolerate."

He paused, and she wondered what that was supposed to mean.

"I want nothing to do with your politics or any kind of coup or war, if that's what you're talking about," she said warily.

"But if the war comes to you, you're going to have to pick a side. You did it once, decisively. There will come a time—perhaps soon—when you'll have a chance to speak up to defend Zenobia and the Azuros and so sway public opinion. I'm asking you to . . ." He shrugged. ". . . not say anything at all. That's it."

She dreaded to think what he could be planning. "I don't have as much influence as you think."

"You have more than you think, and could have still more if you bothered to cultivate it . . . and if you associated less closely with the very people you overthrew by killing Darius."

Every time she lifted the gauze, blood seeped up immediately, sluggish but insistent. She could tear a strip from her T-shirt to fix the gauze in place, but she liked this T-shirt. She could just pull her jeans up, but bloodstains were tough to get out, and Harmony would never let her hear the end of it. She could feel Nico watching her.

"Did I ever tell you how I started all this?" He touched the bumpy rows of scars on his face. "It was your friend Veronica who gave me the idea."

She looked up, startled to hear Vron's name here in this place, from this man.

"I found her once, years ago, cutting little notches up and down her side. I tried to talk to her about it. I mean, she wasn't much older than my daughter, and it was an unnerving thing to see. She said . . . she said she was assigning a memory to each scar and leaving it there. So that she could count with her fingers the things she'd survived." He rubbed both hands over his face. "And hell if that didn't strike me as a perfectly reasonable idea. I was in a bad place, though."

"We all were," she said numbly. *Still are.*

"I tried to tell her she needed to get help, she needed to talk to someone if the pain was so bad. She just looked at me like I was the one who needed help."

"Why are we talking about this?"

"You could cut up your whole body and it won't change what happened. You'll run out of skin, and then what?"

She put down the bloody gauze, stood, and dragged up her jeans. Harmony would know some way to get bloodstains out of jeans, though she'd never stop scolding Jasper about it. "Are you trying to say you *care* about my mental well-being or something? Don't make me laugh. Get to the point."

"You could say I've run out of skin space," he said quietly. "I'm trying something different now. So if you ever find you need a different way of dealing with your pain, or a sense of purpose perhaps, come find me."

"What do you know about what I—?"

"I *know*." He closed a broad, callused hand into a fist and set it on the table. "I see the way you act a fool. Still flamingo-ing after all these years like Darius never died. Gambling, drinking, cutting these scars. You're reckless as shit. You looking to take the easy way out? Is that it? Like Veronica? Is that what this is all about?"

"What makes you think I need a goddamn father figure? I'm not Crane, Nico." Nico's flinch was barely perceptible, but she instantly regretted her words. She took a breath and let it out. "I want that kid. Will you let me have him or not?"

He sat back in his chair and sighed. "I already made you my offer. Take it or leave it."

She left the basement, jeans chafing the wound on her inner thigh.

She let herself be swallowed by the crowd in the church sanctuary. Drinks were pushed into her hands and she drank them. Time slipped past like water, impossible to grasp or stop.

A glass, a bucket, a river of time later found her outside sitting on grass, the black shadows of trees pressed damply against the black sky. The door to the church was propped open a crack, spilling out light and voices and the plaintive ripple of a guitar. Concrete at her back, she was leaning against the side of the steps, a glass in her hand. She was missing a shoe. Crickets scratched furrows into the night.

People stood around in pairs or clumps, smoking and

talking, lit by the glow of their joints and the thread of light from the door. Wana smoke turned the air sharp and dank.

The air rippled and swayed as if she were underwater. Snatches of conversation floated by like seaweed streamers. Light wavered and broke apart in hypnotic shimmers. People appeared and disappeared again like bubbles. She was trapped in a slower time than they were.

Merlot's voice drifted out of the darkness, round with laughter and smudged into softness by the whimsical unreality of long-past-midnight. ". . . so there we were on the roof of the tallest building on the block, like five storeys, and it's raining like the fucking apocalypse and we're across the street from a literal treasure trove of copper and we can't cross because of the fucking bear, right? So Jas turns and says—"

A voice interrupted with a question, a male voice, keen and curious. If she weren't a feather in an ocean, she might swear it was Ryan's voice, but the tides were rising and falling inside her head, and it couldn't be him. She'd told him to leave and he'd left. He wasn't sitting on the other side of the steps in the pillow-soft darkness sharing a joint with Merlot, of all people, and listening to his grav-walking stories.

". . . Ben gives me this look, like *Are you gonna say something?* And there's no way I'm opening my mouth because I wanna see what happens, right? So Jas gets a running start and fucking *jumps* off the roof . . ."

The flavourless liquid in her glass was water. Who'd had the nerve to give her water? Also her missing shoe sat in the grass beside her. She'd drawn carnivorous roses on it in marker and spiders drowning in lava.

". . . shoulda seen the look on her face when Ben told her it had been there the whole time!"

Their laughter curled past her with the scent of grass and smoke.

With Darius sated and lulled to sleep in the crevices under her ribs, she let herself imagine her father standing in the tall grass beside the church, head tilted back to study the stars. Andrew Pine had disappeared into the Tower while Jasper was only a tiny knot of cells in her mother's womb, and she hadn't seen a picture of him since she was five, so when she conjured him from shadow and wish, he always had his back to her; otherwise his face would simply take the shape of Ben's. His hair was a familiar, dishevelled smudge of squid ink, his shoulders broad like Ben's.

Did you know you were going to die? Jasper asked him. *Were you afraid?* She watched him watch the sky, this mist-formed idea of a father. *Ben remembers your hug and your voice and your strawberry pancakes. He remembers that you loved him. You'd love him still if you saw him now. But would you love me?*

According to Zenobia, when Andrew had Shattered in the Tower, a vertical up-gee zone had formed between the tip of the Tower and the outer atmosphere like a drinking straw sucking everything on the earth end up into the maw of hard vacuum.

Ever since Jasper had first heard about that zone, she had been haunted by dreams where she was falling like a spear into a bed of empty darkness prickled with acid-edged stars.

The Tower remained rooted to the planet, but Andrew had fallen along with his alien infestation. The earth hadn't wanted him either. Somewhere out there among the diamond dust stars, his body drifted still, a tiny human vessel in the void. If she Shattered, she'd join him. She wondered if she'd have a chance to see the stars spreading out around her before the vacuum killed her.

A couple argued nearby, nearly lost in the shadows. The man was trying to steal kisses while the girl harangued him. She was looking for somebody, and he was demanding a kiss as payment for telling her. Her laugh was too high pitched to reflect real amusement. Short hair like Jasper's but blond, her face pale in the darkness and familiar.

Their voices were drowned by a wash of light and noise from the church as someone stepped outside, someone with a familiar voice.

". . . but if you're a peddler, you must know just about everybody in the zones." Ryan. What was he still doing here?

"Sure, I meet lots of people," Quick Rick agreed, affable, slightly drunk.

From her shadowy spot beside the stairs, Jasper twisted around to see them. They sat down on the steps to share a smoke.

"You ever meet someone here in the zones who was a microbiologist before the Shattering?"

"Can't say as I have," Quick Rick said after a thoughtful pause. "But people don't necessarily talk about who they used to be. You looking for someone in particular or just anyone who fits that description?"

"Dr. River Lee."

"Doesn't sound familiar. Can I ask why you're looking for this person?"

A pause. The smell of smoke drifted to Jasper's nostrils. "She was a friend of the family and I heard a rumour she was alive. I . . . lost my parents, you see, and so I thought I'd seek out someone who knew them."

"Ah. Yes, I see," Quick Rick said. "Sorry I can't help you. I know where you're coming from. My two oldest were in college across the country, thank God, so I like to think about them going about their lives on the outside and getting married and having kids and such." He sniffed noisily and cleared his throat. "But my youngest, Rachel, she was here visiting me. She was literally down the street at an old school friend's house and . . .

well, our house stayed down-gee, but that friend's house went up-gee."

"I'm sorry," said Ryan.

"Everyone's lost someone. Everyone. You gotta build a family with who's left, you know? You were asking me about Jasper earlier. Her and her brother and Merlot—you were talking to him before—and his sister and a few others, they were my gravving team for a while before I screwed up my knees good. Wouldn't know it to look at me now, but I was into parkour, free running, skateboarding, the whole culture back in the day. Urban exploring too, but let me tell you, a Black kid who wants to trespass onto abandoned properties better know how to run fast—you feel me?" He gave a huff of a laugh, and Ryan grunted in acknowledgement.

Quick Rick continued, "But those kids, I taught them everything I knew, and by the end of it they were teaching me. Kids, they can adapt to anything, and that bunch took to the zones like raccoons to dumpsters. Jas especially. I think if she could manage it, she'd never set foot in down-gee again. Can't replace the people you lost, but those kids, I love 'em like they're my own, you know? So I can't complain."

She hadn't spent nearly enough time with Quick Rick lately, too absorbed with her own life, her own problems. She'd visit him tomorrow, bring him some of Harmony's kimchi, reminisce about their gravving days back when Charlie was there to crack jokes and Merlot laughed freely and Ben wasn't so knotted up in worry over Jasper. Back when Vron was alive.

The damn smoke was making her eyes water and nose run.

"They're lucky to have had you as a father," Ryan said. "I guess you'd do anything for your kids, eh?"

"If you told me right now I could trade places with my Rachel so she'd be alive, I'd do it. No question. That's what it means to be a parent."

"What if you could trade someone else's life for Rachel?" Ryan asked. "Mine, for instance, or that guy's over there. Would you do that?"

"Christ, what a question." Quick Rick sounded taken aback. "A little too deep and dark for me to think about at this time of night."

"But if Rachel and I were both standing in front of you and one of us was going to be shot and you could choose which one, you'd choose me, right? No question."

When Quick Rick spoke again, his voice was heavy and tired. "My boy, I understand you're new around here, but a question like that is exactly the kind of game Darius Dalca used to play with us, and I want no part of it, not even hypothetically."

"I'm sorry, I didn't—"

"No one wants to be the person saved at the price of another soul." A scuff of shoes and then the burst of sound and light as Quick Rick pulled the door open. Quiet and darkness returned as it banged shut behind him.

Jasper took the steps carefully one at a time. She sat on the top step beside Ryan. He looked at her, opened his mouth to speak, and then just exhaled.

"Still think I'm a ghost?" he asked after a while.

"We're all ghosts, but some of us are more attached to our bones than others." It was something Vron used to say. Vron had only ever been very loosely attached to her bones.

"Delightful thought." He held a full glass in his hand but wasn't drinking from it. He lifted it to his nose and sniffed. Then he lowered it again.

"Are your parents really dead, or is that just part of your cover story?"

"Really dead," he said.

"But you have a brother."

"Foster brother, really, but yes. Titus," he said. "How about you? Merlot mentioned you had a brother."

"Yeah. His name is Ben."

"Ben." He looked up at the stars for a while. "You guys close?"

She started to say something flippant but then changed her mind and answered honestly, "I'd choose him over everyone."

He grunted. With the heel of one hand, he rubbed at the line of tattooed blue dots on his arm.

"What about you and your brother?"

It took him a while to answer. "My parents died in a car accident when I was six. I met Titus in the foster care system. I was a scrawny, nerdy Black kid and he was a rough, tough white kid built like a linebacker, and for some reason he took a shine to me. Maybe I was the first person who was ever kind to him. Or wasn't afraid of him. I don't know what it was, but he wouldn't let anyone lay a hand on me. He made me do my homework and stole food for me and kicked my ass if I even looked at a drug or a cigarette sideways."

"Sounds like a good big brother," she said when he fell silent.

"He was good to me." He was still rubbing at his tattoos as if they itched. "But not so much to anyone else. I joined the army to get away from him." He snorted as if at a bitter, private joke. "Not for my own sake but to protect the people around me from him."

His words felt like familiar footsteps on the stairs. "You know how Zenobia said Darius loved me? Well, he did. Sort of. His own twisty version of it. But what people call love doesn't always exactly line up with the real thing. Sometimes it's a very fucked-up mess of barbed wire instead."

The sound he made was to a laugh what a gecko was to a

dragon—distantly related. "You're really not going to make this easy, are you?"

"Make what easy?" When he didn't answer, she nudged him with her elbow. "If it's a real tattoo, it won't come off, you know."

He looked at her in surprise and then down at his arm. He laughed self-consciously and placed both hands around his full glass.

"Are you gonna drink that or not?"

Once again he brought the glass to his nose and inhaled deeply. "Haven't decided yet."

The couple's argument nearby was growing more heated, drawing their attention. The girl said loudly, "If you won't help me, I'll find him myself."

The man grabbed her wrist, his face twisted in irritation. "I'm tellen you what the price is, and it ain't even that high. Don't be acten like such a bitch." His head turned toward the light. It was Dragon with his zigzag blond hair and ritual scars on pale cheekbones and that familiar streak of nastiness.

Back from stealing copper and shooting and kidnapping children, it seemed.

Beside her Ryan tensed, ready to move. But before he or Jasper could react, another figure stalked out of the shadows, skinny and deadly as an assassin's garrotte. Crane removed a wana joint from her sharp lips and blew smoke into Dragon's face.

"You like touchen pretty girls who aren't liken you," Crane observed. She dropped the joint and stomped it out with an oversized boot. "Well, I like cutten ugly boys who aren't liken me. Wanna see?" Blades appeared in her hands; she was spinning and flipping them casually over her knuckles, her smile like a razor blade.

Jasper opened her mouth to utter a warning, an automatic attempt to rein Crane in. But she checked herself. If anyone could teach Dragon a lesson, it was Crane, and Jasper wanted to see it happen.

Dragon's face darkened into an ugly scowl, but before he could respond, the blond girl jerked her wrist free from his grip. She looked at Crane in confusion, lips parted as if about to say something. Crane winked at her.

The blond girl sputtered something, then whirled and stormed away from them both.

"Are you okay?" Ryan asked her, but she clattered up the stairs and swept between him and Jasper as they leaned out of the way. She entered the church.

Jasper twisted around to watch her go. "Oh my God, that's Grace Kornelsen. I didn't recognize her with that hair. How did she even get in? Liam and Ahmed don't serve minors. Not ones with parents anyway." She wondered if Esther had any idea what her innocent little sister was up to. Jeans and a tank top weren't a very Mennonite outfit, and a bar wasn't a place where Mennonites were normally found. And what the hell did she want from a man like Dragon?

Dragon and Crane squared up as conversations died around them.

"Crane," Ryan said warningly.

Still grinning at Dragon, she didn't look at him.

"Hedgehog," Ryan said, "why don't you go ask that girl if she's okay?"

Crane sheathed her smile as she considered this suggestion. Her knives disappeared again. She waggled her fingers at Dragon. "I'll be cutten off your nasty hands some other time."

"Anytime, anywhere, bitch." Dragon glanced around at the people watching and sneered, but he walked away quickly, disappearing into the darkness.

Crane skipped up the steps. She was still wearing her favourite red jeans with the ridiculous yellow patches on the knees. She patted both Ryan and Jasper on the head hard enough to sting and slipped into the church before Jasper could smack her on the ass in retaliation.

Ryan frowned in the direction Dragon had gone.

"Next time you beat up a Damasker, pick him," Jasper said. "Children and women of the zones will thank you."

"Unfortunately, I'm not here to solve your problems. I've got enough of my own."

Startled by the bitterness of his tone, she stared at him. He winced as if hearing his own words, but didn't look at her.

She got up. "So why don't you go home, downie, since being stuck behind quarantine walls for the rest of your life is not one of your problems."

"Wait, ZP. That didn't come out right." He got up too and thrust his glass at her. "Have a drink on me, Zeep, please."

She took the glass, frowning at him, and took a cautious sip. The homemade liquor might not be fancy enough for a downie, but it was no worse than anything she'd drunk before at Liam and Ahmed's bar. She took a healthy swallow and felt slightly more magnanimous.

"So what are these problems you're so worried about?" She wondered whether he'd tell her about the graviteria samples he was after. She didn't want to leave the delicious coolness of the night breeze for the stuffy heat of the crowded bar, so she sat back down on the steps. He sat down too and watched her take another gulp.

Instead of answering, he asked, "Would you leave quarantine if you had a chance?"

"All my friends and family are here. I mean, if everyone was allowed to leave, sure, I'd be curious about downieland, but . . ." Could she live in a place where it was down-gee all the time, everywhere, without a single pocket zone for variety? What hideous monotony that would be. "This is home. Small god knows it's not perfect, but it's where I belong."

"Must be nice," he said. "To feel that way about a place."

She'd probably reached her limit for the night. Her eyes had grown impossibly heavy and so had her tongue. As well as the glass in her hand with its innocently clear liquid.

"I'm sorry," he said after a while.

"For what?" she asked, or tried to, but he didn't answer.

14

TIES THAT BIND

When your reputation precedes you
Reminiscing over a favourite memory and someone reminds
you of details you'd forgotten

~ Veronica Park (*Things I Will Miss/Reasons to Live*)

E ven before she could reach the surface level of consciousness, she was convulsing from the signals her body was sending her, the biological equivalent of flashing red lights and air-raid sirens and faraway screams. She tried to dive back into oblivion, but oblivion wanted no part of her and spat her back out.

World War III in her head and arid roadkill in her mouth and a dozen furnaces baking her to a crisp, and on top of that, an aching bladder made worse by the merciless jolting and bumping of the world around her. She groaned out the worst series of curses she could summon with a brain that felt like week-old porridge. Her mouth didn't seem to work right, and the words came out muffled. Because . . .

Because she was gagged.

Her instinctive move to pull out whatever the hell had been stuffed in her mouth revealed that her hands were bound together. Her legs too. The earth wasn't shaking. She was being dragged on a travois. She forced her eyes open but was instantly assaulted by weaponized sunlight. Her eyeballs tried to crawl back into her skull.

The motion of the travois stopped, and it was lowered so she lay flat on her back on the ground. She tried to sit up but she'd been strapped into it. Only with that realization did panic bubble up like explosive gases in a swamp.

A figure moved around the travois. He untied the straps holding her body to it and removed the gag from her mouth. Then he squatted back on his heels and waited for her to get her bearings. She sat up. She couldn't do much else with her limbs tied, but at least she could breathe. She blinked away the involuntary tears that had formed from the blinding sunlight. The man's face came into focus.

Ryan Latrans.

Shock and denial were closely followed by a surge of humiliation and self-disgust. She couldn't even say she'd been betrayed. Zenobia had warned her in plain terms to avoid him, that he was a soldier on a mission, that he was looking for Jasper even if he didn't know it yet. She hadn't listened, had wilfully chosen to believe his facade of honesty and decency. He'd learned her worst secret and hadn't withdrawn from her, so she —sad, desperate fool—had assumed a connection, a tiny intimacy. He'd made a show of vulnerability to cement that feeling, but all along he'd been playing a role, gathering intel, winning her trust for the sole purpose of exploiting it.

You really think you can reason your way past my ghost?

Darius's voice tasted like tinfoil between the teeth. *I created a pattern for your life, and you're doomed to repeat it for the remainder of your regrettably short lifespan.*

Humiliation twisted into anger, not so much at Ryan as at herself. She'd survived Darius fucking Dalca, the king of sociopathic manipulators. She should have built up a permanent immunity to charming strangers, but instead she'd been careless, and Ryan had gotten past her defences. In the broom closet, he must have realized she was shifted, or he'd learned of her shifts from someone else, Merlot or Quick Rick maybe, after charming them and plying them with alcohol. Either way, her secret was out, and it was the kind of cat that would never suffer being stuffed back into a bag.

He hadn't killed her yet. That meant whoever had sent him wanted her alive as a lab rat, a money-maker, a weapon prototype. Someone more concerned about the safety of humanity would've had her killed, ticking time bomb that she was. Of course, there was no electricity in the zones and therefore no way to preserve a dead body. He could be waiting to get her someplace where she and the alien in her body could be frozen for the scientists to dissect.

"I expected you'd be cussing a blue streak by now," he remarked. He sat on a nearby concrete road divider and pulled out his canteen. His face glistened with sweat. It was midmorning, and he could've been dragging her travois for several hours now.

She twisted around, trying to orient herself. The quarantine walls, their destination, loomed in the near distance. They were off the beaten path, as Ryan would want to skirt the Azuros' trading post to get to the gate without any zoners seeing.

He offered her the canteen. She wanted to gnaw his hand off at the wrist, but she was also so thirsty, she felt faint. She drank.

"I need to pee." Her voice felt hoarse and raw.

"I hope you're not shy, then, because I'll be watching."

She hadn't yet been able to assemble the words to express her opinion of him, but her stare expressed it. He had the nerve to grin, and she was possessed of the urge to peel his face from his skull.

"You made the mistake of impressing me a little too much with your physical skills, Zeep, and I'm not going to turn my back on you." He approached the travois and gestured to his gun to remind her of its presence. He cut her loose from the zip ties.

She stood slowly, her muscles stiff and aching. Her head was a throbbing mess. She had a hangover stacked on top of a hangover with a little hangover sombrero on top. Whatever he'd slipped into her drink wasn't helping matters any. If she ran, he could catch her easily without even drawing his gun. They were in the five-kilometre-wide down-gee buffer zone near the quarantine walls, far from any true zones, so she couldn't use his downie inexperience against him.

A jumble of concrete road dividers lined the road. They were barely higher than her knee, but when she squatted behind them, they allowed her a tiny bit of privacy and dignity while keeping her in Ryan's peripheral vision. With her jeans around her ankles, she took the opportunity to search her pockets for anything useful. Her pouches and knife were gone, of course, but he'd also been thorough in removing everything from her pockets down to the bits of ribbon grav-walkers used to test unknown zones. She still had her belt. The belt buckle, designed by Ben during the long, idle winters, could be broken apart into lock picking tools. Which wouldn't be very effective against zip ties, but it was something.

The tiny square wound on her thigh had scabbed over but still throbbed. The memory of everything Nico had told her niggled at her, but right now she had bigger problems to worry about.

When she was finished, she climbed onto a nearby car and sat on the roof despite the heat of the rusted metal. Ryan remained sitting as well, chewing a piece of jerky. He held it up inquiringly, but she shook her head and looked away. The thought of food was nauseating, and so was his calmness, as if a kidnapping was an ordinary day's work for him.

"Was it the broom closet that gave me away?" she asked.

"Yes, but also your name. We knew Andrew Pine's son had been born before Andrew was infected, but we had no idea there'd been a daughter as well, so I wasn't looking for you specifically. But when I heard you called the Pinegirl, it got my attention. The Azuros wouldn't tell me anything about you, almost like they'd been ordered not to. But Nico told me your full name, and Quick Rick told me your age. You mentioning you had a brother named Ben just confirmed it."

She stared at the quarantine walls in the distance. She couldn't look at his face; it hadn't changed at all, and that was the worst thing. He'd drugged and kidnapped her and was carrying her away from family, friends, and home to deliver her to people who would experiment on her, use her, and kill her, not necessarily in that order. Shouldn't he have dropped his nice guy mask? Shouldn't he be speaking and acting like a robot now, or some cold, pitiless hit man? It'd be easier if he did.

He approached her with a fresh set of zip ties. "Walking or travois?"

She almost considered the travois, if only because it would tire him out and slow their progress, but the thought of being strapped down and immobile brought the bubbles of panic too close to the surface. She held out her wrists for the zip ties. At least with her legs free she could take advantage of any opportunity to run.

He seemed to sense her thought. "If you run and I have to shoot you, we're close enough to the walls that I can probably

get you there before you bleed out, but let's not test that theory."
He held up the gag. "I don't need to use this, do I?" She shook
her head hastily, and he tucked it away. "Also, please don't forget
that I know where to find your friends, Merlot and Quick Rick,
and I'm sure it wouldn't be too difficult to find Ben. So don't try
anything stupid, okay?"

She looked him in the eye, hating him so hard, her head
hurt. Hating herself. Zenobia had warned her of danger, and
she'd jumped in headfirst. How much of that had just been
rebellion against Zenobia, acting out like a child against rules
meant to protect her?

"Why didn't Zenobia kill you?" she wondered aloud.
Zenobia wouldn't have even had to get her own hands dirty; she
would have only needed to drop a hint to Crane. Crane loved
sticking knives in people. He could have disappeared, and if
anyone had even noticed, they would have assumed he'd gone
back to his home on the other side of the city.

"Because I'm the best-case scenario, and she knows it. The
next person or team to be sent would be less surgical and more
scorched earth in their tactics."

He tossed the travois into a ditch and directed her to start
walking ahead of him.

"These people you're bringing me to, will they kill me before
or after they experiment on me?" He was behind her so she
couldn't see his expression. When he said nothing, she
continued, "Zenobia has a cure for me, you know. She's been
trying to perfect it to give me the best chance at surviving it, but
we were never going to let me Shatter. In three months I
would've been either cured or dead." Or cured and as good as
dead. "Anyway, if you cared about stopping a Shattering, you'd
have just killed me."

"Wasn't my mission," he said curtly.

"The easiest way to use me would be to drop me into an

enemy country. Boom. I Shatter and the whole country is devastated. My father's Shattering was a small one, I hope you know, limited but not prevented by the antibac he'd been given. Mine will be massive, but hey, at least there's no radiation like from a nuke. Well, not the kind that gives you cancer anyway. Just the kind that kills electronics and doesn't dissipate, which I'm told is bad enough. Zenobia and I discuss this sometimes, all the ways in which I could be used for evil. You put any thought into it yourself?"

"I was assured that the threat of Shattering would be neutralized," he said. "I take it some version of the cure has been developed. And with better resources than whatever Zenobia has cobbled together by herself here in the zones, don't you want to give it a chance?"

"Surely you're not that naive."

"Would you prefer to be killed instead?" he snapped.

She stopped and turned so abruptly, he nearly walked into her. He took a step back to keep a small wary distance between them. "You think I'd rather be responsible for millions of deaths instead? If you do this, you'll be responsible too."

He looked away. His eyes were bloodshot with dark hollows beneath them, as if he hadn't slept all night. The set of his jaw was rigid, brittle. His apparent calmness didn't come from coldness so much as from the inertia of having committed to a decision, no matter how ugly or damning.

What kind of man would make that decision? Not any kind of man she should ever have trusted. But maybe Darius was right and she had a type she'd always be vulnerable to, even with eyes wide open.

"Is it money?"

"What does it matter why?" he said harshly. "You think there's something I could tell you that would make this okay? There isn't. Just keep moving."

She walked as slowly as she thought she could get away with, scuffing her feet through the knee-high grass that sprouted from cracks in the asphalt. Her head throbbed in time to her steps. After a short while, she stopped again.

"I need a drink."

He handed over the canteen without a word, even though she'd had a drink fifteen minutes ago. A real pushover of a kidnapper, or else one with a heavy burden of guilt. She didn't think Ryan was a pushover. If he thought this was his only option, he'd grit his teeth and carry through.

Funny how she was back to thinking she knew him. Dangerous, that. Still, he'd revealed the lines he was willing to cross, and she wouldn't easily trust him again. She had little to lose in probing his commitment to his mission. Small god only knew what would happen to her after she went through the quarantine gates. This might be her last chance to obtain real information.

"Do you trust whoever hired you?" she asked. "Do you think they'll use me for good?"

"Of course not. But—" He stopped, lips tightening.

"But you have no choice."

"You don't know my brother. He's . . ." He stopped. "Well, maybe you do. He likes games too, you see. But they're not games to him. They're a way to get what he wants—whatever he wants. In the beginning it was just a way to survive, and he used it to help me, get me set up in life. But I joined the army and got out from under his thumb, didn't need him anymore. He didn't like that."

"I don't understand. What does your brother have to do with anything?"

"Titus works for a massive corporation that does pharmaceutical research, weapons research, biological warfare, all kinds of things. He intercepted Zenobia's messages to someone within the company. He did some digging and figured out there was still graviteria in the zones, probably in the Tower. When confronted, Zenobia agreed this was true but insisted the Tower was inaccessible. Crane was supposed to prove that to me. Zenobia's been less than cooperative."

"Yeah, I'll bet. Why has she been cooperative at all? What do you have on her?"

He seemed to be considering how to answer, and her thoughts jumped around, wondering what point of pressure Ryan's brother could have brought to bear on Zenobia.

"Oh my God, the kid." Had he somehow gotten his hands on Grammar? But in that case, why wouldn't Zenobia do a straight exchange and give up Jasper for Grammar's sake? Surely that would be the logical move for a mother, even one like Zenobia. Especially one like Zenobia.

But Ryan frowned. "Kid? What kid are you talking about?"

Ryan had been in the zones for several months already, but a week ago Grammar had been running free with his pack.

"Never mind."

Suspicion appeared on his face. "Wait, do you have a kid?"

"Me? Jesus, no. How stupid do you think I am? Any kid of mine would be infected too." She pressed her fingers to her temples as her headache threatened to burst out of her skin. "I can never have children."

Her hangover finally overflowed, and she turned away to retch. Unlike in the church, he didn't move to hold her steady. She sank to a crouch while her digestive system tried to turn itself inside out. She tried to think around the blinding obstacles thrown up by her pain-racked brain.

When the vomiting had settled into intermittent dry heaves, she said hoarsely, "What exactly did your brother want you to bring back?"

"The graviteria host. Failing that, some form of graviteria

sample. And my brother really wants this microbiologist called River Lee, who he thinks is still alive in the zones somewhere. Apparently, she had some unique ideas about the capabilities of an infected host that he wanted to test out."

She spat and spat again to try to clear her mouth of the taste of bile. Then she let herself tip backwards to sit on the warm pavement. Bees hummed in the clover by the side of the road. A row of starlings sat on a sagging telephone wire like beads on a necklace. Farther down the road a rabbit hopped slowly along, occasionally stopping to nibble on the greenery. Just another lazy summer day in the zones. Her last summer. And maybe her last day in the zones.

"So tell me, Ryan, what does your brother have on you? Why are you doing this when you know it's wrong?"

"You think you fucking know me?" But he sounded tired, not venomous. She took tiny sips of water while she waited. "I have my reasons."

"So you need to bring your brother something," she said when it became apparent he wouldn't elaborate. "It doesn't necessarily have to be me."

His face hardened. "Let's get moving."

She got up but turned her back on the quarantine walls and began walking toward Yorky instead.

"Where do you think you're going?" He didn't immediately move to stop her, thrown off by her calm pace.

"Forcing you to shoot me."

He was behind her now. Her back crawled, waiting for the slam of a bullet into her spine. She kept walking, kept her eyes on the ragged horizon, on home.

"I don't have to shoot you. I'll just knock you unconscious and carry you."

"You do what you have to, Ryan. I'll do the same."

She listened for footsteps behind her and heard nothing.

Each stride carried her farther away from him, but he could catch her easily if he wanted to. Or shoot her even more easily.

What kind of man was he? He didn't trust Titus but had let himself be convinced that his brother had a cure for Jasper and because of that was willing to risk a Shattering. She'd been Darius's pet long enough to know that games like this were never simple. She didn't expect him to be able to put into words the hold his brother had over him, even when he thought he'd freed himself, any more than she could explain how deeply Darius still lived in her bones and blood and psyche long after his death.

"What would you suggest?" he asked finally.

His tone turned her around. He hadn't taken a step toward her or drawn his gun.

"Why turn over a Shattering time bomb to your brother, who you clearly don't trust, when instead you could let me take the cure first and *then* turn me over. I'd still be graviteria-infected but harmless. You could claim to your brother I was like that when you found me. The threat of the Shattering would be over. Your conscience would be clear ... ish."

"And you want me to believe you'd just quietly come with me after that?"

"You know where to find my family and friends. It would be too easy for you to apply pressure if you needed to. Anyway, there's a good chance the cure will leave me a drooling vegetable, so . . ." She shrugged. "I won't care much at that point."

"Yeah, and out here on your turf there'll be plenty of opportunities for me to conveniently, accidentally end up dead. What's my guarantee that won't happen?"

"Because I have an alternative to kidnapping me. If we're going to the Tower anyway, there are some graviteria samples still stored there—it's how the prototypes are tested. In addition, I think I know who that microbiologist you're looking for is."

"River Lee? Really? No one else knew who I was talking about."

"I didn't even know River Lee was her name. She's known as the Guardian. She's the leader of the ReGeneration, and she stays in the deep zones so no one ever sees her, but the other day Zenobia met with her. That was the conversation I overheard."

Ryan cursed. "*That's* why Zenobia sent me to talk to the Damaskers that morning, to get me out of the way. I can't believe I was that close."

"The ReGeneration guard the Tower. We wouldn't get in without their help anyway, so you'll get a chance to talk to the Guardian. What do you think? Would your brother be satisfied with a graviteria sample and this microbiologist instead of me?"

He considered the horizon. "He might. If I convinced him."

"Which is why it's in my best interests to keep you alive. Because I don't want Titus sending anyone else into the zones, and who better to persuade him than his little brother?"

His jaw flexed. "It's not like I have any influence over him."

"But neither does he believe you'll lie to him. Isn't that right?"

He stared at her, then swore under his breath.

"Face it, if you didn't want to be talked out of it, you'd have given me enough drug to stay asleep until you got me outside the walls."

"You think you know me."

Against all logic and past experience, she did. "What I *don't* know is why you're really doing this. You know my ugly secrets. I think you owe me a little reciprocal truth, don't you?"

He inhaled and his lips pinched. For a second Jasper felt as if a furnace door had been flung open in front of her face, releasing a blast of heat and a glimpse of a tightly contained rage she hadn't even suspected until now. But just as swiftly, the furnace was relocked and in its chilly absence was fear. He rubbed the back of his neck and swallowed.

"He has my son," he said.

It was like jumping into a zone and finding yourself hurled in the direction opposite to the one you'd expected, a whiplash of the whole body.

"You're a father?"

"Will be. She's due in a couple of months." He studied the ground, avoiding her eyes. "Titus is watching over her while I'm here."

"As a hostage." Things were becoming painfully clear.

"Titus got Allison a job with his company. So now she has benefits and health insurance and maternity leave and daycare —all of it. But he could take that away just as easily. I would have told her not to take the job, that I'd find some other way to support her and the kid, but she doesn't believe me about Titus. She thinks he's great. And it doesn't matter. Either way, Titus will find a way to hurt her and the kid if I don't do what he told me to. He's playing the part of indulgent uncle, which Allison loves, but all I can think about is the damage he could do to an impressionable kid . . ." He stopped speaking for several moments. "It's the perfect way to keep me in his control."

Man after my own heart, this Titus. Darius chuckled.

Jasper turned her back on Ryan so she could reorder her face, her emotions, her perspective. It was cold comfort that she'd been right about Ryan's character all along. Either that or his acting abilities were unreal and he was ensuring Jasper was too sympathetic to his plight to consider his death a possible solution to her problems. Too paranoid? Better than too trusting.

Offspring: a truly stunning weakness that no rational adult should allow themselves.

"You see why I can't go through those gates empty-handed," he said.

"Yes, I see." She resumed walking toward Yorky and this time heard him follow. She slowed down enough to let him catch up. When he did, she held out her bound wrists for him to cut the tie. "But don't expect me to trust you again anytime soon."

He rubbed a hand over his face, the stubble rasping. "That's fair."

"So's this." She stepped close and punched him in the stomach. For a moment she watched him doubled over and groaning. Then she turned away.

"That's for fucking gagging me."

15

THE ROAD TO DAMASCUS

Scars, the evidence of everything you've survived

~ Veronica Park (*Things I Will Miss/Reasons to Live*)

The original Saints of Damascus cult had settled in several suburban blocks dense with townhouses, many with fenced yards. These fences had been reinforced and heightened. In other places, with their outer-facing windows and doors boarded up, the attached townhouses formed part of the wall, with the partial exception of upper windows, which were used as lookouts and defensible positions. In this way a fully walled compound was created, with all open space inside the compounds used for agriculture or communal activities.

After the death of their eccentric prophet, many of the cult members had drifted away, but Nico Mavuto had seen an opportunity and taken over the training of the younger, more fanatical cultists, redirecting their energies to aims that suited him and creating an army in the process.

Jasper and Ryan took up positions on opposite sides of the compound throughout the day and then met up again in the evening to compare notes about the frequency of ganger patrols around the walls, and the inspections the guards performed on everyone who passed into the gates. The only people who'd left the compound were animal herders and field workers. The gangers patrolled the walls and a squad of teenagers in identical black shirts engaged in training manoeuvres in an open field.

Dusk fell and fires were lit. The field workers trudged back through the gates, where the guards checked them before allowing them through, then the cows and goats in a lowing, bleating, dusty haze, along with their herders and a few dogs. The squad of recruits had re-entered the compound hours ago.

Jasper lowered her binocs and glanced over at Ryan, who sat at ease on a moss-covered mattress on the third floor of this abandoned townhouse. He'd napped while she kept watch and now looked irritatingly well rested. Despite his relaxed appearance, he was breaking down and cleaning his gun for the third time that evening. Jasper didn't know whether she wanted to throw the damn gun out the window or let herself be lulled by the methodical, hypnotic motions of his hands. Any light could give them away, so he accomplished his ritual by feel and habit in heavy shadow.

She tossed the binocs on the bed. "My eyes hurt. Your turn."

She left the room before he could say anything and made her way down the dark hallway by memory. At the back of the house, where she'd be hidden from the Damasker compound, she climbed out of the window onto the roof of the adjoining garage and did push-ups until the taut jitteriness in her muscles subsided.

"Still not sure why we have to break this kid out," Ryan said, leaning out of the window to watch her. "I'm in favour of helping abducted kids, of course, but it sounds like there's a lot of them here, so why this one in particular? Aren't there other ways to find the ReGeneration?"

"You're supposed to be watching the compound."

"They've closed their gates for the night."

Jasper put one hand behind her back and continued her push-ups. "This kid knows how to find the ReGeneration," she said between breaths.

That was a blatant lie, but it should be enough to satisfy him. She saw no reason to get into the story of her mother stealing something Zenobia didn't want her to find. At best he'd find it irrelevant to his mission. At worst he'd be too interested. She might be a slow learner in the trusting Ryan department, but she did learn.

The truth might come out later, but as long as Grammar was free and provided her with the information she needed, she didn't much care. The zones were her territory. If she wanted to take a detour to find her mother's body on the way to the Tower, Ryan was hardly in a position to protest. He might not even notice, since it was impossible to travel in a straight line in the zones.

"There must be other ways of finding the ReGeneration," he said doubtfully. "I don't think we can afford side quests, especially one as risky as this. As you said yourself, there's some time pressure here. This looks like a delaying action on your part. We had an agreement."

"I don't care what you think." Despite the sudden hot streak of anger, she kept her voice down. They were a quarter mile from the compound, but sound carried in still night air. "I'm getting that kid. You can help or not, but the only way you're stopping me is to knock me out again."

Her challenge heated the air between them. Finally, he said, "I'd like to look my son in the eye one day with a clear conscience, but mainly I'd like the chance to look him in the eye at all. I don't want to kidnap or kill anyone, and I don't want to deliver a potential Shattering to my brother. But I'll do what I have to."

"We're already super clear on that point, downie." She tipped over into a handstand and kicked idly at the stars.

Ryan withdrew from the window and disappeared back into the house.

When the darkness had thickened to midnight, they moved toward the compound. They carried no light, navigating by the torches along the compound walls. Without too many stumbles in the dark, they reached the stretch of boarded-up townhouses that Jasper had marked in her mind's eye.

As she'd expected, the Damasker gangers focused their patrols and watchfulness on the lower walls and considered the boarded-up townhouses to be more solid barriers.

Ryan waited below as Jasper climbed freehand up the side of a townhouse. Candlelight filtered from a few of the boarded-up windows, but she should go unnoticed in the dark, and hopefully whatever scuffling sounds she made would be attributed to squirrels or mice in the walls. Once at the top she tied her rope around a chimney and tossed the end down to Ryan. He attached it to the makeshift harness she'd made him wear and climbed slowly but carefully till he reached the roof.

So he could climb a simple wall in down-gee; that was nothing to be impressed about. The gravity zones would be the real test.

Jasper turned to descending the other side into the compound. Firelight flared on a few street corners, tended by gangers on patrol, but otherwise the streets were empty, and only a few scattered windows still held candlelight. From their vantage point on the roof, Jasper studied the compound layout. Ryan touched her shoulder and pointed.

She nodded. Of course, the school. What better place to imprison a bunch of unwilling kids?

Windows were not boarded up on the inner-facing side of the townhouses, but most people would be asleep by now. They dropped down onto a garage roof and from there into a narrow alley between buildings. Keeping to the shadows, they made their way toward the school. They hid behind a dumpster while two gangers shared a smoke. When the gangers re-entered the school, Ryan, swift and silent, darted after them and kept the door from swinging shut. The gangers disappeared down the locker-lined hall, and Jasper slipped inside with Ryan behind her.

Ryan pointed out the exit sign that marked a stairwell. They descended the dark, echoing stairs as quietly as possible into the basement where, according to the stories she'd heard, the newest recruits would be kept. A murmur rose as they approached the last set of stairwell doors. Torchlight filtered from under the doors.

"I thought they were supposed to be asleep at this time," Ryan murmured into her ear.

Jasper listened, a bad feeling growing in her gut. She pulled the door open and peered into the hallway. A single hall torch flickered spookily over bare concrete and tile. Doors that should've been shut, locking recruits inside, were ajar, revealing empty bunk beds. No ganger guards were visible.

Instead all the recruits were crowded into one of the rooms, with more gathered outside peering in. She heard a ripple of sound, a murmur of voices. The mood lifted the hair on Jasper's spine. The unmistakable thud of fists on flesh and the grunt and ragged gasps of the combatants carried clearly through the electric tension of the spectators.

Jasper ducked back and turned to see Ryan's face falling into grim lines. "Listen to me, downie. If we're going to get ourselves and the kid out of here alive, you're going to follow my lead, see?"

He gave her a flat stare but gestured curtly for her to go ahead. She'd already tied on a black bandanna to cover her distinctive short hair. She couldn't do anything about her face except hope the lighting was dim and that no one here had met her before. She dug out a wana joint from a pouch and stuck it between her lips unlit. Then she pushed open the doors and stepped into the hallway. Ryan followed.

The kids in the hall turned to see them, their faces wary and hostile and closed. Nearly all of them had triple scars across each cheekbone. Jasper kept her expression bland, shoulders slouched, strolling in with as much insouciance as she could muster. At their presence a murmur moved through the crowd; Jasper and Ryan were causing a stir, turning heads and savage eyes, though the sounds of the fight didn't abate. Suspicious glances slid over her and settled on Ryan's towering presence behind her. Eyes widened, but nobody raised an alarm. The kids parted without protest and let her and Ryan slip into the room.

The crowd closed back around them, cutting off their escape.

Jasper loosened her shoulders and moved as if she'd been thrown into Darius's dog pit—*I'm not here for trouble, but if you start it, I'll fucking finish it*. It was the only way to handle strange dogs and a potentially murderous swarm of feral teenagers. She didn't know what Ryan's face showed, but having him right behind her, covering her back, was reassuring. This room alone probably contained more shivs than an entire downieland prison.

"Where the fuck are the adults in charge?" Ryan whispered in her ear.

She jerked her chin to indicate a trio of older teenagers leaning against the far wall, smoking. They were armed, unlike the crowd of raw recruits. The gangers stared in their direction, perplexed, as if struggling to recognize them but not yet alarmed by their presence. This might be an underground fight club, but Damaskers weren't the only ones invited. Jasper spotted several faces in the crowd who were clearly not Damaskers.

One was Crane.

Her heart froze for an instant and her step stuttered. It was certainly Crane's kind of scene. It wasn't shocking to see her, but it wasn't welcome. Crane saw her an instant later and her sharp eyebrows rose. Jasper tapped a casual finger against her lips and winked. Crane frowned but shrugged.

Was there a chance Zenobia had sent Crane to retrieve Grammar and they were here for the same reason? If so, this could get messy.

"Is that . . . ?" Ryan began, but she quelled him with a gesture. Crane was a wild card, but nothing could be done about it now.

With Ryan behind her, Jasper pushed to the front of the crowd and got her first look at the combatants.

Grammar and a boy twice his size rolled on the floor, trading punches. Grammar's face was nearly unrecognizable, swollen and covered in blood, and only his furious speed and agility prevented the bigger boy from pinning him.

Jasper cursed.

"I take it that's the kid," Ryan said.

If Grammar had just been a spectator, she could've sneaked him away while everyone's attention was on the fight. But now she'd have to wait for it to be over.

If he even survived it. The bigger boy slammed his forehead into Grammar's, and Grammar went slack. The other boy straddled him and lifted his fist. Behind her, Ryan made a convulsive movement, and she planted an elbow in his stomach.

Jasper stepped forward and clapped her hands together

limply, drawing all eyes to her. "Mildly entertaining, I'm supposen," she said, pitching her voice to be heard above the guttural buzz of the crowd. "I'm hopen the next fight is a little better matched. Makes for more excitement, dontcha think?" She gestured disdainfully, indicating the size difference of the combatants. "Anyway, I been comen too late to be betten on this one. So who's the next pair, eh? Be bringen 'em out so I can be spenden my good copper."

The hulking boy's fist still hovered over Grammar's face. He twisted around to look uncertainly at the three Damasker gangers.

Jasper had everybody's attention in the room and she could feel their eyes crawling over her skin. The three gangers looked at each other. Then their leader, a tall white girl with crooked teeth and beautiful blue eyes, stepped forward. She had the shape of a supermodel and the cruel smile of an alpha.

"Fight's not done yet." Her eyes raked Jasper from head to toe.

"Is looken done to me," Jasper said derisively. Grammar was blinking but seemed only half conscious. "Unless this is a fight to the death or something."

As soon as she'd said the words, she wished she hadn't.

The blond alpha's lips curled upward. "You're new," she said. "You're not knowen how this worken. How is it you're comen here?"

Jasper gambled. "Crane's been tellen me about it, of course."

Crane had disappeared; Jasper couldn't see her anywhere in the crowd.

"Well, you're knowen how Crane is," Jasper said hastily, waving her joint in the air to distract the alpha from Crane's untimely departure. "Just been tellen me it'd be fun. Why don't you be explainen it so I can be layen my bets." She pulled out a thin strand of copper wire that she'd managed to salvage from the basement of the otherwise looted house she and Ryan had camped in.

One of the other gangers appeared at the alpha's shoulder. "Vic, I'm thinken she's—"

"I know," Vic said. Her blue eyes hadn't left Jasper's face. She grabbed Jasper's wrist and pulled her forward. Before Jasper could resist, the alpha jerked her T-shirt up, revealing the pine tree scars cut into her abdomen.

A gasp and a whisper spread through the crowd.

"Be looken at that, younglings. We're haven a celebrity with us," Vic said, jeering.

It wasn't hostility that animated the faces that stared at her; neither was it awe nor adoration like she might find among younger pack kids. Instead it was a kind of avidity, an eagerness to see what would happen, a hunger for spectacle, for violence. Jasper's heart pounded and her skin prickled with the volatile wash of emotion in the room. She was the Pinegirl, but the Pinegirl was a legend, and legends couldn't show weakness. Here, showing weakness meant death.

She waved at the crowd modestly. "Oh, I'm just here to see the fights. Never mind me. Carry on. But please tell me these two are done. I was expecting to see a real fight."

Vic's smile held all the warmth of a praying mantis. "Long ago, you been given us the rules of the pack, Pinegirl. Here—now—*I'm* maken a rule. Same rule as every night. If he's winnen, he's liven. If he's losen, well ..."

Jasper looked again at Grammar and realized that the bruises visible through streaks of blood were not only black and blue but also purple, yellow, and green, in the various stages of healing. Grammar must have been fighting for his life every day for almost a week. Behind her, Ryan made an inarticulate sound, as if from the same realization.

But somehow the kid was still alive.

"Doesn't seem like the most effective way to keep recruits," Jasper said as her mind raced for a way out of this. "Wouldn't Nico notice if recruits were dying every single night?"

"Oh, no. Not all recruits are fighten. Just the special ones." Vic's smile turned ugly. Ugli*er*. "Just the ones with attitude. The alpha-brains who're not knowen when to give up. Those ones, they'll never be belongen anyway."

Ryan said, his voice deadly calm, "In that case you won't mind if we just take him off your hands, right?"

Vic glanced at him and then over at Grammar. "It's the boy you're wanten, then?"

"You clearly don't. We'd be doing you a service," Ryan said.

Jasper controlled the urge to kick Ryan in the shin, but barely. Now Vic knew what they wanted, but they were in no position to bargain. They had nothing to bargain with. The strand of copper was pocket change to an alpha who, above all else, would love to show her dominance over the Pinegirl in front of her followers. If she could make Jasper look weak or foolish or like a supplicant, Vic's status would rise and Jasper's legend would erode.

Vic cocked a thumb at Ryan. "Maybe I'm traden you the kid for your tall boytoy."

Some of the kids laughed. Jasper felt her fingernails dig into her palms as she controlled the urge to bop Vic a sharp one on the nose. She opened her mouth.

"I think you sadly overestimate what you can handle," Ryan drawled. His words seemed to come longer and looser the angrier he was.

Vic only laughed, self-satisfied and cocky here on her own turf. She turned back to Jasper. "What are you wanten the kid for?"

"The little runt owes me, and I'd like a chance to collect on that debt before he's dead. So if you could leave him a little bit alive, I'd appreciate it." Jasper let her eyes fall on Grammar. His swollen eyes wandered over her face blankly.

Vic crossed her arms over her chest. "Not gonna just be given him to you. Wanna be watchen him fight."

Negotiations had begun.

"I wouldn't want to see you lose your entertainment," Jasper said. "Of course you'll be compensated."

"How about a wager? I'm hearen you're liken wagers." Vic's smile turned sly and predatory. "How about you and me fighten, Pinegirl? If you're winnen, you can be haven the kid. If you're losen . . ." Her breath smelled like rot as she leaned into Jasper's face. ". . . I'll be carven my name into your belly."

It was all Jasper could do to keep her face still as the kids whooped and cheered, a sudden clamour of noise, a surge of awful, bloody excitement. To see the Pinegirl fight, to see her possibly defeated and humiliated, they'd be witness to a new legend rising and an old one dying.

Vic matched her in size and weight, but it had been over a year since Jasper had last fought with her fists. It just wasn't her scene anymore. But Vic wouldn't be out of practice.

You can't fight her on her terms, pet. You know what you have to do.

Her knife sat heavy on her hip. It dragged at her belt, dragged at her gut, dragged the blood from her chest.

She's not a worthy opponent. She's beneath you. You need to show them that.

She needed to respond or lose face. The longer she hesitated, the further the crowd's support would swing away from her. She searched desperately for words, for a plan, and couldn't find either. All she had was the oversized weight of her knife.

Put her down, pet, quick and bloody. Right now. Stomp on her like a cockroach. It's the only way.

Vic slapped her in the face with the back of her hand. Jasper gasped as the sting made her eyes water. The watching kids cried out in surprise and anticipation.

"Not much of a legend, it's looken like," Vic said contemptuously.

Jasper punched her in the face, grabbed Vic's head, brought up her knee, and slammed Vic's face into it.

Adrenalin rocketed through her.

This was a dog pit. There were no rules. In a dog pit you dominated or you died.

Vic reeled, blood pouring from her face, as the crowd roared.

Jasper found her fist full of Vic's shirt. Found a knife in her hand. A knife pressed to Vic's throat, carving a thin red line into white skin.

That's it, pet. You've been here before. You know how this goes.

Her stomach lurched and bile crawled up her throat.

Doesn't she deserve it, pet? Didn't I?

She was frozen. White blinded her eyes and her legs wouldn't hold her.

Remembering a knife in her hand and blood on the floor . . .

"Pinegirl, don't!" Ryan's voice.

Couldn't he see she was a thin skin of ice over water, seconds from collapsing? Couldn't they all see? She'd fall and they'd devour her. The dogs were always waiting for her to fall.

She could feel him beside her, solid and rooted as a tree. "Come on, Pinegirl. Last time you did this, we were cleaning blood and brains out of our hair for weeks."

What? She couldn't understand what he was saying and why his voice sounded impatient, long suffering. But the white was receding from her eyes.

Everyone was staring at Ryan now.

"Remember how long it took us to scrub the blood off the walls, and the ceiling too?" Ryan gave her a pointed look. "But I guess that's what happens when you jerk someone's heart out of their chest with your bare hand and then stomp on it."

Oh. Jasper struggled to swallow down the sour burn in her throat. Her hand was frozen to the knife, the knife she had used to slice a narrow line through Vic's throat. But she forced her voice to work. "I suspect Vic's heart will be much smaller and more shrivelled. Less of a mess."

The kids' eyes widened as they clutched their amulets. Some looked excited at the promise of a spectacle but others shrank backwards.

Vic held still as stone, but fury was replacing the stunned look in her eyes. "Not afraid of you. You're just a girl."

"A girl who's killen the devil," somebody mumbled, loud enough to be heard but quiet enough to remain unidentified. Jasper wouldn't have sworn it was Grammar, but the voice sure seemed to have come from near the floor.

Vic glowered, but the anger in her face wavered.

"The real problem," Ryan said, "was that the Pinegirl stomped so hard that the room shook." He scanned the ceiling anxiously. "If she were to do that now, this whole ceiling would collapse. Look at those cracks in the walls. And no windows to escape." He sucked in his breath through his teeth, shaking his head in dismay. "Shoddy construction. This whole building would come down on top of us."

Kids lifted their heads, twisted around to study the walls and low concrete ceiling. Murmurs took on the higher pitch of alarm.

Jasper sighed theatrically. "I know, but Vic wanted a fight." The tremble was working its way down her arm. In moments the knife would be rattling in her hand, destroying any intimidation factor she'd gained. "Is that what you want, Vic? Or shall we go about this a different way?"

Vic stared at her with hatred and then at the kids, who

seemed moments away from stampeding from the room. Her mouth worked and finally she said, "You're talken compensation?"

"Compensation?" Ryan snorted. "We'll let you all live and we'll take the kid. How about that?"

Even with a knife to her throat, Vic's lip curled. "Is your magic strong enough to be stoppen crossbow bolts?"

It certainly was not. "Oh, let's not get unfriendly," Jasper said. "I'm a reasonable person, Vic. And I'm not the one who started this." As a show of good faith, she removed the knife from Vic's neck and lowered it to her side; she wouldn't be able to sheathe it cleanly with her hand shaking this much.

Vic took a step back, pressing her hand to the cut on her throat. Caution was now mixed with hatred as she narrowed her eyes at Jasper.

"You're entitled to compensation, of course," Jasper said, putting condescension in her voice as if generously granting a favour, not bluffing from a position of weakness. Because her mind was a blank. They had nothing of value to trade. "I've got good credit with the Azuros," she began, knowing how weak it sounded.

But Vic was eyeing Ryan. "I'll be letten you take the kid," she said, "for that gun."

Ryan made a face like he'd swallowed a mouthful of gasoline. "Wow, kids are a real bargain these days, huh? What do toddlers go for? Two butter knives and some pocket lint?"

"Nothing. Toddlers are useless." Vic held out her hand and waited. A narrow slash of a smile curved across her face at Ryan's reluctance.

Ryan looked at Jasper, his feelings briefly transparent. He didn't want to buy a child and he didn't want to give up his gun. She grimaced in answer. Did he have any better ideas?

Ryan inhaled deeply through his nose and glanced at

Grammar, bloody and motionless under the weight of the bigger boy. Grudgingly, he unholstered his gun. With precise, emphatic movements he unloaded it and pocketed the bullets. He slapped the empty gun into Vic's hand.

"Bullets too," Vic said, lips white with fury.

Jasper clicked her tongue in disapproval. "Look at the kid! He's beat to shit! I'm not giving you a gun *and* bullets for a kid who's barely functional. Don't tell me there's a single useless recruit here that you'd pay that much for."

Vic's smile was uglier than her scowl. She gave a mocking bow of acquiescence and tucked the gun into her waistband. She walked back to join her two lieutenants, only now belatedly fumbling to load their crossbows.

Jasper used both hands to slide her knife back into its sheath and was relieved to succeed without too much fumbling. She pushed her hands into her pockets to hide their trembling and approached Grammar. Awareness had filtered back into his eyes, though he remained unmoving beneath his opponent.

"Hope you don't have much to pack, kid."

"Not so fast," said Vic.

Vic's two gangers aimed loaded crossbows at them.

Jasper's knife was sheathed and Ryan was no longer armed, and the three Damaskers were across the room out of reach.

"We had a deal," Jasper said.

"I hope you're ready to be crushed by a thousand pounds of concrete," Ryan said in a tone of resignation.

The crowd thinned as recruits closer to the door edged into the hall. Others reached for their amulets and cast uneasy glances between Jasper and Vic. Jasper tried to smile like someone who'd held a beating human heart in her hand before and might like to again.

Vic held steady, her smile vindictive. "The deal's standen. But I been maken a previous promise to all these fine younglings

—I been promisen a fight. So you can be haven the boy, yes. But only if he's winnen."

Jasper glanced at Grammar, still supine on the concrete. His wandering eyes focused on her and narrowed. The boy on top of him raised his bloody fist to finish the fight. The room swayed as if she were on the flamingo and dogs prowled beneath her.

"Fine," she said. "Deal."

16

FIGHT AND FLIGHT

Things we have to tell our children:
Keep an eye on the sky
Down is a state of mind
Wear a helmet when it's windy out

~ Veronica Park (*Lists of the Apocalypse*)

"Jasper . . ." Ryan said, barely moving his lips. He looked a breath away from snatching Grammar and running.

At this range, they'd sprout crossbow quarrels like pincushions. So would the unlucky kids standing near them in the crowded room.

She grabbed a handful of his shirt, pulling him back. She could've chipped her nails against the coiled steel tension in his muscles. "Trust me, Ryan!" she said, trying to keep the fear out of her voice. Fear and doubt, because what if she was wrong about the spark of alertness and understanding she'd seen in Grammar's eyes?

Vic nodded to the boy on top of Grammar.

The boy's fist descended.

Grammar twisted like a fish and jabbed his elbow into the other boy's crotch. The boy howled and Grammar lunged upward and sank his teeth into the boy's jaw, biting and tearing skin and flesh. The boy screamed, shrill and awful.

A second later Grammar was on top, hands wrapped around the other boy's throat, and the only sound in the room was the savage scarlet growl coming from Grammar and the other boy choking, heels kicking a tattoo on the floor.

Jasper gripped Ryan's shirt with both hands now, leaning into him to hold him back.

"I'm not watching any kid get killed here today." He moved her aside with insulting ease.

The mood in the room shifted. A groan and a rising murmur.

Grammar's opponent slapped the ground feebly, his face purple. Grammar snarled in his face, his grip not slackening.

"*Dalca,*" Jasper heard the kids around her whisper. "*Devilman.*"

"Grammar!" she cried.

Ryan stepped forward.

Grammar released the boy and jumped to his feet, teeth bared in a bloody grimace.

Jasper grabbed Ryan by the belt and pulled him to a stop. The boy on the floor gasped raggedly for breath, moaning with pain and shock. Ryan hesitated.

"Easy." Jasper didn't know whether she was talking to Ryan or Darius's bloody child.

Grammar paced back and forth, raw fists clenched at his side, blood dripping in syrupy streamers down his chin. One eye was swollen shut and only a glint of blue showed in the other.

He opened his mouth and screamed at the silent crowd, a harsh, wordless sound.

His challenge was answered only by silence.

He stopped in front of the alpha and stared at her with an arrogance shocking in someone who'd nearly been pulped into unconsciousness. "Be fighten me," he said to her.

Vic's brow creased in black fury. "I'm not fighten worms. I'm only killen them."

"Afraid," Grammar said through raw lips.

A knife was in Vic's hand and she was stabbing before Jasper could inhale.

Ryan lunged forward. Clutching a handful of the boy's shirt, he jerked him out of the way. With a chop of his other hand, Ryan sent Vic's knife flying. The clatter echoed loudly in the abrupt, frozen silence.

Ryan loomed over Vic, ignoring the two gangers who pointed crossbows at him with shaking hands. His glare was searing, but his expression was rigidly, ferociously controlled.

Jasper stepped forward, praying her voice wouldn't squeak. "He won. The boy's mine."

Vic edged back from Ryan without taking her eyes from him. "He's Dalca spawn," she spat. "He's *bad*, Pinegirl. Better never be turnen your back. Better never be trusten."

Alas, if only someone had warned me about you, Darius mused. *But would I have listened? Probably not.*

I need him, Jasper said silently.

Need's a boggy swamp, pet. A place to lure others, not get trapped yourself.

Ryan still had a grip on Grammar's shirt. Stunned, the boy made no attempt to pull free, the fury and bloodlust gone out of him. Ryan's hand may have been all that was holding him on his feet.

"Let's go," Jasper said. Tension scraped her throat raw.

Vic made no move to stop them. The crowd parted and they left in eerie silence, Grammar stumbling at Ryan's side, leaving a trail of his blood behind them.

The silence lasted until they reached the stairwell. The letter of the promise had been fulfilled. Shouts broke out, echoing through the basement.

"Go, go, go," Jasper cried, alarmed by the way Grammar was swaying and tripping over the stairs.

Ryan hoisted the boy and tossed him over his shoulder. They raced up the stairs and then slammed to a halt as a pair of gangers ran down the hall toward them. Ryan spun and Jasper followed. They ran in the other direction around the corner and toward the exit doors at the far end.

But there'd be guards at those doors too.

Ahead of them Crane poked her head out of a classroom and looked around inquisitively.

"Jasper, what's goen—?"

Jasper grabbed Ryan, and they dodged sideways through the classroom door, pushing Crane with them. In the darkness they stood frozen as the Damasker gangers ran past in the hallway.

With a scrape and some sparks, Crane lit a candle.

"Never mind what happened," Jasper said when Crane opened her mouth. "We need to get out of here."

"And blow out the damn light," Ryan whispered.

Crane ignored him. She was wearing jeans covered in various sizes of asymmetrical patches of purple and green and blue. Her T-shirt had KNIFE TO MEET YOU embroidered on it, a gift from Jasper a few Christmases ago.

Jasper registered the room's other occupant.

"*Grace?*" Seeing a sixteen-year-old Mennonite girl at an underground Damasker fight club in the company of Crane, of all people, wasn't the unlikeliest thing Jasper had ever seen, but it made the top ten. First in the church with Dragon, and now here with Crane?

"What are you two doing here in the dark?" Jasper asked blankly, registering a pile of half-eaten strawberries beside the candle. Her brain scrambled for possible explanations and came up only with a string of exclamation marks. "What is this, a date? In the middle of the night at a fight club in Damascus, Crane? Are you kidding me?"

Was it possible Crane wasn't here for Grammar at Zenobia's behest?

Grace flushed. "This isn't—it's not—we were just—"

"She been sayen she's wanten to come here," Crane said indignantly. "Can't be sayen no to a pretty girl. Ha, look at her face!" Delightedly, she prodded Grace's cheek with a fingertip. "It's pink! She's turnen pink. How's she doen that?"

Grace once again wore distinctly non-Mennonite garb, jeans and a sweatshirt, and her cropped blond hair was hidden under a knit hat. When had she chopped off her long blond braids? That must have caused a ruckus in her family. She had a grav-walker's pouch strapped to her thigh, decorated with vampiric kittens and zombie rabbits.

Jasper recognized that pouch. She had decorated it and given it to Vron long ago. She hadn't seen it in years. But it was the least of her concerns right now.

Jasper smacked Crane's hand away. She grabbed Grace's shoulders. "Grace Kornelsen, tell me what the fuck you're doing here this instant or I'll tell Esther and Merlot everything."

Grace looked horrified. "Don't tell my sister. Are you crazy? And Merlot would kill me." She caught Jasper's glare and hurried on. "I came here looking for someone named Grammar. I know he's here because Merlot told me what happened on your gravving trip and he mentioned Grammar's name. I tried to get Dragon to help me see him, but he wouldn't unless I—he wanted . . ." She stopped and bit her lip. "Anyway, that's why I asked Crane instead to get me in."

The string of exclamation marks in Jasper's head grew longer. She pointed at the blood-covered boy draped over Ryan's arm as Ryan stood by the door, listening. "You mean that Grammar?"

Grace's eyes grew round. "That's Grammar? Is he alive? Why do you have him? How did you find him? No one here would answer my questions."

"Because you're talken too pretty and never sayen fuck," Crane said.

"Can we maybe, just maybe, do this later?" Ryan asked.

"One second," Jasper snapped. Her brain was going to explode if she didn't get some instant answers. She glared into Grace's wide blue eyes. "Why are *you* looking for Grammar? Speak!"

"Because Vron talked about him in her journal," Grace blurted.

"What?"

"Yeah, what?" Crane was suddenly frowning. "What journal? All Vron's journals been burnen after she been dyen."

"Not this one," Grace said and patted the pouch on her thigh. "She gave it to me the day before she . . . before she died. I only started reading it recently, though."

"We need to move. Now," said Ryan and opened the door.

When Crane only stood there and frowned at Grace, Jasper blew out the candle and tugged on Crane's arm. They all hurried after Ryan into an empty hallway. Shouts came from outside and echoed in the building.

"This way," said Crane. They followed her into a different room and out a window with a loose board.

They ran for the townhouse where they'd left the rope. Light bloomed in a few more windows as shouts echoed down the street. Ryan climbed first, with Grammar clinging to his back.

"Why you not been tellen me you been haven Vron's notebook?" Crane demanded to Grace as they waited.

"Why would it matter?" Grace asked.

"I'm thinken you're wanten—" Crane cut herself off. She made a sharp, dismissive gesture that included rippling a knife over her knuckles before sheathing it.

Grace frowned at her uncertainly.

Ryan and Grammar reached the rooftop.

"You next," Jasper said to Grace.

"No," Crane said. "They never seen us with you. We'll be maken a distraction and you can be goen."

"Are you sure?" Jasper asked, surprised by the offer, although Crane wasn't wrong.

"What kind of distraction?" Grace demanded, looking alarmed.

"Fighten or kissen, you choose," Crane said with her toothiest grin.

Grace smacked Crane's arm with the back of her hand, and Jasper was reassured. Grace still had the spunk that had so amused and won over Merlot when he was unwillingly fostered by the Kornelsen family years earlier. Maybe she could handle Crane. As much as Crane could be handled without inflicting injury.

"Okay, you're choosen fighten." Crane's smile grew wider. "Let's be goen." She hustled Grace out of the alley.

Jasper grabbed Crane's arm for a last word. "I better see her in Yorky tomorrow in one piece, Crane. She's not a feral or a ganger. She's never been in a fight in her life. Take care of her."

Crane pulled her arm away with an unfriendly grin. "What's that Zenobia's always sayen and sayen? Oh yeah, *consequences*.

Choices are haven consequences. This little pink cheek girl is maken the choice to be here."

"Crane..."

"Jasper," Crane said, mimicking her tone. She pulled a horrible face at Jasper and ran after Grace.

Jasper hesitated. Could she really leave Grace in Crane's indifferent, dangerous hands in the heart of Damasker territory? Did she have any choice?

Ryan hissed her name from the roof. She climbed rapidly and helped guide Grammar down the other side of the roof in the dark. As their feet hit the ground outside the walls, voices bubbled out from the gates. Dogs barked and howled. Whatever distraction Crane and Grace had undertaken had only delayed the inevitable by a minute or two.

With Grammar on his back, Ryan headed toward Yorky. Jasper seized his arm.

"They've got dogs. The only way we're going to lose them is if we go into the zones where the dogs can't follow."

He followed her without question. They ran through the dark, grass whipping their legs and branches stinging their faces, stumbling and tripping over unseen obstacles.

Jasper had marked out the zone borders during her day of reconnaissance, and navigating by moonlight she aimed for the nearest one. It was west-draw side-gee, which meant that when the warning buzz and tingle of the zone border brought them to a halt, they were standing at the top of a gravity cliff, although the ground continued to stretch out with apparently innocent flatness before them. The ground extended westward a dozen metres to the crumbling wall of a car dealership. Crumpled fallen cars hunched against the wall.

Behind them dogs yipped and bayed in excitement. Fear clawed its fingers through Jasper's bloodstream, causing her to fumble as she looped the rope around a tree on the down-gee side of the border.

"Take the kid down to the wall and hide inside," she said. "Hurry. I'll have to untie or cut the rope so they don't notice it." She forestalled his protest. "I'll climb freehand. Go!"

Ryan didn't waste time arguing. With the boy clinging to his neck, he edged clumsily over the zone border. He grunted and jerked as gravity changed, dragging away from the surface of the earth and westward instead. A dozen metres across flat ground had become a dozen-metre drop to a concrete wall. He froze.

"What are you waiting for?" Her voice threatened to rise an octave.

Ryan was breathing fast and ragged. Too fast. The one and only time he'd been in the zones he'd nearly died and Crane had been badly injured.

"Look, it's not even a rib-cracker of a distance. It's a bruise-and-roll at most." He didn't respond. "The kid's life depends on you. You need to move!"

He muttered a string of panicky profanities under his breath but slowly began rappelling downward toward the car dealership. She wasn't sure in the dark, but she thought his eyes were closed. It was one way for a zones rookie to cope. He picked up speed as he adjusted, but his pace still seemed painfully slow to Jasper's eyes.

She remained crouched in down-gee beside the rope anchor point, feeling exposed and afraid. The dogs were getting closer. Their voices crowded her ears, pummelling her with urgency. She had only seconds. Did Ryan and Grammar have their feet on a solid wall yet? In the dark she could barely make out their shapes.

She changed her mind about unknotting the rope and drew her knife instead. The dogs were almost on top of her, and the voices of their human pursuers were farther away but closing in.

She strained to see the boys' progress. Were they close enough? They had to be.

She cut the rope. Thuds and a grunt, scuffling sounds. No cry of pain. They were on their own now.

She ran parallel to the zone border, dangerously fast in the dark. She kept her left arm extended toward the border. If the tingling sensation moved from her fingertips to her wrist and up her arm, she veered to the right to always maintain an arm's-length distance from the border.

Behind her the dogs' voices rose in confusion. They'd be lingering at the edge of the side-gee zone, sensibly refusing to set foot over the border.

Then the baying began again. The scent trail had forked, and they'd picked up on the one they could actually follow— Jasper's. Hopefully their human handlers wouldn't even notice the moment of confusion; they would assume that no reasonable person would dare to negotiate the zones in the dark.

Now the dogs were chasing her alone. Great.

She came upon a tree that had fallen in a storm, half of its massive trunk extending from down-gee into—she extended a hand across the zone border—east-draw side-gee. The opposite draw of the zone Ryan and Grammar were in.

She hopped onto the tree trunk and climbed it through the hair-lifting tingle of the border, with barely a pause for the blood rush as gravity changed. She was now climbing the fallen tree *up* as the ground became an upwardly vertical cliff face, her weight drawing her down back toward the zone border.

She climbed a few metres until she came to what had once been a roadside ditch but was now oriented as a ledge in a cliff face, a lengthwise cross-section of a tunnel. She crawled along this ditch as the baying grew closer and torches came into view. Jasper flattened herself behind a stubby little pine tree that had aimed itself for the sky regardless of gravity's orientation, its roots dug stubbornly into the earth. She swiped a handful of dirt over her face and then lay still.

Two torches and three dogs. The dogs yapped in excitement, nosing around where she'd crossed the border. The two men lifted their torches and scanned the area. The light barely reached her where she lay hidden in the ditch, but if they looked very closely or dared to enter the side-gee zone even a little way they'd see her.

"They're just chasing coyotes," one man said, sounding disgruntled. An adult, not one of the feral gangers.

"The kids are swearen there been intruders." The other ganger sounded younger, barely more than a teenager. "Right in the school."

"Yeah, they said it was the Pinegirl. And she nearly collapsed the ceiling by stomping her foot. And stole a recruit who's apparently Darius Dalca's son. I mean, Jesus. Is that a story you want to repeat back to Nico? Damn pack kids see a shadow move, and all of a sudden, the Pinegirl herself is rampaging through the streets. We're wasting our time."

"Yeah, sir, but all the kids are sayen the same thing."

"You know how fast stories spread in those dorms. The guards are covering their asses because they let a recruit escape, and the other kids are parroting the story because anything to do with the Pinegirl they'll repeat as gospel. Jasper Pine did *not* sneak into our compound tonight. At most a recruit escaped. If he's in the zones, he's either dead or long gone. In any case, we can't follow him in the dark and without equipment. Let's go."

The man was sensible but wrong. If Nico heard this story, he'd know instantly Jasper had stolen one of his recruits, the one she'd asked him about. If he listened to the whole story, he'd realize for the first time that he'd had Zenobia's son in his grip and lost him. And then he'd come after Jasper.

The dogs pointed their noses in her direction, barking insistently. The older man shouted at them to shut up.

Jasper waited until the torches had disappeared into the distance before finally stirring and climbing out of side-gee. Her legs shook at the close call. She hurried back to the zone where she'd left Ryan and Grammar.

"Guys," she called in a loud whisper from the border, "it's safe. They're gone."

No response.

Muttering a curse under her breath, she tapped a toe behind her other foot, crouched, and slipped into side-gee. It wasn't the first time she'd ever climbed freehand in the dark, but she always hoped it was the last. At least it was a clear night with a nearly full moon.

Slowly, she descended toward the car dealership where the boys were supposed to be sheltering. She was sweating by the time she dropped the last few feet onto the outer wall. It creaked beneath her feet but held.

Half of the dealership's outer walls had once been made of glass, which was shattered now and open to the weather. She dropped through the opening and fell to an inner wall. She landed amid pebbly chunks of safety glass and rolled to her feet. She listened but heard nothing.

She was standing on the inner wall, a hand braced against the perpendicular floor. Ahead of her, at her feet, a door in the wall formed a rectangular cut-out of darkness a shade deeper than the shadows around her.

The rope they'd descended had been tied to the frame of a smashed-up SUV that balanced against the wall on its nose. The other end dangled into the door in the wall where Ryan and Grammar must have gone to hide.

She stepped to the edge of the door frame and looked down through the doorway. She could make out nothing inside the room. Was the sound of breathing coming only from her or from others?

Thoughts of bears, outlaws, a hostile kid pack, and the Upgee Witch flitted through her mind. She knew tinylings weren't really demons; Vron had made them up. But sometimes giving the monsters a name was what brought them to life.

"Ryan!" Her voice came out too loud but was instantly muffled by layers upon layers of darkness.

"Jasper?"

She exhaled hard. "You guys okay? It's safe. I'll pull you up."

His voice was tired. "I think we're going to need a minute."

"What's wrong? Are you hurt? How's the kid?"

"I don't know. He stabbed me, won't let me near him."

"He *stabbed* you? Jesus. Are you okay?"

A long pause. "It's superficial. Can't see anything, though."

"Hold on. I'm coming down."

Holding on to the rope, she lowered herself hand over hand through the doorway, descending into the darkness.

17

THE DEVILMAN'S SON

Walking barefoot through grass
Winning

~ Veronica Park (*Things I Will Miss/Reasons to Live*)

With each breath she drew in the black, the suffocating lightlessness. She didn't know what kind of room it was, surely just an average office, but her descent seemed to take forever.

"Hey, downie." She needed to hear a voice, any voice. She needed Ben scolding her for forgetting her helmet or Vron chanting some nonsense rhyme about tinylings and hedgehogs. She even needed Merlot scoffing at her fear.

"Yeah, Zeep?" Ryan's voice was close, almost in her ear.

She closed her eyes and let go of the rope. For half a breath she fell. Her feet hit the wall. She rolled to absorb the impact and landed up against Ryan. She knew it was him and not

Grammar because, one, he didn't stab her, and two, he smelled like sweat and crushed grass, not blood.

Though she strained her eyes, she couldn't make out where the boy was. She pulled a candle stub and a flint striker from her thigh pouch. Light flared like the ringing of a silent bell or the turning of a key in a lock. Light brought air back into the room.

They were in what had once been an office. Desks and chairs and computer monitors and potted plants and filing cabinets had fallen and smashed against the west wall, along with a litter of paper and pens and staplers and wobbly-headed figurines. She and Ryan were seated on the wall beside a whiteboard that still had "Top Weekly Sales" written at the top with a list of smudged names.

Grammar huddled with his back against the north-facing wall, arms wrapped around his knees, as far away from Ryan and Jasper as he could get. The light caught a glint from his eyes as he watched them but didn't illuminate the bloody, bruised wreckage of his face.

Ryan gave a choked-off exclamation. He'd just noticed the human skull lying companionably a few feet away from him, still adorned in the papery remnants of skin. Jasper crossed herself and muttered Vron's ghost-away incantation. By the end, Ryan was eyeing her rather than the skull.

The cut on his arm was maybe three inches long and shallow and already beginning to crust over.

"Oh, you'll live." She eyed Grammar huddled unmoving in his corner. "Does he still have a knife on him?"

"I disarmed him. He wasn't trying to kill me, just wanted me to let go. Now he won't let me near him."

"Maybe he thinks you'll pull out his heart and stomp on it," Jasper said pointedly. "Where did that story come from anyway?"

"I talked to a lot of people at the church the other night,"

Ryan said. "Everyone had a different Pinegirl story, each more outlandish than the last. So I invented my own. It seemed to suit a grown-up Zombie Princess."

"It was delightful. I'll probably have nightmares. Thank you for that." He'd saved her from that standoff with Vic, that soul-sickening moment when she'd teetered between murder and collapse. He deserved more than sarcasm. "Seriously, Ryan," she said. "Thank you."

His expression didn't change, but his eyes warmed. "You're welcome, Zeep," he said. "Next time I want my own superhero name, though."

"All I can think of right now is RyGuy."

"*RyGuy?* Jesus."

"Jesus is already taken, I think."

He laughed, which had the same effect on her insides as hot soup or a cup of cinnamon tea after waking up from a nightmare.

She was delaying the inevitable, the need to deal somehow with the battered, bloody son of Darius. Jasper picked up the candle and started toward Grammar.

"It was my own knife he stole and stabbed me with," Ryan said grudgingly.

"Damn, soldier boy."

"Shut up. He's quick."

She handed him her knife for safekeeping. "Try to hold on to this one."

Without moving, Grammar watched her approach. She crouched a metre away, candle lifted so she could see the bloody mess of his face. One eye was swollen shut, and only a spark of blue showed from the other. His face was too lumpy and mottled with bruising to show expression, but his raw-knuckled hands gripped each other around his knees with palpable tension. The

Damaskers had shaved off his mohawk, revealing the naked, vulnerable curve of his skull.

Face to face with him, she was at a loss for words. How did one talk to the spawn of Darius and Zenobia, five feet nothing and ninety pounds of scrappiness and rage? How much of his father's bloodlust and ruthlessness lived under his ribs? How much of his mother's cold calculation?

He was a pack alpha, used to commanding obedience, used to trusting no one, and he wasn't even thirteen years old.

She set down the candle on the floor between them, and he followed the motion like a dog backed into a corner. No anger was left in the taut lines of his body. It was exhaustion and tension and fear that made him quiver.

A memory. Jasper hiding on the sticky, stained floor under Martha Abebe's surgical table. Martha had pulled up the sheet and crouched to see her. Jasper had shrunk away from her, terrified by those deft, terrible butcher's hands that wielded saw and scalpel on human flesh. The doctor's round brown face had seemed a twisted reflection, a mirror showing Jasper's own guilt and desperation. But from somewhere Martha had found and dusted off a smile for her, riddled with cracks but still a homely, reassuring sight in the midst of horror.

"Peace, little tadpole," Jasper said to Grammar as Martha had said to her. "You're safe. I'll not hurt you."

A shudder went through him, bone deep. He began shaking. He clenched his hands into fists but couldn't stop trembling.

"I can be killen you," he said. He clenched his jaw to stop his teeth from chattering.

"Yes, I know." She dug around in her pouches and came up with a multi-purpose cloth that could be folded down into a tiny square. She wet it with water from her canteen. "I'm going to clean up some of that blood on your face. Is that okay?"

He thought about it. Then he reached out an imperious hand for the cloth. "Myself."

She sat cross-legged while he dabbed at his face, fumbling with the cloth when his hand shook too badly. "You remember me?" she asked.

He shot her a one-eyed glance that said he wasn't an idiot.

She jerked her thumb over her shoulder. "That's Ryan. He saved your life earlier tonight, if you recall, when you made the stunningly brilliant move of challenging Vic on her own turf."

Grammar glanced past her at Ryan. "Fast like a demon," he observed.

"Let's stick to all of us being human, okay? I'm not magic and you're not invincible and he's not a demon."

Grammar grunted. "I'm knowen that. He's bleeden."

"If that's the test, then I guess we can be pretty sure you're not a demon either," Ryan said. "You're bleeding enough to feed a whole family of vampires and their dog."

"Vampires are not real," Grammar said, frowning.

"Oh, vampires are where we draw the line, is it?" Ryan laughed. "Good to know."

Grammar lowered his knees so he was sitting cross-legged like Jasper. His face without a coating of dried blood wasn't much improved, but at least his features were discernible now. He dug under the neck of his T-shirt and pulled out a handful of amulets. Against his grimy palm the clay bird gleamed palely. He gave a sharp tug, breaking the thong. "You wanten this? Be taken it."

He dropped it into her cupped hands. It still held her mother's fingerprints, baked into its wings. It was real, the first concrete evidence of her mother's existence other than fallible memories and the photograph on Harmony's fridge.

"Where did you find it?"

"Not rememberen."

She closed her hand around the amulet. "Don't give me that. You must know."

He didn't respond, his gaze dropping down to the floor, which was actually a wall. She wanted to shake him until the words he seemed to be hoarding fell out of his mouth.

"I know the zones are hard to explain, but could you show me?" she tried. "Can you bring me there?"

He twined the bloodied cloth through his fingers. His pinky stood out at an angle, clearly broken, but he didn't seem to notice. "I'm never maken a deal with you."

"You stole my copper," she reminded him with an edge of anger. "And I just rescued you from that hellhole. I would suggest you owe me."

"Dangerous."

She didn't believe for a second he was scared of the zones, the way he and his pack had moved through them as easily as thought. Which meant he was scared of something else. She grimaced and made a guess. "Whatever bad magic you're afraid of, you'll be protected with me. I'm the Pinegirl." Even though she'd just told him she wasn't magic. No pack kid would believe her anyway.

He darted her a quick look, uncertain and skeptical. His jaw set and he shook his head. "Be asken me something different. Another favour I can be doen for you. Not this."

"But this is the only thing I want from you. Please, Grammar."

He was hooked unerringly by the need in her voice. Of course Darius's child would home in on weakness, on vulnerability. "Why so important?"

She weighed her answer. Everything in her screamed that no Dalca, no matter how young, could be trusted with truth. What games could he play with her if she gave him honesty?

"You da Pinegirl," Grammar said. "But you're a biggie now

too. You been given us the rules: never trusten biggies. You been killen da bad man." His throat bobbed as he swallowed. "Da bad man was my papa. I'm Devilman's son. So why should I be trusten you?"

This admission rocked her backwards. He'd confirmed his identity to his father's killer. He had real reason to fear that her grudge against his father might extend to him. Christ, the kid had nerve. She didn't know whether to fear him less because he was afraid of her too, or more because he was willing to show it just to provoke a reaction.

Was he Darius Dalca's son? Abso-fucking-lutely he was. But by the small god, maybe he was also something else entirely.

She showed him the amulet. "My mama made this and she wore it all the time. I know she's dead, but I want to find her body."

Ryan was listening, probably wondering what she was talking about, but right now she didn't care. Once they were in the zones, Ryan would be forced to trust her as his guide, and if she wanted to take them to the Tower via her mother's body, he couldn't stop her. All she needed was to convince Grammar to tell her the truth.

"Why?" Grammar asked. "If she been dead."

"Before she died in the Shattering, she went to find something. A cure."

This was the story that Zenobia had told her and Ben. Jasper's gravity had begun malfunctioning not long after she learned to walk. Worried about a future where Jasper would be taken away from her and turned into a lab rat or worse, Catherine Pine had concealed her daughter's condition, made up excuses for the injuries she suffered—bruises and cuts, and even a broken arm from her falls. They moved several times to avoid visits from social services. Jasper had memories of being always leashed to something, of harnesses and straps, of mattresses leaned against the walls to cushion her falls.

Finally, after Jasper shifted up-gee while outside, barely avoiding a fall into the upper atmosphere by grabbing on to the branches of a nearby tree, her mother, at her wit's end, contacted her husband's former colleague, Dr. Zenobia Allan, to ask for help.

Unbeknownst to Catherine, her husband was still alive in the Tower. Since his initial infection five years before, Zenobia and her team had been working to develop an antibac to cleanse the graviteria from Andrew's system. According to Zenobia, his participation in these secret experiments was voluntary, though Jasper had always been skeptical that her father would agree to let his family think he was dead. But Zenobia was the only one left alive who knew the truth, and she would only tell Jasper what suited her own purposes.

When Catherine met with Zenobia, Zenobia gave her a syringe of this potential cure for Jasper and advised her to bring Jasper to the Tower for treatment. It was too late for Andrew Pine, however; his graviteria had matured past the point of no return. Catherine, unaware her husband was even still alive, had barely exited the Tower when the graviteria inhabiting Andrew's body Shattered.

She and the antibac never made it home.

"Cure?" Grammar's attention sharpened. "For what?"

"For me. It'd be useless after all this time, of course. But she found something else. Some information or clue or idea that . . . that might save my life." It was hard to say those words that reflected the tiny secret hope that had bloomed ever since she'd overheard that conversation between Zenobia and the Guardian. Her mother had found something Zenobia didn't want her to find. Zenobia wanted to cure Jasper but she wanted to do it her way, and that involved an antibac with a 50 percent chance of killing or crippling Jasper. The Guardian had a different idea. Maybe her mother had too.

Grammar slumped back a little. Whatever he'd been expecting, it wasn't this. He studied her face for truth and seemed satisfied. His wariness settled but didn't disappear.

She could feel Ryan's narrow-eyed stare burning into her head, but he hadn't spoken up, so she ignored him.

"Everyone says I'm a hero for killing your father, but I don't feel I am. I did an awful thing to stop him from doing awful things. I never want to do such a thing again." She met his eyes. "Does it make me nervous that you're his son? Yes, it does. But you're not him. And I won't hurt you."

"Because you're needen me." A jab of cynicism in his voice.

At his age would she have been convinced by mere words? "Sure. That's true too."

She let the silence puddle between them. He was thinking but also fighting exhaustion, his narrow shoulders drooping. She handed him her canteen, and he drank gingerly through raw lips.

Ryan crouched beside her with a plastic bag of nuts, which he extended to Grammar. Grammar just stared, so Ryan placed it on the floor and then sat several feet away from Jasper so it didn't seem as if they were cornering Grammar against the wall.

"Looks like you got a broken finger there, buddy," Ryan said.

Grammar looked down at his hand, appearing to notice the injury for the first time. "Phalanges," he said almost dreamily. "Metacarpal fracture."

She'd have been less surprised if he'd suddenly quoted *Hamlet*, but it wasn't his words so much as the thickening of a silken burr that had lain hidden in his voice. A familiar flavour she couldn't place.

"Yeah, that's right," Ryan said. "I can splint that up for you if you like."

Grammar eyed him as if he hadn't quite given up the notion that Ryan might be a demon, but weariness won over suspicion. A shift of posture offered consent, and Ryan kneeled beside him, Jasper's small first aid kit in hand. He talked as he grasped the boy's hand, a flow of words hypnotic as river water. Grammar barely reacted as Ryan pulled the broken finger straight.

"I hear you know where to find the ReGeneration," Ryan said easily, never changing his tone.

Jasper opened her mouth, but Grammar shrugged. "Yeah, maybe. Why?"

Ryan shot Jasper an unreadable look. "Just wondering."

It had been a lie on her part, an excuse to rescue Grammar. But kid packs spent most of their time in the zones, so it wouldn't be surprising if they knew more about the ReGeneration's movements than even grav-walkers like Jasper.

Ryan left it at that, but she suspected she'd hear a great deal more on the subject later.

Her mind went back to Grace's revelation that she was also looking for Grammar. "Do you know who Grace Kornelsen is?"

"Soup kitchen lady," he said after a moment's reflection.

"Do you know why she'd be looking for you?"

A blank stare was her answer.

"What about Vron? Veronica Park? Did you ever meet her? It'd be over three years ago."

Grammar flinched. It could've been from the pain of his broken finger as Ryan taped the pinky to the ring finger. After a long pause, he said, "The Storytalker. Dead."

"So you know who she is? How did you meet her?"

Grammar's tension reappeared, his shoulders hunching almost to his ears. He lifted his free hand palm up in a warding gesture. "Bad idea," he muttered. "Was a bad idea. She's maken me."

"What do you mean? What was a bad idea?"

He dodged Ryan's efforts to deal with the cuts on his face. He grasped his amulets with both hands and muttered something under his breath.

"What did you say?"

"Curse!" he blurted. "Was a curse and she been dyen."

"Curse? The only curse Vron had was called depression." Her voice came out harsher than she'd meant. "Just tell me how you met her."

He shook his head. In denial, perhaps, rather than refusal.

Ryan frowned at Jasper. "Maybe this can wait."

She wanted to shake answers out of him, but Ryan was right. The boy's agitation was clear. Perhaps he'd never even met Vron. To the pack kids Vron was known as the Storytalker. Her stories and rhymes and incantations formed the framework, the hidden bones of kid pack worldviews. Inevitably, they'd have formed their own ideas about how she died.

Why had Vron mentioned Grammar in her journal, then? She might not have known that he was Darius's son, but she must have met him to know his name. What had she written about him to send Grace investigating years later? Why had she given Grace the journal and not Merlot or her other friends?

It was Grace that Jasper needed to talk to for sensible answers.

She fought to keep her eyes open as the adrenalin of the night's escapades finally subsided. She took a handful of nuts from Ryan's bag, chewing to stay awake. Ryan also took a nut for form's sake, then tilted the bag toward Grammar, who accepted it automatically. Ryan probed Grammar's face, asking questions as he went.

"And what's this bone called?"

"Man—man—dibbles."

"Well done. Let's see if you have any broken teeth. Open up. You know what the back teeth are called?"

"Wise tooths. But they're just dumb like other tooths."

"It's a con game, I know. Take a deep breath for me. That hurts, eh? A cracked rib maybe. Lovely." Somehow he was keeping his voice mild even as anger dug a furrow beneath the surface.

Jasper leaned forward. "Grammar, who raised you before you joined the packs?"

"Auntie." His response was prompt, unguarded.

"Auntie who? What was her name?"

His one visible eye fluttered shut. "Auntie Martha."

"Martha *Abebe*?"

"Mmm. Nev's mama. She been callen me tadpole too."

Then he was asleep as suddenly and deeply as an infant. Ryan caught him and lowered him to a horizontal position, straightening his limbs gently.

Shock muddied Jasper's already exhausted thoughts. If he'd truly been raised by the doctor from Sierra Leone, it would explain the flavour of his hidden accent and his unexpected knowledge of anatomy. He had no reason to lie, and Martha's reclusive lifestyle explained why he'd gone unnoticed.

Nev's mama. Martha had had another daughter? She'd been estranged from Nico by the time Jasper killed Darius, so who was Neverwhen's father? Jasper couldn't even begin to guess.

Did Sparrow even know she had another niece?

After Darius's death Martha had lived as a hermit far from Yorky, drowning her memories in solitude. Jasper had brought her occasional gifts and supplies in gratitude for helping Ben survive his amputation and treating Harmony's acid burns. She wasn't the only one to do so. Martha decreed that gifts were to be left some distance from her house so she could avoid direct contact with people. Not even her sister, Sparrow, was allowed to visit, and definitely not her husband, Nico.

Jasper did recall now that there'd been a kid or two around

the place, unremarkable to her eyes at the time, just a few of the many family-less feral waifs that were either adopted by adults or left to band together into packs. When Martha's body was found months after her death, Ibtisam had guessed the cause was a sudden illness or heart attack, as there was no sign of injury or violence. The kids under her care had disappeared by the time she was found, and no one had given them any thought.

But why—*why*—would Zenobia entrust her son to a traumatized, bitter surgeon who had more reason than most to hate both Darius and her? And why in all the small god's realm would Martha have agreed? What pressure could Zenobia have brought to bear?

The answer to that had hair like an explosion and too many knives to count: Crane. A child for a child. A trade of hostages in a sense, though not exactly, for Crane had refused to rejoin her mother or father even when given the choice. She'd tied her loyalty to the two people who taken her away from her parents, and when Zenobia had tried to cut her loose after Darius's death, Crane wouldn't go. Martha had been rejected by her daughter, but she could raise Zenobia's son as insurance for Crane's good treatment. Had it been any consolation? How had Martha borne it, looking every day into Grammar's face and seeing her two worst enemies and the loss of her daughter staring back at her?

Did Nico know his wife—ex-wife—had been raising his enemy's son? Or, for that matter, that she'd had another child by a different man? Probably not. If he knew Grammar existed, as he soon would, he'd tear the zones apart looking for him.

She wondered how he'd react to Neverwhen's existence. That might depend on who the girl's father was. An inkling of his identity swam up from the depths of her subconscious, but an overwhelming weariness dragged it back into the deep.

Jasper became vaguely aware that she'd curled up on the wall and someone was tucking a blanket around her. Harmony had always tucked her in with her wrinkled old hands every night, even when Jasper had been bad—thrown dishes or kicked the cats or screamed for hours. Darius had melted Harmony's face half off because Jasper and the other kids had escaped the cages, and yet she'd brushed away Jasper's hair from her face and kissed her cheek and said long prayers to bless the room, and she'd burned a match in every corner to chase away the tinylings lurking in the shadows.

What made old women love and adopt horrible children that they should really hate?

"You shouldn't love me," she mumbled to Harmony.

"I'll take that under advisement," she heard Ryan reply dryly from far away, but sleep had already swallowed Jasper into its treacherous maw.

18

WHEN WE WERE YOUNG

The drag of your fingers
Over metal bars.
The words in your mouth
Like spoken scars.
The dogs in your heart
Under howling stars.

~ Veronica Park (*Story of a Monster*)

She dreamed of spiders marching, climbing, crawling under the skin of faces, twitching muscles, staring out of eyes, opening mouths. She dreamed of spiders pulling strings behind Ben's eyes, spiders crawling out of Harmony's mouth.

But in her hand was the sharp, the bloody, bloody sharp, and she was stabbing their spider-eaten faces, bloody, bloody stabs, and the spiders were gone, all gone, had never existed. And now only their faces, their bloody, bloody faces, empty and screaming, but still she held the bloody, bloody sharp and she swung—

"Jasper! Wake up, Jasper."

—and stabbed and cut until—

She opened her eyes as she sat up, arm swinging. Ryan caught her wrist, her blade inches from his eye.

"I understand your feelings about spiders," he said. "But your shoe would be more effective than your knife."

"What?" She felt drunk. She lowered the knife, pushed her other hand through her hair.

"You were mumbling about spiders in your sleep," Ryan said.

Morning light filtered into the office, lightening shadows into grey.

She looked around. "Where's the kid?"

The blanket Ryan had draped over Grammar still lay on the wall, but the bag of nuts and Jasper's canteen were gone. So was the rope she'd left dangling from the doorway above their heads. She whirled to stare at Ryan, hoping against hope that he hadn't escaped, hoping for an alternate explanation.

He winced at her expression. "He was gone when I woke up. I'm sorry."

"No!" She leaped to her feet, looking around wildly as if she might find him hiding in the rubble. "No, no, no, no."

"Maybe he's exploring," Ryan said. "Maybe he'll come back."

He'd taken the rope. If he was just out taking a leak or foraging for food or having a look around, he wouldn't have stolen Jasper's rope. Grammar had taken the rope because he needed it to move through the zones and because he wanted to give himself a head start on any pursuers.

"Grammar!" she screamed at the doorway. "Get back here, you alpha-brained little bastard!"

Her voice faded along with her rage, replaced by horror and self-loathing. He'd *played* her. She'd been Darius's pet; she knew better than anyone what Dalca manipulation looked like. *She should've known better*. She'd had full knowledge of his heritage, had witnessed his ruthless rage in battle, and then freely told him the truth of what she needed most and why. Stupid, stupid, stupid. How could she have been so stupid? He had absorbed everything she'd said, had acted vulnerable so she'd let her guard down. He'd waited for his chance and then taken it.

First Ryan and now Darius's goddamn *son*. What was wrong with her? Darius was right; she had some kind of congenital weakness, something irreversibly broken inside that doomed her to fall for this shit over and over again.

"He didn't play you," said Ryan, making her start. She didn't realize she'd spoken aloud. "He said straight out he didn't want to do it. He offered to do something else instead. He's already been kidnapped once. Maybe he was afraid we'd force him."

"Well, maybe he's right because there is, in fact, a kidnapper in this room and it isn't me!"

"I'm just saying—"

"What kind of soldier are you anyway, if this kid can sneak right by you?" He scowled and she forced herself to take a deep breath. If she didn't, she'd scream. "You didn't know his father. And Christ, he's got his mother in him too. The game is in his blood. You have no idea how fucking terrifying this kid is."

Blood will out, Darius agreed smugly.

"You're right. I don't. All I saw was a kid who was abducted, forced to fight for his life every night, then snatched away by the person who killed his father and pressured to do something he's afraid of. Something you lied to me about, by the way."

"Wow, you're so sympathetic to kidnapping victims suddenly."

He glared and she glared back.

"Finding your mother's body?" he asked pointedly. "Is that what freeing this kid was about all along? We don't have time to get distracted by a side quest."

"Side quest? Because the only kid that matters is yours, right?"

His face hardened. He folded his arms across his chest. "You risked my life along with yours when we walked into Damascus and you didn't tell me why. I don't regret saving the kid, but I don't enjoy being lied to. Also, you owe me a gun."

"Oh, how could I forget! I'm so sorry. Was it a special gun? Did you name it? Sleep with it at night?"

His impassive face and the sourness of her own voice struck her with enough shame that she couldn't deflect it with anger. She turned away, swearing under her breath. After the risks she —*they*—had taken to rescue Grammar, she had nothing more than when they'd started. Except now Nico was guaranteed to hear about the Devilman's son he'd briefly had in his grasp, and her chances of extracting the information she needed from Grammar were slimmer than ever.

"We don't have any reason to trust each other—I get it," Ryan said. "But the sooner we get to the Tower, the sooner you can get rid of me."

"That's fine for you, downie, but either way, my life is still on the line." The muscles across her shoulders ached with tension, and she forced herself to drag in a deep breath. "If I want to find my mom before I die, I only have a couple of months to do so. You want to get out of here, but I don't think your deadline is as unforgiving as mine."

His forehead knotted and he looked away. He rubbed a hand over the back of his neck.

In the end, what did it matter that they both hated the position they'd been forced into? Here they were, regardless. It was all a moot point anyway when Grammar had taken off. Gone was gone.

"We need to get out of here," she said.

They stacked one desk on top of another, and then a filing cabinet and then a chair. Ryan steadied the chair while Jasper tried to leap up to catch the door frame. It was still too far.

Finally, Ryan climbed onto the chair, slowly, as the rickety pile teetered and threatened to crumple under his weight. His height brought him closer, but they were still a foot short. So Jasper climbed onto his back, agonizingly slowly, to keep the precarious pyramid from toppling from her additional weight. He made stirrups with his hands for her feet and then boosted her high enough to catch the edge of the door frame and pull herself out of the room.

Pulling him out was trickier. She salvaged a seat belt from one of the crashed cars, tied a carabiner to one end, and attached it to the harness ring at her waist. She dangled the other end into the doorway while she lay flat on the wall with her feet braced against the door frame to counterbalance his weight.

Ryan at least was fast, catching hold of the seat belt and pulling himself up hand over hand in just a few seconds to where he could lunge and grab the door frame instead.

Thank the small god for the fitness level of downie soldiers. She wondered if they all had the biceps and abs Ryan had displayed in pulling himself upward.

She smacked the thought on the wrist and sent it to a corner.

"Maybe he climbed back to regular gravity and is waiting for us," Ryan suggested once he was up. He rubbed his knuckles restlessly along his breastbone as he looked around, seeing the building for the first time in daylight.

Grammar would not be waiting in down-gee. He'd probably taken off through the zones where he could outrun anyone but a grav-walker.

"No such thing as *regular* gravity in the zones, downie. Call it down-gee like a normal non-moron."

She climbed up the vertical dealership floor toward the outer wall, empty of glass, above them. Enough of the tiling had cracked and pitted and buckled for her to find handholds and toeholds, and she could climb over the jumble of once-new cars that had fallen against the wall and each other.

She was nearly outside when she realized Ryan hadn't followed.

He stood on the inner wall, digging a thumb into the palm of his left hand, looking around as if he'd forgotten something. Even from several metres above him, she could see how deliberately he was inhaling and exhaling.

He'd rappelled down here in the middle of the night, barely able to see anything of his surroundings. But now in daylight it was impossible to ignore that he was standing on a wall. She was climbing *up* a floor. What should've been flat ground presented itself as a sheer cliff face. Reality was tilted over on its side.

It had been a long time since the zones had disoriented her, but his face reminded her of the sensation.

"Hey, downie," she said crossly. "Look at me."

He gave her a distracted glance and went back to surveying his surroundings, his jaw rigid.

"No, hey, hey, coyote boy, *look* at me." She climbed back down partway. "Put your hands and feet where I do."

He looked past her at the route they'd have to climb and shook his head fast, lips pinched. "No. Nope. Freehand? That's craziness. Sorry. You'll have to come back for me with rope. This is—I can't."

She could leave him here, just walk away. She was tempted, but rationality asserted itself. Killing Ryan, as he'd pointed out, would only encourage his brother to send a more ruthless and violent team into the zones. Besides, Ryan would never stay here and wait to die. He'd eventually push past his fear and drag himself out of the zone. She knew survivors, and he was one. Which didn't help her exasperation.

"Yeah, you can. I've already seen you climb," she said. "You were in the zones for a couple of days with Crane, weren't you?"

"We had ropes."

"Look, forget the gravity. Focus on me and the next step and that's it. Got it? We'll be in down-gee before you know it."

He took a deep breath. He stepped close enough to the floor to put his hands on the tile. From her angle she could just see the mass of his locs spilling over his shoulders. He took a few more breaths.

"Why did you call me Coyote Boy?" he asked. He reached for the first handhold, set his foot into a crack, and hoisted himself upward. "Is that meant to be my new superhero name? Pinegirl and Coyote Boy."

"You named yourself after the coyote and thought no one would notice? *Canis latrans*. At least I'm assuming you made up your last name."

"I did. But how do you know the Latin name for the coyote?"

"We may not have fancy schools or the interwebnet or whatever, but we've still got books in the zones."

"No offence meant. Most people wouldn't know."

"So why did you name yourself after the coyote?" She didn't care, but distractions tended to be helpful against the existential terror of dealing with gravity that all your senses screamed was *wrong*.

"I had a foster father who used to take me camping to watch a nearby pack of coyotes. He was fascinated by them. They can adapt to any environment, including urban areas. They're clever and tough and they're survivors." He stopped to wipe his face on his shoulder but didn't look up at her. "I remember the sound of them yipping and howling with their families and thinking that's all I wanted to be. I wanted to cut off my human skin and grow fur and find a pack and run so fast that no one could ever catch me."

They climbed in silence for a few breaths.

"We didn't stay at that home long," Ryan said. "We found

traps set for the coyotes. My foster father thought it was farmers setting them, but I knew it was Titus. Jealous, maybe. So I asked our social worker to move us. Never forgot those coyotes, though."

"The name suits you," she said without thinking, and then wanted to bite her tongue out. Because she could see him, long and rangy as a coyote, loping over endless prairie, part of the land and sky, but hell if she was going to tell him that. And he was playing on her sympathies again. He'd already demonstrated how convincingly he could make up stories.

"Those kids, they actually believed the story I made up about you," Ryan said, as if sensing the direction of her thoughts.

"They also believe the Up-gee Witch is real, and so are tinylings and demons, and that there's a fairy who will steal the teeth from your mouth if you don't sleep with a coin under your pillow. They have more stories than the zones have plastic. Doesn't mean anything."

"But is it just because you killed Darius Dalca? That was over ten years ago. They're too young to remember him, surely."

"Stories, man. They tell stories and pass them down to the younglings. The story of the Pinegirl and da bad man is ancient legend by now. All the kids grow up hearing it, and new stories crop up all the time like weeds. Sparrow calls it post-apocalyptic meme culture, if that makes sense to you."

He snorted, surprised and amused. "It does, actually."

"It's how kid packs survive and pass along knowledge. That and the rules."

"What rules are those?"

He was climbing painfully slowly but more steadily now. If he could play for her sympathies, she could do the same. Her sob story at least had the benefit of being true and verifiable, and should do the job of distracting him.

"We escaped from the cages, a bunch of us—me and my brother, Ben; Merlot Park and his sister, Vron; Charlie Grey; Crane; and a few others. Ben and Charlie were the oldest, eleven. We were the first true kid pack, and the first rule was not to trust adults. We learned that the hard way."

Many of them had already spent weeks or months roaming the zones right after the Shattering, so they knew how to break into buildings and find food and other supplies. There was still a lot of loot to find in those days. Ben had been in Scouts, and Charlie used to go camping with his cousins. They collected books from libraries and bookstores to learn about edible plants and setting snares and traps. Vron made up songs and rhymes to canonize important information.

"It wasn't a bad life, actually. At least in the summer. Winter was harder. There wasn't a lot of wildlife yet, so we lived on rats and pigeons. So did the dogs . . . except they figured out human children had a lot more meat on them than rats and were frankly easier to catch. Until we figured out the same thing and started hunting them right back."

He threw her an appalled glance. "Dogs don't—dogs wouldn't—that's horrible!"

He'd accepted that she'd killed a man with hardly a blink, she noted cynically, but couldn't imagine dogs acting like rational predators. What an odd world downieland was, where dogs were held to a higher standard than humans. So he'd never had to fear a dog. How very goddamn nice for him. Some people didn't get to be that lucky.

Gradually, more kids had escaped and joined them, and they taught them too. There were some arguments about letting the littlest kids join, because they were a drain on resources and not very useful to the group.

"They'd be dumb and not listen or not understand and get themselves killed or injured, so we had to put the fear of the devil in them to make them obey so they could keep alive. But we decided early that adults were the enemy, and so kids, all kids, had to take care of each other and never turn anyone away. The rules evolved from those principles."

"And what are the rules?"

"Kids take care of kids. Never trust biggies. Always teach. Always share. Always protect the younglings." She could almost hear the ring of Vron's voice as she led the younglings in the nighttime chant. "Those were the original ones."

"Do they really live by those rules? That was a harsh crowd watching Grammar get beaten to shit. Not much protecting or taking care of each other there."

"Like any religion, interpretations vary. It depends a lot on the pack alpha and what kind of tone they set. It can be a violent life in the zones, and for many kids the rules don't apply outside their pack. Except for the one about not trusting adults. That one's universal."

"So I get that Darius and the Azuros treated kids horribly, but why the universal hatred of all adults? Surely some adults must have helped the kids."

"Some did but, well . . . many of the older generation were convinced they'd one day be let out of quarantine. So they stayed with Darius despite everything, because at least it was down-gee. They were terrified of the zones. Still are." Jasper strained for the next handhold, inching her way left across the parking lot so she could take advantage of the buckling of the pavement. "But they also stayed because of the cages. Darius kept kids in cages for entertainment, dog food, and punishment for adults."

"Jesus."

"Entertainment wasn't so bad. Contests, races, fights, the flamingo, that kind of thing. He and his men would place bets on who would win. But if the hunters hadn't brought in enough game or if a kid was already sick and dying, the kid might get thrown in with Darius's dogs. The same cuddly mutts Zenobia keeps at the trading post, actually—the ones who've lived this long."

He was starting to look ill, but she barrelled on without sympathy. He hadn't experienced the Dalca regime himself; the least he could do was endure a retelling of its horrors. Besides, it was doing the job of distracting him from the climb.

"Mostly we were there so Darius could control the adults. If anyone disobeyed or resisted him, he'd hurt a kid. Didn't matter if the kid belonged to that particular adult or not. Very few people had survived the Shattering with an intact family anyway. He'd assign adults to kids in a weird little adoption program. From then on, the adult would know that the particular kid would be hurt if they themselves stepped out of line. It was effective. People did some pretty amazing shit to protect their cage kid. And some awful shit too. That's how our pack eventually got rounded up. Some adult betrayed us to protect their cage kid."

They were nearly to the zone border of down-gee, but the last stretch was the unbroken pavement of the parking lot. Jasper stopped talking to concentrate on finding the easiest route. Her fingers ached and her hands were scraped raw from jamming them into rough pavement cracks and supporting her whole weight that way. She suspected Ryan had heard enough anyway.

That one short year of pack life still brimmed with vividness in her memory. Lazy golden summer days of running near naked through fragrant grass. The sharp crispness of autumn mornings when it seemed they were the only ones left on earth. The pleasure of fresh roasted meat they'd caught themselves. Vron telling stories around the fire, spinning magic with her voice and hands. The sated warmth of piling together to sleep, surrounded by the comforting warmth and smell of the pack.

A slice of honey-tinted skies and cloudy dandelion fluff, bracketed on either side by shit-smeared cages and misery.

If she hadn't had that taste of freedom, would she have been able to resist the spiderweb Darius had woven around her? Would she have decided that being his pet was the best life she could hope for? For certain if Harmony's horribly scarred face hadn't reminded her of the price of that freedom, she wouldn't have summoned the rage to fight the seduction of Darius's games.

Then there was the incident with Crane and her pet dog, in which Jasper had watched another of Darius's pets broken like cheap glass. And of course, as soon as he'd made Martha Abebe cut off Ben's leg, it was all over. After that it had just been a question of who she'd use the knife on: Darius or herself.

There was something fierce and pure and free about pack life that the do-gooders at the soup kitchen could never grasp. The utter loyalty that stemmed from codependence, the haunting contentment almost too big to contain when she could reach out in her sleep and touch Ben's arm, Merlot's cheek, Crane's springy hair, Charlie's leg, and Vron's hand squeezing back an acknowledgement—*I'm here, you're not alone, I'll guard your dreams for you.* She could search her whole life and never recapture that wordless sense of connection and belonging.

They'd regained a hint of it as teenagers in Quick Rick's gravving team, but it wasn't the same and it didn't last. Adolescence hit them all in different ways. Crane had joined the Azuros, linking her loyalty to Zenobia and turning her back on her parents with finality. Jasper and Merlot had collided into each other like meteors and been struck temporarily deaf and blind to the rest of the world. Ben had become gun-shy of relationships after two consecutive bad breakups, one with a girl and the next with Charlie, prior to Charlie's abrupt departure from Yorky. Charlie had joined the ReGeneration, choosing their mission to restore the land over his friends; they'd seen little of him after that.

But Vron, always bubbling with midnight rainbows and sly jokes and hypnotic stories, their guardian against the dark, their myth-spinner, spellcaster, dream interpreter—she was the one who had succumbed. If the strongest and bravest of them couldn't fight off the spider demons in her mind, what hope did the rest of them have?

Maybe Grammar and the pack kids were right and Vron had taken the brunt of a curse that should have been distributed equally among all of them.

Vron had been cursed, all right. Cursed with friends who hadn't seen what was right in front of them. Friends who blithely assumed she'd always be strong and never falter, never break.

Jasper pulled herself up the last metre of side-gee and rolled through the static tingle of the border and came to rest on flat ground in down-gee. For that instant of relief, she could imagine the earth embraced her, welcomed her back. But it wouldn't last. Now that she was back in down-gee, the alien seeds inside her would eventually stutter and twitch, and the earth would flick her skin like a horse shooing a fly with its tail and Jasper would fall. Like the earth was trying to get rid of her before she Shattered. Like the graviteria were impatient to drag her out of this unaccustomed gravity well and lift her into space where they belonged.

Fighting a planet's disdain was exhausting, as was defying the deadly destiny living and growing in her veins.

She reached across the tingle of the zone border, and Ryan caught hold of her hand. He tumbled into down-gee with such eagerness that he rolled right on top of her. For the smallest moment she let him lie there, as if his weight and warmth pinning her down could force the earth to accept her.

She pushed him off and sat up.

"Let's not do that again anytime soon," he said, lying in the grass with his eyes closed.

She snorted. "You're welcome to walk straight back through the gates if you can't handle a weak-ass climb like that, soldier boy. The Tower's in the heart of the zones. It's not exactly going to be safe."

"Oh, joy."

"Anyway, safe is for people who want to get old."

"What's wrong with getting old?"

The improbability of it.

She got up and shaded her eyes, scanning the surrounding area in case the Damaskers had decided to investigate the runaway recruit in daylight. "We better stay off the roads today."

He stood and brushed dirt and grass from his jeans. "You said Grammar is Darius's son. But you also said Zenobia was Darius's girlfriend. I asked some of the Azuros if Zenobia had any kids, and they said she had one who died as a baby." He paused but she only gave him a blank expression. He asked bluntly, "Is Grammar Zenobia's son or another woman's?"

The intentness of his stare put her off. Why should she tell him anything? She shrugged. "I don't know who Darius fucked besides Zenobia. I was just a kid. I doubt he was a one-woman guy, but stranger things have happened. Ask *her* if you really want to know."

She walked off before he could persist. She had more important things to worry about— mostly that Grammar had been her only chance of finding her mother and whatever essential secret Zenobia didn't want her to know about.

"Why are we going back to Yorky? Shouldn't we be heading for the Tower?" Ryan asked.

"First of all, I need more than this basic gear. And proper equipment for you too. Second of all, Ben's coming with us. I'm not telling him about what you did to me because he'd freak out and kill you, probably, if not have a heart attack. So keep your mouth shut about it, got it? We're going to find my mother, and you're just tagging along for the adventure."

"Shoot, I was totally planning to tell your family and friends I kidnapped you," he said dryly. "But without Grammar, how does your story about finding your mother hold up?"

"Let me worry about that."

She looked up at the sun and stopped, realizing what day it was.

Ryan nearly bumped into her. "What is it?"

"Nothing." She resumed walking. "We won't be leaving today, though."

Because today was Zones Day. Probably her last. She wasn't going to miss it.

19

ZONES DAY

Dancing is
The closest we get
To transcendence or to sex
Without the commitment
To either religion
Or intimacy.

~ Veronica Park

"Welcome to the eighth annual Zones Day Parkour Games," Quick Rick announced to the crowd. "Are y'all ready for some incredible feats of athleticism and acrobatics, some real circus shit—I mean, stuff? Eh? I can't hear you! That's better. Okay, okay, calm down. Geez. All right, the first contestant..."

Jasper sat with her legs dangling over the tallest platform, waiting her turn with the other contestants. A bottle of hooch was being passed around, and she took a healthy gulp when it came to her, even though she'd consumed the contents of a flask earlier in the day. Zones Day wasn't a day for sobriety, especially not this one, though normally she'd have waited until after the competition.

Ryan sat in the stands, chatting with Quick Rick between contestants. He'd been impatient to head out into the zones immediately to find either Grammar or the ReGeneration some other way. Jasper had put her foot down. No way was she missing Zones Day. He could accuse of her delaying and he'd be right, but what did one day matter when they had no idea where Grammar had gone?

For the competition an obstacle course had been set up in the park with scaffolding bars, ramps, and platforms of varying sizes scattered about like children's blocks. The stands were filled with people, this being one of the more popular events of Zones Day. Beyond the parkour obstacle course, rubber mats and mattresses had been laid out for children and aspiring grav-walkers to practise their tumbles and somersaults on. Kids hopped and flipped and bumped into each other on the trampolines like kernels of corn on a hot pan.

"You're up, Pine," someone called.

She scrambled to her feet, adrenalin spiking through her veins. She stepped to the edge of the platform and scanned the course as the promise of movement muttered like thunder in her bones. The gathered spectators murmured at the sight of her, heads turning to watch. She snapped shut her helmet strap under her chin and rewrapped her wrist guards.

"Our next contestant needs no introduction. She's won four of the six games she's participated in. Her creative and downright reckless stunts have made her a fan favourite in this event and turned my hair grey despite my youth. Let's hear it for *Jasper Pine!*"

The crowd roared, and the sound shivered through her muscles. But she wasn't here for them.

The other grav-walkers on the platform continued to stretch and loosen up as if nothing was happening, but she could feel their attention as sharply as needles to the skin. Even Merlot, slouched into the depths of his Batman hoodie, glanced at her once, heavy lidded and impassive. Her grin at him was more of a cat's snarl, and she saw the jolt in his spine as surely as she felt it in her own.

Before she drank the potion that would either kill or cure her, she had a few things she was going to say to him. The words were lined up in the back of her throat, waiting. But now was not the time.

She tapped her right foot on the platform behind her left and then balanced with her toes hanging over the edge, teasing the crowd with her hesitation. This moment before the leap was the purest drug she'd ever encountered, a narcotic express train roaring through her blood, and she wanted to savour every last drop of it.

Her last Zones Day. At least the last one she'd likely be able to participate in.

The thought chilled the supernova explosions in her veins. She was too loose from the alcohol, her muscles slippery and distracted. A bee swarm buzz filled her head and a jitter danced over her nerves.

Better make it one to remember.

She didn't leap. She dived headfirst.

The crowd's gasp hung suspended as she flipped, knees tucked to her chest, slow as the movement of the earth. Then the gritty surface of a platform filled her palms, her toes pushing off, launching back into flight.

Movement was a wolf's howl, a rebellion, a storm unleashed. Walls were made to be defied, the tic tac of her toes kissing wood, the twist of her body against gravity, a flying side flip. Leaping gulfs, precision jumps from ledge to ledge without pause. Running across the bars as if they were open ground. Adding a somersault, landing on the bar on the balls of her feet. Dropping from railing to railing, feet only, no hands. Making a final dismount, a double sideways flip that felt eternal, the spiral at the heart of the galaxy . . .

Too slow, too slow, too caught up in the syrupy nostalgia of her farewell tour. The ground came too hard, too soon. Unforgiving. Immovable. Final.

The crowd gasped, drawing in all the air, leaving her lungs empty and straining. Light sparkled in front of her eyes.

Not a bad way to go out in the end.

She kept her eyes open, filling herself to the brim with sky, sky, sky, with the blue and eternal, with all the air she would no longer breathe.

Ten out of ten for flair and dare and flawlessly styled hair, Vron whispered in her ear. *All hail the lean, mean, coffee bean queen of gravitation, levitation, prestidigitation. Look at her, defeated at last.*

"I am not . . . defeated." Jasper croaked the words, annoyed, and with the return of her voice she knew that she was alive after all.

"That remains to be seen, chickie." Quick Rick's weathered brown face and greying locs under his baseball cap appeared in her field of vision. "Nobody'll beat your run, but that was a hell of a landing. Could've gone better."

"Oh, hey, you're alive," Ben noted with sharp sarcasm, kneeling on her other side. His worry dimples dug grooves in his cheeks.

"Was it the best wipeout in history or what?" Jasper asked. Air only had to fight a small skirmish to win entry into her lungs now.

"Not sure it even makes your top ten, honestly." Ben sniffed.

"Jesus *Christ*, Jas. Did you drink a whole brewery? Before gravving? Are you fucking kidding me? That's it. I'm going to kill you. For my mental health, you see. And then Harmony's going to kill you, and then I'm going to kill you again. And then Sparrow will want a turn and then—"

"Dude, chill." Jasper struggled to sit up. Pain slammed into her like a falling building, but pain was an old acquaintance, a first cousin, a regular drinking buddy. Pain could be classified, ranked, greeted politely, and then ignored.

Muttering under his breath, Ben took a firm grip of her arm as she waited for the shuddering ground to settle beneath her feet. Seeing her stand, the crowd roared its approval, and she raised her arms in salute.

Quick Rick waved to the crowd. "She's okay! Y'all know by now it'd take an act of God to kill Jasper Pine!"

The act of an alien god, maybe.

People settled back into their seats, and normal chatter resumed. Ryan leaned forward in his seat, elbows on his knees, watching her. He didn't come over to see if she was okay.

Ben's hand dug into her arm so deeply it would leave bruises. She tugged but he wouldn't release her. His skin was sickly pale under his tan and his lips tight. He was very angry. He had been ever since she'd told him that morning about what had happened in Damascus. About the fact that she'd gone without telling him, leaving him to worry for a day and night. About the fact that the Damaskers could have killed her. He'd tried to hide it, push it away, focus on what they were going to do next, but she could feel it simmering under his worry.

She hadn't told him anything about Ryan kidnapping her or about the deal they'd made— nor would she if she could help it. Ben would have a meltdown, and it was the last thing she needed.

"It was an accident, Ben. My run was flawless. I just landed wrong."

"You're drunk. *That's* not an accident."

"I'm mildly buzzed. On Zones Day. You're being dramatic."

That accusation went over as well as could be expected, and he stormed away.

She spotted Esther Kornelsen sitting on the bottom row of the stands and on impulse walked over and sat beside her. Esther glanced over distractedly, then looked surprised to see her. She was holding a little boy on her lap, a blond one this time.

"Whose kid is that?" Jasper asked by way of small talk.

"Lily's. She had a migraine today." Esther's older sister Lily had fallen from the barn roof years ago trying to rescue a cat and was now confined to a wheelchair. Her post-concussion migraines also gave her a low tolerance for crowds or noise, which included her own children. Fortunately, she had a wealth of sisters to pick up the slack.

"That fall looked bad. Are you all right?" Esther asked politely. Her expression said, *Why are you talking to me?*

"Sometimes gravity likes to remind me who's boss. I'll live." Though not for much longer.

Harmony liked to point to Lily's accident as an example of why Jasper should be more careful. Jasper's response that Lily should've left the climbing to professionals hadn't gone over well. The words "professional dumbass" had been thrown around.

"So where's the Graceling today?" Jasper asked, looking around. There were plenty of Mennonites in the crowd, women in long handmade dresses, their hair pinned up under black *duaks*, blond children, men with button-front shirts and suspenders. She spotted Esther's other older sister Sarah with her husband and children, but no sign of Grace with her jeans and defiantly shorn hair.

Esther shot her an anxious glance. Dark rings circled her eyes. "She didn't come home last night. Have you seen her?"

Last she'd seen Grace, she'd been in the company of Crane, about to create a distraction for a bunch of riled-up Damaskers. She could hardly tell Esther that.

She'd seen Crane earlier today coming in the gates with Zenobia and Tom. If Crane had gotten away from the Damaskers unscathed, why hadn't Grace made it home?

Esther grabbed her arm. "What aren't you telling me? Where is she?"

"Relax. Last I saw her, she was fine. She was . . . with a friend."

Esther looked at her, relief warring with suspicion. "You mean a boyfriend?"

Jasper thought of Grace arguing with Dragon at the church. *God, I hope not.* "She's a smart girl. She'll be fine. Just committing her obligatory teenage rebellion, I'm sure."

Esther glared. "You're covering up for her, aren't you? You and Merlot always took her side and—and encouraged her to misbehave. She's not like you. She's good and sweet and she has a future."

Unlike me, eh? Well, that was true on all counts, truer than Esther could know. That and a stab of guilt kept Jasper's smart remarks locked up.

After Darius's death there'd been a lot of talk about all the orphaned children running wild, but not much corresponding action. The Kornelsen family had practised what they preached and taken in Merlot and Vron. Vron was wary but tolerant of her foster family, but Merlot never fit in or made any effort to. Looking back, Jasper could admit that she hadn't helped matters any. She'd been jealous of that big cheerful family with a mother and father and sisters and a horde of nieces and nephews who were indiscriminately loved and taken care of. She'd poked fun at them, their conservativeness, their religion, their old-fashioned clothes and habits, and Merlot had followed her lead as he always did. He'd left the Kornelsen home as soon as he could, as soon as Jasper agreed to live with him.

Which was ironic, because after Vron's death the Kornelsens had been there for Merlot, while Jasper had run away.

"Grace is apprenticing with Ibtisam," Esther was saying. "She has stacks of medical books in her room. She uses my cushions to practise stitching up cuts. This acting up, being out at all hours, disappearing for days and not telling us what she's doing—it's not like her. I don't care if she wants to wear pants and cut her hair. I want her to be safe. I know you don't think much of us, Jasper, but I thought you at least had a soft spot for Grace."

Jasper squirmed a little. She'd hardly had any contact with Grace and the rest of the Kornelsens since her breakup with Merlot. "Have you asked Merlot?"

"I told you. He won't talk to me." Esther looked away. "He thinks I'm a controlling, joyless, self-righteous conformist who wants to crush Grace's spirit."

"Jesus, what an ass," Jasper said guiltily. At least part of that quote smacked of her own teenage tirades. The little boy on Esther's lap looked at her with interest. She revised her words hastily. "I mean, geez, what a meanie."

Esther ignored her and leaned forward to speak to her nephew in Low German, gesturing for him to look at the parkour platform where Merlot had just been announced as the next contestant.

The crowd hushed.

Jasper loved watching Merlot run, dark and lean as a hawk,

the slash of his elbows and the length of his jumps, each footstep placed like the notes of a song.

When he landed, light and final, a spear coming to rest, it was all she could do not to run to him. There was a time she would have. She'd have grabbed him and kissed him, and they'd have laughed like lunatics, high on movement, high on flight. She'd almost forgotten how that unfettered grin of his sank thunder into her heart and fishhooks into the marrow of her bones. She'd almost forgotten that a shovel had scooped out half her insides when they'd broken up, when he'd decided to hate her and she'd decided to let him.

She didn't miss him. She missed the past. There was a difference; she was sure of it.

She froze her face, afraid it had revealed too much, and glanced sideways at Esther to see if she'd noticed. But Esther was watching Merlot with an expression that was impossible to interpret, at least in any way that made sense.

Jasper slipped away. She bumped into Sparrow, who promptly pulled her into a giant hug. "That was a scary-looking fall, you know, missy."

Jasper sank into the hug gratefully. The Yorky ganglord smelled like iron and peppermint gum. "Just lucky, I guess."

Sparrow had been a superhero to Jasper once, the rebel leader who'd repeatedly dared to defy Darius when no one else would. Jasper would never forget Sparrow scooping up her blood-covered eight-year-old self in her powerful arms and carrying her away from the scene, the body, the nightmare. If the Pinegirl was the wave that had brought change, Sparrow was the rocky shore that had held steady and dissipated her destruction. The Pinegirl had broken the back of a regime, but Sparrow had picked up the pieces and built something new.

People called Jasper a hero, but she was an imposter. She knew what a real hero looked like.

Sparrow pushed her back and studied her critically. "I hate to tell you, babe, but there's a massive rip in the ass of your leggings."

"Wonderful." Jasper twisted around, trying to see the rip. Esther could've pointed it out. She hadn't. She'd probably learned that level of pettiness from Merlot.

"You know, the thing about luck is that it always, always runs out eventually," Sparrow said.

Not when it was a curse. "Wanna bet?"

Sparrow narrowed her eyes. "You need a kid."

Jasper laughed, startled. "Excuse me? Who was it who personally delivered a dozen boxes of condoms when Merlot and I moved in together?"

"I don't mean an infant—are you crazy? No, more like an apprentice. Just some dumbass kid to worry over. It'd serve you right."

Jasper thought of Neverwhen's angry, disillusioned face before she ran away, Grammar demanding whether she would kill him like she'd killed his father. "Excellent idea. I don't think the younger generation's been fucked up enough yet, but just leave it to me."

Since the damage to her leggings seemed irreparable and left nothing to the imagination anyway, Jasper kicked off her shoes and stripped off the leggings.

"Uh, you want my scarf to tie around your waist?"

"No, my T-shirt's long enough."

"If 'long enough' means covering your crotch, sure. I hope by the time Ippy persuades me to have a child you'll have adopted the human custom of wearing pants. You know, to set a good example."

"It sounds like she's already persuaded you."

Sparrow smiled as she looked over to where her wife was taking a break from the first aid station to paint children's faces, transforming them into butterflies and tigers and superheroes. With her pink head scarf and surrounded by children, she looked like a flower swarmed by bees. "Yeah, but I enjoy the buttering-up process."

"That's an image."

"It wasn't meant literally, sicko. I take back what I said about you having a kid."

"Common sense prevails, then. Well, there's never any shortage of free-range younglings around here to adopt. They practically grow on trees."

"But why should I have a kid when I have my hands full worrying about your dumb ass?"

"So you'll have lots of practice. Mom. Mommy. Mama Sparrow. General Mother. Motha frickin' gang mama."

"See, this is why you're single." Sparrow tilted her sunglasses down her nose and peered over them. "Speaking of which, is tall, dark, and handsome flirting with Merlot or your brother?"

Ryan Latrans had joined Ben and Merlot near the finish line. Ryan animatedly gestured to the course as he talked. Ben and Merlot were laughing, damn them. Now Ryan was reaching over to shake hands with Ben, introducing himself, flashing that goddamn smile of his.

"They're not flirting."

Ryan knew who Ben was now, his insurance if Jasper reneged on their deal. Maybe she needed to warn her brother after all about the treachery behind Ryan's smile. Except seeing Ben's dimples appear, free of worry or anger, was almost worth it. If Jasper kept her part of the bargain, he'd never have to know better.

"You sure?" Sparrow said dubiously. "Last time I saw Ben smile like that, Charlie was still in town."

"Don't say his name," Jasper said automatically.

Sparrow refrained from rolling her eyes. "Still? People are allowed to leave, Jas."

"Not when it comes to my brother, they're not. Anyway, Ryan's not flirting." He was gathering trust for potential exploitation later. "He has a girlfriend." Or wife, fiancée, whatever she was. Mother of his child. Ryan hadn't explained the relationship. He'd focused mostly on the danger to his son. Jasper wondered what that meant, if anything.

Sparrow raised an eyebrow but didn't comment. "Listen, missy, I need to go do leaderly things like make sure my brother-in-law's Damaskers don't start fights with the Azuros. Do I need to assign a ganger to keep you out of trouble?" She glanced pointedly at Jasper's bare legs.

"Relax. I'm not going to do anything stupid."

"Empty words coming from someone who did Merlot."

"Oh, *ouch*." Jasper glared.

Laughing, Sparrow left her with a wave, the tremendous corona of her afro bobbing above the crowd.

A nearby group of drunk gangers noticed Jasper's state of undress and erupted with hoots and wolf whistles. She waved her leggings over her head like a flag and gave them the finger at the same time. The boys glanced over at the commotion. Ben took one look, clapped a hand to his face in disgusted embarrassment, and turned away. Merlot rolled his eyes, but Ryan just waved in cheerful greeting.

"I need a drink," she announced to nobody in particular. Her current attire or lack of it certainly had one advantage. Three different guys were offering her hooch almost before the words had left her mouth. She challenged one of them to a rock, paper, scissors battle and upon winning demanded payment of the bet. To the jeers of his friends, the ganger good-naturedly stripped off his jeans and handed them over.

She slung them over her shoulder and bowed extravagantly

to the group. Declining the ganger's offer for a round two, she aimed her steps toward the market square, where Harmony and her team were setting up the barbeques for supper.

She was briefly swarmed by a horde of children, so loud and wild and shrill that it was hard to believe they weren't pack kids but had parents and bedtimes and regular baths. They invented a game on the fly that involved high-fiving Jasper's bare thighs as they streaked past. She high-fived the backs of their heads in return, but they were fast for shoe-wearing townie turds.

"Filthy little brats," she shouted after them as they raced away in a cloud of dust and shrieks and laughter. "I'll barbeque your nasty hands and serve them as hamburgers! Hand-burgers, ha!"

She bumped into someone. "Watch where you're . . . oh, hi, Pastor Tim."

Pastor Tim McCleary was long and ungainly and often looked as if he were about to fall down, though he never quite did. His beard was as dark and shiny as a beaver's pelt on his gaunt, pale jaws, and his eye sockets looked as if they'd been carved out with spoons, raw and craggy and tired but always kind. His left arm ended at the wrist.

"Hello, Jasper, my dear," he said, smiling at a point somewhere above her head.

"Oh. Uh, yeah." Hastily, she kicked off her shoes and scrambled into the jeans she'd just won. They were tight over the hips and a little short but otherwise a decent fit. She'd chosen her target well. "I can't believe Sparrow thinks I should have a kid," she said to distract from the fact that the pastor had seen her in her underwear. "They're rude and noisy little animals. I should know—I was one very recently."

"That may be," he said mildly, "but then you get to watch them grow up into wonderful young men and women who—"

"Still run around without their pants on," Jasper said, grinning.

He laughed. "Apparently so. I was going to say watching a wild child grow up into a thoughtful and worthwhile young adult is the reward that warms us in our old age."

"But they'll make you suffer first, though," Jasper said skeptically. "I mean, I used to run away from Harmony whenever she wanted me to do chores, and I'd stay away till it was dark. I'd wake up screaming from nightmares five nights a week so she never got any sleep. And when I got mad, I used to kick her in the shins. God, I was awful."

"But ask her if she thought it was worth it."

Jasper couldn't think of anything to say to that. She kicked at the dirt with the toe of her shoe and stared for a minute at the hole she'd made. She knew what Harmony's answer would be, but wouldn't she have been better off without the worry and heartache Jasper had caused her and would yet, before it was all over?

"Something on your mind?" he asked gently.

Does your God listen to alien-human hybrid girls? Is full human being status required to get into heaven? Or am I a blind spot in the eye of God, just like the earth?

"Will you be available for confessions tomorrow?" she asked.

Pastor Tim wasn't a priest or Catholic, but for the sake of his Catholic parishioners he made himself available to anyone who wanted to confess, although this more often turned into a comfortable chat with tea and biscuits.

"I'm always available. How does seven a.m. sound?"

"You're very funny for a minister."

"I think so. Are you expecting to have a lot to confess?"

"I certainly hope so."

He shook his head but smiled. "May your bones remain

unbroken, your heart unwounded, and your liver in recoverable shape by tomorrow morning."

Jasper crossed herself. "Amen."

"And may you leave everyone around you in the same condition," he said dryly.

She continued on her way. In the market square Harmony was at the centre of a bustle of activity. Meat roasted on braziers over coals. Platters of shiny brown buns and roti and bowls of egg and potato salad, coleslaw, kimchi, and curried rice were being set out on long tables along with plates of sliced tomatoes, cucumber, and carrots. Pitchers of cold tea and fruit juice sweated beside stacks of plastic cups. Desserts were being preserved in coolers full of precious ice from the community ice cellar.

A group of older townie kids had been roped into setting up rows of chairs in front of the stage for the talent show and concert. The band was warming up their instruments: two guitars, a fiddle, drums, and a flute. Old women sat near the tables and waved off flies, stray dogs, and opportunistic kids.

Not long after she killed Darius Dalca, Jasper had stopped talking. Her throat had rusted shut. Words became dandelion puffs falling apart at the merest breath. She let the words of others sail past her like badly aimed arrows, and in the pit of her stomach her own words lay in a rotting heap without grave marker or monument.

She and Ben had been Harmony's cage kids. Her good behaviour was guaranteed by their imprisonment, but in turn she was punished for their bad behaviour. Despite that, after it was all over, Harmony gathered them up and adopted them by the force of her will, even though Jasper wouldn't talk and ran away repeatedly.

Harmony began signing to her instead, using the swoop and flutter of her knobby old fingers to underscore her spoken words and ensnare Jasper's attention. Though her vocal cords remained as silent and abandoned as the city around them, Jasper found her fingers twitching in response, forming words out of air and releasing them like little birds. Her body, it seemed, still had things to say.

Catching Harmony's eye across the square, she formed the words that Harmony had signed to her every night before bed: *Family always.*

Harmony smiled her lopsided smile and signed it back. She was distracted by a commotion caused by a stray dog who had crept close and upended a rack of cooking meat.

In the ensuing commotion, Jasper slipped away and left the festivities behind.

20

OF DOGS AND GIRLS

That warm heavy buzz when you've drunk just the right
*   amount*
Good hair days

~ Veronica Park (*Things I Will Miss/Reasons to Live*)

C heers and the screams of children at play drifted to Jasper's ears as she wandered the empty streets and alleys away from the park and the town square, where the bulk of the festivities were taking place.

She'd planned to live this Zones Day to the fullest, to play every game, to talk to every friend, to eat every ounce of food she could stuff into her belly, to maintain a constant alcoholic buzz, to dance till her legs no longer supported her. She had planned to be a glutton, only to find she had no appetite at all.

She'd traded a kiss for a ganger's flask, so at least now her aches and bruises were receding into a warm fuzz.

A dog's high-pitched whimper cut through her pleasant

haze. She turned warily in the middle of the street. The street was empty but for a ganger who was ducking into an alley, probably to take a leak. Seeing nothing else, she followed the sound down the alley and into an empty, overgrown lot.

The dog, an indeterminate mix of breeds that granted it size and long tangled brown fur, was crouched against a wire fence, holding one paw up in pain. Blocking his escape from the fenced-in lot was a familiar figure, skinny and long limbed as a cartoon and with hair big enough to hide knives in. As Jasper approached, Crane picked up a rock and hurled it at the dog. She missed by inches, and the dog wheeled in the other direction. Crane bent in a leisurely fashion to pick out another rock.

"Hey, Crane. I see you made it out of Damascus alive. What about Grace?"

Crane barely spared her a glance. "How about some fun, Pinegirl? Five throws each. Most hits is getten—"

"Grace didn't come home last night. What happened?"

Crane shrugged. "How should I know? I been asken if she's liken me and she's sayen no. Okay, fine. So I been goen home and I guess she been goen too."

Jasper rubbed at her forehead. A most unlikely crush, and not one she could ever see working out. "Oh, Crane. She's sixteen. And a Mennonite." Crane gave her a blank look. "You know what? Never mind. You left her out there by herself in the middle of the night? Why didn't you at least walk her home, for gravity's sake?"

Crane's eyes were simmering cauldrons of trouble. "I'm bodyguard for Zenobia, not little pink cheek girl."

"What are you doing here, then? Last I saw, Zenobia was watching the concert."

"Tom's with her. She been tellen me to go have fun." Crane hefted the rock and smiled toothily. "So I am."

Crane in an ordinary mood and Crane in a bad mood were virtually indistinguishable on the surface. The difference lay in the prickling sensation in the back of Jasper's neck and the electric edge to Crane's smile.

The dog limped along the edge of the fence, searching for a way out that wouldn't take him past the two humans. Crane wound up like a baseball pitcher and hurled the rock as hard as she could. But not before Jasper jogged her elbow.

Crane whirled and lashed out in instant rage. Jasper dodged backwards, but Crane's fingernails scored bloody lines of pain across her jaw.

"What's the cardinal rule?" Jasper backpedalled into the lot as Crane advanced.

"Zenobia's not here." Crane stalked after her. Unlike Jasper, she'd have a multitude of hidden knives to reach for, despite the Zones Day rules against weapons. "And you'll be tellen her nothing."

"I won't. What's to tell?" Jasper's backing away had drawn Crane away from the gate. The dog, sidling away from their approach, spotted the opening.

Crane saw Jasper's gaze flicker past her. She scooped up a stone, whirled, and threw it. It struck the dog square in the side and elicited a piercing yelp. He shied away from the gate and slunk back toward the fence.

"Come on, just let him go," Jasper said.

"What, you feelen sorry for a dog? Why? Just stupid animal. Ugly, dumb thing. Ugly, dirty, stupid, dumb piece of shit thing with pathetic, stupid, boo-hoo voice. Good for nothing! Useless!"

Rage was increasing in Crane's voice with every word as she entered that liminal space where anger rose like the tide and her fists did the talking her heart couldn't manage.

Jasper edged backwards again, casting about for a way to

distract Crane and snap her out of this violent vortex of a mood. "You had a puppy once, Crane. Don't you remember?"

Crane froze. "What?"

"You called him Shadow. He followed you everywhere. You loved him more than anything."

"You're *lyen*. I never been haven a dog. Never!" But Crane couldn't seem to move. Her cheek twitched.

Jasper was stomping on thin rotten ice, but she was already far enough from shore to shrug off the consequences. She had never mentioned Shadow to Crane before. She suspected no one had. Who would dare? Was it possible Crane truly didn't remember? She had been young. But then, so had Jasper, and she remembered. More clearly, in fact, than she remembered killing Darius.

She remembered an unmoving puddle of silky white fur and a silence without a yap or a yelp to brighten it. Dark splotches on the floor. Tiny Crane, a painting in sepia with crimson fingers, all expression draining slowly from her face like warmth from a cup of tea. Tear tracks fossilizing on her cheeks. She remembered a knife on the floor with small bloody fingerprints. And Darius, always Darius, crouched beside her like a blue-eyed spider, casting a monster-sized shadow on the wall.

"Shadow." The name seemed to escape Crane's lips involuntarily. Her eyes snapped back into focus, and the desperation in them sent Jasper reeling.

Crane whirled and advanced on the dog, hurling everything she could get her hands on. Rocks, juice box cartons, an old shoe. Blind fury affected her aim, but the rain of items sent the dog running back and forth against the fence, whimpering and howling, pawing at the wire.

Turn and fight, pathetic beast, Jasper willed it. *You've got a mouthful of weapons, and I've got nothing.*

A piercing whistle. Then a *thwack* as something small hit

Crane's arm. She yelped and stopped in her tracks. A small figure stood in the gate, aiming a slingshot at Crane, eyes glittering behind a spill of soft plaits.

"Neverwhen?" Jasper said incredulously.

"Little rat," Crane snarled. She altered direction to bear down on the girl.

Neverwhen released the shot. The pebble hit Crane square in the abdomen. She shouted with fury and pain and clamped her arms around her middle.

Neverwhen whistled again. The dog slunk low and fast in her direction. He slipped past her and out the gate. Neverwhen already had another pebble in her sling.

"You gonna pay," Crane promised.

Even before her fingers flicked to the knife at her hip, Jasper was moving. She bore Crane to the ground in a full body tackle.

"Run, Neverwhen," she yelled in the single moment when Crane was too stunned to react. She didn't have time to see whether the pack girl obeyed as Crane writhed back to life. Jasper had several dozen pounds on Crane, but that meant nothing against the other girl's cat-like speed and savagery. In seconds Jasper was on her back, fighting with all her strength to keep Crane's hands from wrapping around her throat like a steel collar.

"Come on, Craney, it's me," she gasped out. "We're pack, remember?"

"Long time ago."

"If I hadn't tackled you, you might have killed that girl and Zen would've put you in a cage forever!"

"Just a rat. Nobody's caren."

Crane's fingers reached closer to her throat. She pushed down with all her weight while Jasper gripped her wrists, straining to hold her back. Jasper choked out, "I care. I don't want to see you in a cage again."

Crane released her. She sat on Jasper's torso and stared down at her. When she spoke, her voice was tiny, almost surprised. "He was a puppy. He was haven white fur."

"Yes."

Crane was an object lesson in the foolishness of loving something Darius could hurt. His pets could only be loyal to him. He would carve away everything else—no, he'd put the knife in your hand and make you do it yourself.

Crane said, "He been sayen if I didn't, he'd be kill—"

Abruptly Crane stood. She shoved a hand into the single thigh pouch she wore over jeans with flowered patches. She pulled out a crumpled square of paper and began folding.

Jasper got up slowly. Her hands were shaking. The freckles and scars, the nicks and scratches and calluses, the raw-bitten nails seemed distant and detached from her body. Perhaps they'd been cut off long ago and these were ghost hands she'd lived with since. She tucked them into her pockets so she didn't have to look at them anymore.

Crane's slender fingers moved without hesitation. Her small pointed face held the same cooling remoteness that Jasper could feel settling inside the cage bars of her own ribs.

"Crane, what happened with Grace?"

"She's not wanten me." Crane's voice was eerily calm, her eyes absorbed in her paper folding.

"That must've hurt your feelings," Jasper said cautiously.

Crane shrugged absently. "Is consequence."

"Consequence of what?"

Crane stared at her finished creation, a crane. "Of breaken the rules." She tossed the crane to the ground and walked away.

"What rule did you break?" Jasper called after her.

Crane didn't answer.

Jasper picked up the paper bird and dusted it off. How often had she and Crane sat side by side, seeing who could fold cranes the fastest? *Whoever folds a thousand cranes will receive a wish*, Zenobia had told them. While they were folding, all became silent. That silence swallowed the screams, the pleading, the laughter, the sobbing. They could fold the paper—the sounds, their hearts, their fear—fold it smaller and smaller until it made sense. Until it was beautiful.

And then they'd throw it away.

Crane stopped near the gate and turned as if she'd remembered something. "Hey, you haven any of Vron's notebooks too?"

"What? No. Merlot burned them all."

"Yeah. Except pink cheek girl's haven one. So you sure?"

"Of course I'm sure. Why? Why do you care?"

Crane bared her teeth. "No reason." Then she was gone.

Perhaps it was a mercy Crane didn't remember much about Shadow, that flop-eared, yap-voiced, drooly-tongued little fur-fluff who'd slept every night on Crane's chest with his muzzle tucked across her soft throat. A dumb little mutt who'd trusted his dumb little human because neither of them knew yet that humans could never be trusted.

Darius had gotten what he wanted from Crane—a broken, loyal weapon whose forging had torn her parents into shredded shadows of their former selves. It wouldn't have taken him long to do the same to Jasper. Ben's leg would've been only the beginning.

Wandering aimlessly, Jasper realized she'd come to the Raleigh apartment building. At ten storeys it was the tallest building in the Yorky community, which otherwise mostly consisted of townhouses and single-family detached homes, shops, and restaurants. She could've gone inside and taken the stairs to the top. Instead she climbed the drainpipes on the outside.

Gravving focused her, returned sensation to her body, filled her with air. Maybe it was gravity that smothered her when her feet touched the ground, or maybe it was the earth that sucked oxygen from her lungs, unwilling to share her gifts with those tainted by the extraterrestrial. But when Jasper climbed, she could breathe.

Even if she survived the cure, it could take all this away from her. It could take her body and her movement. It could take her ability to breathe.

She reached the roof and sat at the edge with her legs dangling over the side. From there she could see all of Yorky, the geometric patterns of backyard gardens and outhouses and clotheslines and goat and chicken pens. The quarantine wall glimmered in the distance, facing the broken buildings of downtown, pinned in place by the Tower's arrogant spire.

Music drifted to her from the park, the plaintive strains of guitar and violin stretched on a skeleton of percussion. A swell of voices as people sang along to old favourites from pre-Shattering. Hymns to an irretrievable past.

The wind blew the grass below into waves of green and silver.

Jasper pulled out the flask and took a swig.

Her memories of killing Darius were as slippery as bars of soap under her feet and as insubstantial as blown bubbles. If there hadn't been so many witnesses, maybe she'd have forgotten the whole day as much as Crane had forgotten Shadow. People remembered, and with their words and stories they kept Darius's ghost alive, kept her fragmented recollections fresh and bloody. Were the memories even her own or bestowed on her like a grisly second-hand bouquet?

She remembered Sparrow picking her up and carrying her away. She remembered Martha washing the blood from her body, scrubbing her over and over with soap. She remembered lying in bed with Harmony curled around her on one side and

Ben on the other, smothered by their warmth and breath and barely hidden devastation. She'd lain awake after they'd fallen asleep, alone in the dark, alone but for the silent, laughing, inescapable voice in her head. *Now we'll be together forever, my pet. Forever and ever and ever.*

She tilted back the flask and let the promise of temporary oblivion rush down her throat. She leaned forward, elbows on knees, and kicked her heels against the building side. Wind swooped through her hair and flattened her clothes to her body with the hands of the dead. A sway and a slip, and she'd tumble like a leaf on the wind.

A tragic accident, they'd say. Too drunk, too cocky, too close to the edge.

No one would be overly surprised.

And then I win, Darius said.

"Oh, fuck you. This isn't about you." She took another swallow. "Anyway, I won. How long before you'd have made me kill Ben? Huh?"

He'd had Jasper—all of them—so wrapped up in his webs that who could know what she would've done under his influence. His game was so full of choices—right hand or left, flamingo or dog pit, this life or that life—it might never have occurred to her that she didn't have to play the game at all.

He'd done it to Crane.

You were always much smarter than Crane. That's why you were my favourite.

"Shadow was your biggest mistake. I saw you then for real. I saw the game. I saw what you would do to me."

So she'd ended it the only way she could. Permanently. *I beat you.*

Did you? His voice was so faint she could hardly make it out. *You did what Crane never could. You saw the truth and you broke the rules and you took over the game. You made your final move, your endgame, with such ruthlessness that you surprised even me. This is not defeat for me; this is victory. You surpassed your teacher. You won because of how I made you, not in spite of it. Oh, pet, I was so proud.*

Jasper tilted her head back and swallowed the rest of the flask's contents, welcoming the volatile burn in her throat. Fire to cleanse and to scour, and to chase out the shadows and burn the corpses.

Her life had felt borrowed from the moment she'd taken Darius's, an overdue library book she'd soon return.

She hurled the empty flask into the streets, where a couple of kids were running past. They stopped to look up. A dog barked. She stood, balancing at the roof edge as she had balanced on the parkour platform that morning.

In the days after she killed Darius, Merlot and Vron and Charlie and Ben had surrounded her and braided her hair. It was much longer in those days. For hours she sat, unspeaking, as they separated her hair and formed it into hundreds of tiny plaits. The gentle tug of their hands wove her, strand by strand, back into the warp and weft of the universe. Vron lifted Jasper's (bloody, bloody) hands to her mouth and spoke stories into them. She rewrote Jasper's hands back into existence, etched with the fairy gold witchery and tinyling soot sorcery of her words.

The first time Zenobia had been allowed to see her, she took both of Jasper's rewritten hands in hers and kissed them. Tom Jitters kneeled to tie her laces and then took a marker and drew a bird on her shoe. Nico Mavuto caught her eye across a crowded room, silently straightened, and saluted.

Crane had punched her in the stomach. *How could you kill him?* Betrayal and loss wrapped up in a tornado twist of fury. She punched and kicked Jasper until Jasper could only curl up in a ball on the ground and wait to either die or for Crane's rage to pass. The words rang as clearly as tiny bells in her head: *I did it for you because you couldn't*. But like all words at that time, they dissolved before they reached her tongue, and so she said nothing. It was the last time she ever saw Crane cry.

Jasper stepped off the ledge, back onto the roof.

The wind blew itself out, and the earth was quiet. For once, so was Darius.

A footstep scraped on concrete behind her, and a boy's voice asked, "So what kinda sick are you?"

21

A SECRET UNMASKED

We're all of us cosmic eggs,
Containing nestled universes,
Defying the laws of physics.
But are they really laws?
Or are they poetry?

~ Veronica Park

The voice startled Jasper so much, she tripped as she turned and stumbled backwards toward the edge of the roof. She windmilled for balance, teetering over open air.

She caught a snapshot glimpse of Grammar and Neverwhen in front of the roof access door, staring at her with open mouths. Jasper hurled herself sideways as she fell and hit the gravelled concrete with her shoulder, even as her weight and momentum dragged her over the edge.

She clawed for purchase in the gravel to arrest her slide.

Kicking, she found some traction against the side of the building and stopped her momentum.

"Well, this is embarrassing," she noted.

She propelled herself back up onto the roof just as Grammar and Neverwhen finally moved to help her.

"I'm fine, I'm fine." She stood hastily and dusted herself off, feeling scraped and bruised and raw and shaken. "I never fall, you see," she told them. "It was an unplanned jump, but I changed my mind."

Grammar and Neverwhen exchanged a glance. What were they doing here in Yorky, much less up on this roof with her? Was she hallucinating?

A dog stood beside Neverwhen, tall enough to comfortably lick her neck, and with enough fur to hide a family of squirrels in. He watched Jasper with unnervingly close attention. It was the same dog Crane had been throwing rocks at earlier.

Jasper stepped away from the roof edge. The dog trotted over to investigate favouring an injured paw. She growled at him, but he seemed unfazed, sniffing around her legs with his gaping, panting, toothy mouth. Her skin crawled with the anticipation of crunching teeth and tearing jaws.

"Get away from me, or I'll punch you in the head." She didn't dare move.

"Okuru, come," said Neverwhen. The dog limped back to Neverwhen's side.

Jasper sat abruptly in the gravel and cradled her head in her hands, feeling the first ominous precursors of tomorrow morning's hangover. Finally, she looked up to confirm that Grammar was indeed standing in front of her in the flesh, tense as coiled wire, an unlikely harbinger of hope.

"Why are you here?"

"We seen you up here. Thinken you'll be fallen," said Neverwhen. Nice of her to say *fall* rather than *jump*.

"Oh. No, I mean . . ." She gestured at Grammar.

He crossed his arms tightly across his chest. The bruises on his face clashed in a violent rainbow of blue and green and yellow and violet, crisscrossed with barely scabbed cuts. The swelling had gone down enough that both eyes were visible, if thoroughly blackened.

"You tellen me you're sick?" he said. "What kinda sick?"

"Let's call it gravity sick."

"Maybe Auntie been haven medicine for that." Grammar glanced at Neverwhen. "In our house."

Neverwhen shook her head doubtfully.

"This isn't the kind of sick that doctors and regular medicine can help," Jasper said. "Zenobia is making a cure, but it could just as easily kill me as help. I think maybe my mother had a different idea for a cure, and I want to know what it was."

Grammar stared out over the darkening city. Jasper bit her lip to keep herself from pleading. He was here, wasn't he? Here with Darius's desert sky eyes and Zenobia's haunted forest mouth.

Neverwhen leaned her forehead against Grammar's shoulder, and he glanced down at her. A whole conversation was exchanged in that look, Grammar's reluctance answered by Neverwhen's encouragement.

"I'll be helpen you," he said at last, his whole face sharp and tight and raw. "I'll be showen you where I been finden the amulet."

The strain left her body in a whoosh. She let herself flop over onto her back with nothing between her and the stars but the earth's fickle gravity.

"Why?" she asked, looking up at the sky. "Why did you decide to come back?"

Unexpectedly, he approached. He crouched and touched her forehead with the back of his knuckles, brief and impersonal but so reminiscent of Harmony checking her for fever in her childhood that she nearly cried. He peered at her face intently, as if looking for the sickness she claimed. Or for lies. Or for the young monster who'd killed his father.

He shrugged and straightened. "Nev's maken me."

If he was being flippant, he had Zenobia's poker face to disguise it. She wasn't sure what she'd even expected him to say.

She sat up and looked at Neverwhen. The last time Jasper had seen her, Neverwhen had pleaded for her help and Jasper had proven how cold and cruel biggies could be. After all that, she'd still persuaded Grammar to help Jasper.

"Thank you, Neverwhen." The words seemed hopelessly inadequate.

Neverwhen regarded her solemnly, her gloved hand resting on Okuru's neck. "Doen the right thing," she said. It wasn't clear if she meant Jasper or herself.

Grammar made a sound that might have been disagreement or a complaint about the cost of doing the right thing, but Neverwhen patted his arm, and he sighed. They turned and headed for the roof access door.

Jasper scrambled to her feet. "Wait, where are you going?"

"Too many Damaskers in Yorky today," Grammar said. "Not safe. I'll be meeten you morrow-day." This was a pack kid term for some vague future time; it could mean a few days or weeks.

"So, what? I'm supposed to just . . . ?" Watch him casually walk away? Trust a pack kid to keep his word without threat or promise of reward? She followed them into the stairwell. "You can stay at my house. We have lots of food. No Damaskers will find you there."

"No." Grammar didn't slow down.

Neverwhen, moving at a more sedate pace beside the limping dog, peeked at Jasper and gave her a cautious smile.

"Let's at least arrange a time to meet. Not tomorrow—I'll be too hungover, and so will Ben. How about the day after? We're going into the zones, I take it. How many days should we pack for?"

"Many," Grammar said.

Heroically, Jasper refrained from rolling her eyes. She addressed Neverwhen instead. "You coming too?"

"No," said Grammar.

"Yes," said Neverwhen.

"It'll be nice to have another girl along," Jasper said. "You know, someone sensible." They exchanged smirks. Grammar managed to convey a glower without turning around.

"What about your pack?" Jasper asked.

"Comen too," Neverwhen said cheerfully.

"Not comen," Grammar said with some heat.

"Might be dangerous for younglings." Jasper had to agree with Grammar on this point.

Neverwhen shrugged. "Damaskers are dangerous too. Deep zones are better, maybe."

An entourage of feral children was not her idea of an effective gravving team, but she wasn't inclined to argue with the girl who'd persuaded Grammar to help her.

Neverwhen tucked her gloved hand into Jasper's. "You're rescuen him."

"Doesn't make me a hero if I'm just doing it to help myself."

Grammar was now several flights below them, out of sight in the gathering dark with only the staccato echo of his footsteps to mark his passage.

"True, maybe," said Neverwhen. "But not a villain either."

"Yeah, put that on my tombstone."

Neverwhen squeezed her hand and then released it. "Anyway, I been meanen the dog."

They emerged from the Raleigh building into shadow-tinted dusk. Grammar waited at the end of the street. Neverwhen gave

Jasper a wave and skipped after him. The dog followed more slowly, distracted by smells in the roadside weeds and bushes.

Jasper watched the kids round the corner and move out of sight, still half debating whether to follow them to their hideout so she didn't lose Grammar for a third time.

Suddenly, the dog's head went up. He barked furiously and raced after the kids despite his limp. Neverwhen cried out. A man's voice carried on the evening air.

Jasper ran after the dog and careened around the corner.

And there was Dragon with one arm circling Grammar's throat, pinning the boy against him. The gun in his other hand was pressed against Grammar's skull.

Neverwhen had her slingshot loaded and aimed. Beside her the dog growled, a menacing buzz.

"Get lost, girlie," Dragon was saying. "Not caren about you, see?" He saw Jasper and pointed the gun at her instead. "Look, it's the thieven Pinegirl herself!"

Jasper raised her hands, stunned and infuriated by this turn of events. This was exactly why she hadn't wanted to let Grammar out of her sight, because the boy attracted even more trouble than she did. They both had malicious tinylings tripping along in their shadows.

"I been followen you," Dragon said to Jasper with a triumphant smirk. "I been knowen you'd lead me to him."

Jasper edged in front of Neverwhen. Pack kids could use slingshots to deadly effect, but a single slip of Dragon's finger on the trigger would be fatal to Grammar.

"Let him go, Dragon. This is Yorky. You have no right to grab one of our citizens. And how did you get a gun through the gates?"

"You're knowen very well who this ratling is, and you're stealen him from us. Not nice, Pinegirl. Boss was very upset after hearen we been losen Zenobia's little snake spawn."

She swallowed a curse. He knew who Grammar was, and so apparently did Nico. The news was out; Grammar would never be safe again.

"I don't know what you're talking about. This kid is my apprentice and has been for a year. Why don't I call Sparrow and we can sort this out."

"I'd be putten you down right now like the Azuro-loven whore you are, but I'm still haven plans for you."

"Like you had plans for Grace?" she asked, hoping to catch him off balance. "Where is she? Why didn't she come home last night? She said no to you at the church. Did you decide to find her and take what you felt you were owed?"

She'd surprised him, but only for a moment. "She's a worse cocktease than you. She'll be getten what she's deserven. You both'll be."

But there was an echo of irritation and frustration on his face. Wherever Grace was, she'd escaped his clutches.

Jasper took a step forward.

Dragon fired a shot at the dirt at her feet.

Jasper jumped back as Neverwhen screamed and dropped her slingshot. The dog snarled, his body rigid with menace. With a grin, Dragon pointed his gun at the dog. Neverwhen shrieked and threw herself between them.

In the excitement Grammar's hand slid into his jeans pocket and emerged palming a tiny blade.

Double shit with bird turd icing on top. He'd get himself and possibly all of them killed.

"Stop!" Hands up, Jasper edged forward until the gun muzzle gaped in front of her eyes. *"Bloody blue moons and dusty bone ruins; small god see you and take you, curse you, eat you and remake you; lost voice, lost bones, lost soul among the stones—"*

"What're you—?"

"Cursing you," Jasper said in her most ominous voice. "Also distracting you."

Dragon froze as Ryan loomed up behind him.

"Drop the gun or I'll blow your brains out," Ryan said softly in his ear.

Dragon dropped the gun.

Grammar tore free, turned, and kicked him viciously in the crotch. Dragon shrieked and doubled over.

Ryan tossed aside the empty beer bottle he'd been holding. Its mouth, when pressed against a person's head, was apparently indistinguishable from a gun muzzle.

"Everybody all right?" He shoved a moaning Dragon to his knees and bent to pick up the gun.

Neverwhen hugged Grammar, who still looked in the mood to stomp kneecaps and break noses. The dog nuzzled his children worriedly.

"Look, you have a gun again, soldier boy," Jasper said. "It's fate." She wanted desperately to retch into the bushes, but she'd be damned if she'd show an ounce of weakness in front of a shit receptacle like Dragon.

"Mine was better." Ryan frowned at the gun in his hand. He ejected the magazine to check how full it was, then snapped it back in.

In that moment of inattention, Dragon attacked. He tackled Ryan's legs, knocking him over. After a brief, ugly struggle, the gun came loose.

Dragon landed a punch. Ryan's head snapped back and his limbs slackened.

Dragon lunged for the gun.

Jasper threw herself onto his back. She wrapped an arm around his throat to drag him back. He jabbed a vicious elbow into her belly, and the stunning burst of pain loosened her grip.

He shoved her off and she fell on her back. Jasper scrambled for the gun and so did he. She grabbed the back of his shirt and hauled him back and they rolled in the dust.

Dragon's weight pinned her down and his hands closed over her throat. She scrabbled at his arms, but he was cutting off her airway and she couldn't breathe, couldn't fight back.

Through her blackening vision she saw a figure looming over them both, skinny and ominous and grinning, knives in both hands.

Crane crouched and held her blades delicately over Dragon's throat.

He froze. His hands loosened fractionally, enough for Jasper to drag in a desperate breath.

"How about it, Piney?" Crane said. "This time's my turn for stabben?"

22

LEAP OF FAITH

Things we lost in the Shattering:
Our homes
Our trust
Our way

~ Veronica Park (*Lists of the Apocalypse*)

"No, Crane," Jasper gasped out, winded by Dragon's weight on top of her.

"Easy, hedgehog," Ryan said. He winced as he held his side, but his eyes glittered with barely controlled annoyance. "Whatever passes for the law here can deal with this asshole." He retrieved the gun, which he fully unloaded this time before shoving it into his pocket.

Crane glared into Dragon's eyes. "Come on, Pinegirl, one little stab."

"No," Jasper and Ryan said at the same time.

Gripping Dragon's shirt with one hand, Ryan hauled him off

Jasper and gave him a shake. "Try that again, asshole—I'm begging you." He shoved Dragon to his knees this time and twisted his arm up behind him at a painful angle.

Jasper got up stiffly and dusted herself off. Her legs felt shaky and her ribs would be bruised.

Crane still had her knives in her hands and her eyes on Dragon. Without warning, she punched Dragon full in the face. He cried out, his head jerking back.

She sheathed her knives and smiled widely, unnervingly. "Little shit piece, I'm hearen you been talken badness to pretty pink cheek girl. Ever be talken to her again and I'll be killen you. See?"

He glared at her with hatred and spat blood. "I won't be forgetten this."

"Good!" Crane said cheerily. Her gaze snagged on Neverwhen and Grammar. She frowned at them, and Neverwhen shrank behind Grammar. But Crane dismissed them with a blink. "This been fun! Now I'm goen to be stealen some ice cream."

She skipped off into the dusk.

"Crane, wait," Ryan called after her. "Zenobia was looking for you."

Three people were running down the street toward them, having caught the end of the altercation. Tom Jitters carried a torch in the gathering dusk. He was closely followed by Socrates and Zenobia, who was limping as fast as she could with her cane, strands of hair straggling loose from her coiled updo.

"Crane, get back here!" Zenobia called, but Crane was already gone. "Jasper, what's going on? Who's this?"

"One of Nico's Damaskers. He knew who Grammar was and tried to kidnap him."

Zenobia stiffened as if she'd been stabbed. Slowly, she

turned to face the kids, seeing them for the first time. "You found him," she whispered.

For over a decade Jasper had watched Zenobia hoard her facial expressions like a potentially explosive hand of poker, her life as the stakes. But now Zenobia was caught off guard, her elbow bumped and her cards spilled carelessly over the table.

"Well, that answers that," Jasper muttered to herself, deeply unsettled.

"He had a gun on him," Ryan said. "I thought that wasn't allowed within the Yorky walls." He'd hauled off his belt one handed and was now efficiently trussing up Dragon's arms.

"It sure as hell isn't," Socrates said. "How'd he manage that?"

Dragon sneered and spat.

"He can explain it to the Yorky gangers," Tom said. "We passed a patrol a block past. Socrates, can you take him?"

"With pleasure." Socrates's grin flexed his facial tattoos. He hauled Dragon to his feet. "Try any shit with me, and you'll find out first-hand what I used to do to little ass-lickers like you in prison."

As Socrates pushed him, stumbling, down the street, Dragon twisted around to grin savagely at them. "You'll be getten what's comen to you, whore-bitch, you and all the Azuros. Soon." And he laughed.

Jasper felt a chill at his malicious certainty, but Zenobia barely seemed to notice Dragon's words or his departure.

"Hello, Grammar," Zenobia said a little hoarsely, her face once again under control, though with a spiderweb of hairline fractures in it.

Grammar had drawn Neverwhen several steps away from the group, his body angled in front of hers as if he expected an attack from any of them. Whatever emotions he felt at the sight of his mother, he displayed only tension and wariness. He didn't speak.

"Grammar," Tom said with a grave nod. "Neverwhen. Good to see you again." He managed a better semblance of normalcy than Zenobia, but there was an odd look in his eye as he studied the children.

Grammar gave him a single nod of acknowledgement. Neverwhen waved. "Hi, Tom."

It made sense they'd respond to him more readily. Tom would have accompanied Zenobia on all her visits to Martha's hermitage, but probably he'd gone without her too, to check on them, since Zenobia would have found the long walk too difficult to do often.

"You came back, Grammar," Ryan said. "Look at that. I told Zeep you would." In slow motion, he extended a long arm to Grammar.

Grammar stared at Ryan's proffered fist as if it were a snake. Finally, Neverwhen reached around Grammar and cautiously patted Ryan's hand as she might an overly friendly but probably harmless dog.

Zenobia had sprung a leak in her bucket of words. Jasper had never expected to feel a stirring of pity for Zenobia, and she despised the sensation intensely. Acting like she cared about a kid she'd abandoned. Like she'd had real feelings for him all along. It was nauseating. She wanted to slap Zenobia and tell her to pull herself together.

"The boy should have a protection detail," Tom said, filling the awkward gap. "If the Damaskers know who he is, soon others will as well."

Zenobia regained her faculties. She looked sharply at Ryan and then at Tom and shook her head. She drew Jasper aside. "The boy isn't safe here," she said quietly.

He never would be again, so long as people remembered his parents.

"We'll head into the zones tomorrow probably," Jasper said.

Zenobia searched her face. "To find your mother?"

Jasper shrugged.

"Time's running out," Zenobia warned, lowering her voice further so Ryan wouldn't hear. "Three months is just an estimate. I strongly advise you to get yourself to the Tower soon in preparation for taking the antibac. Take Grammar too—he'll certainly be safe there. And for the love of gravity, make sure *this one* doesn't notice you leave."

This one was busy trying to make friends with the dog. Kneeling, Ryan held out his hand, encouraging "Pupper" to give him his paw to shake. With the same sense of impending doom that any adult feels when watching small children hurtle down stairs, Jasper wanted to drag the large downie idiot to his feet. *You're going to get your damn fool throat ripped out.*

Zenobia didn't know that Ryan already knew all Jasper's secrets and would be joining the expedition into the zones. Much as Jasper would love to see the original ice queen have a true meltdown, she knew Zenobia was all too capable of finding a way to interfere, so Jasper would take a page out of her book and keep secrets.

Grammar murmured something into Neverwhen's ear, and she nodded. They took off running down the street with the dog at their heels.

Zenobia sputtered in shock. "What are they—? Come back! Stop them! Tom, go after them!"

"No!" Jasper grabbed his arm. "If you try to force them to do anything, you'll scare them off for good. They're very good at hiding. They'll be okay."

"You don't know that," Zenobia said wildly, still staring after the kids who'd disappeared into the night, out of her control, taking the secret of Catherine Pine's location with them.

Jasper had to force down her own lurch of fear. What if Grammar didn't come back?

But he'd already come back once, she reminded herself, and he'd promised to bring her to her mother. The thought of trusting Darius's son tasted like ashes in her mouth, but what choice did she have?

"They've been surviving just fine in the zones for years now," Jasper said. "Honestly, the best thing you can do for him is what you've been doing all along: ignore him and pretend he doesn't exist."

Zenobia flinched, which was satisfying in a shameful way. Tom frowned at Jasper.

Ryan dusted his hands off and asked too casually, "That isn't your kid, is it, Zenobia?"

It was unnerving watching Zenobia rebuild her facade, brick by brick, facial muscle by facial muscle. She pinned her hair back up with blue-nailed fingers that only shook slightly, then smoothed down the long-sleeved blouse she wore over black leggings. Her lips returned to their enigmatic half-moon curve. Her eyebrows flattened and her forehead unknitted. She folded both hands over the top of her cane.

"What kind of question is that?" she said at last. "Of course not. I have no living children."

"Of course not," he said. "That would be reckless."

Zenobia's face remained porcelain smooth. "Ryan, thank you for helping us search for Crane. I'm sorry to have pulled you away from your friends."

Ryan saluted mockingly.

"If either of you see Crane, tell her she's back on duty and to come see me at once," Zenobia said. "I just hope she doesn't get into the ice cream again, or she'll be in the outhouse all night."

With a curt nod, Zenobia left, leaning on the arm of her faithful shadow.

Jasper could just make out Ryan's shape in the gathering

dusk as the torchlight receded. "Grammar is Zenobia's kid, isn't he?" he said.

"If he were, a lot of people would want to kill him. So let's say no for his sake."

He didn't move for a while. "It would explain a lot."

"Would it?" She felt weary and bruised inside with a lingering nausea and desire to cry. She wished she'd let Crane stab Dragon multiple times with each of her many knives. "You have any booze on you?"

"I don't drink."

That startled her. "Then how do you cope with all this shit?"

"With great difficulty, to be honest."

She laughed. After a moment, so did he.

"You'll be the only person tomorrow morning without a hangover," she said. "That's too much power for one person."

"It's a good thing I'm so very, very trustworthy," he said dryly.

She pointed at him. "Stop making me laugh. Laughter builds trust."

"Alas, you've uncovered my evil plan."

"I knew it!"

The feeling of being on the rooftop receded, the edge that had seemed perpetually inches from her feet. In the darkness she couldn't see far in front of her, but for now she could trust it was solid ground.

He glanced in the direction Grammar and Neverwhen had gone. "I told you he'd come back."

"He said it was Neverwhen's idea."

Ryan shook his head. "No one could make that boy do anything he didn't decide to do. He came back because he decided to trust you."

"A terrible decision, really." But the thought jumbled her insides, and she could make no sense of it. "Why would he trust me? I don't even trust him, and I think he knows that."

"I know why," he said but didn't elaborate.

It made her chest feel dense and warm. "Maybe it's like me and you."

He tipped his head to the side. "What do you mean?"

"I can't trust you, downie, because you need something from me that I don't want to give you. Same as me and Grammar," she said. "But I find your anger reassuring."

"Oh? That seems a little upside down. Which, come to think of it, is very on brand for Jasper Pine, the Zombie Princess."

"You get angry about the right things. I think . . . I think Darius's reign would've ended a lot quicker if you'd been around. And that I do trust."

He opened his mouth and then closed it. He studied her with unreadable eyes.

"It's good you can still get angry." She closed her eyes, feeling familiar weariness, the kind that sank deep into your bones. After anger flickered out, only emptiness remained. And in that cold void, you became Crane or you became Vron: lost either way. "If you're still angry, it means you're still alive," she said. "Still human."

He gave a soft grunt as if the air had been forced from his lungs. "Stop that, Zeep."

"Stop what, coyote boy?"

"Making me forget my mission."

She looked at him. He looked back. Somewhere outside the walls in downieland waited a woman named Allison and an unborn son. And a foster brother willing to threaten a baby to get his hands on a graviteria sample. If Ryan abandoned his mission and left the zones, it would solve nothing. Not for him. Not for her.

"I've got it," she said. "Grav-walker's UNO. It's the perfect way to destroy trust and ruin friendships."

"Ben and Merlot were teaching me to play when Zenobia

asked me to help her find Crane." He lifted his eyebrows at her. "I'm pretty good at UNO. Are you sure you can handle it?"

She raised her eyebrows in return. "Is that a dare? Because I should warn you, I never turn down a dare."

"Somehow this doesn't shock me." His mouth curled up at the corners.

But the real dare wasn't winning a game of cards or climbing a telephone pole. The real dare was trust. The real dare was a leap into an unknown zone, knowing it could kill you or throw you onto another path entirely. It was falling with nothing but hope on the other side.

Jasper walked into the night, and Ryan fell in step beside her, his stride matching hers.

Above them the stars emerged one by one, brave sparks tiptoeing across the vast unknown.

Jasper's story continues in GRAVITY CURSE,
book 2 of the Gravity Shattered series,
available June 2021.

THANK YOU!

Thank you so much for reading GRAVITY GIRL. I hope you enjoyed your time in the gravity zones with Jasper and her friends.

You can buy the next book in the Gravity Shattered series, GRAVITY CURSE, wherever books are sold.

Please consider leaving a review of GRAVITY GIRL wherever you find reviews. Your review can help other readers find books they'll enjoy. I love to hear from you and appreciate all feedback. It helps me improve and encourages me to keep writing.

You can learn more about me and my books at www.vrfriesen.com.

For a FREE copy of the prequel novella RULES OF CRANE and exclusive bonus scenes for each book, sign up for my newsletter on my website.

Thank you for reading!

SNEAK PEEK

Don't miss Book 2 of the Gravity Shattered series: GRAVITY CURSE

A shocking revelation. An explosive coup. It's harder than ever to decide who to trust.

Left reeling by the events of Zones Day, Jasper flees into the treacherous gravity zones with the outsider, Ryan, and the feral boy, Grammar, who will lead her to a location only he knows and a secret she hopes will save her life. But now they are being hunted by a fanatical army and a leader who will stop at nothing to get his revenge.

At the heart of the zones the mysterious figure of the Guardian awaits them. She holds the key to the Tower and Jasper's untested, dangerous cure. Jasper needs her help, but the Guardian has her own plans.

Meanwhile Jasper grows closer to troubled ex-soldier Ryan Latrans, though she knows she shouldn't. Her future is too uncertain, and Ryan is fighting demons of his own. If he can't find a solution to his dilemma, Jasper will pay the price.

Old hatreds, relationships, and nightmares from Jasper's dark past are stirring up turmoil in her plans and her heart. How can she fight for hope when her past threatens to drown her?

Available June 2021!

BONUS SCENE EXCERPT

SNEAK PEEK

Get the FULL exclusive bonus scene from Crane's perspective for FREE when you sign up for my newsletter at www.vrfriesen.com.

Dogs barked and men shouted. Torches flared under the night sky.

Crane ran. Grass whipped her legs and twigs snapped against her face as she squeezed through trees and hedges. She could hear the pink cheek girl running after her, making a lot more noise than Crane as she flailed through bushes and stumbled over unseen curbs and fallen fences.

The pink cheek girl's name was Grace, but she was clumsier than her name suggested. She couldn't even balance one of Crane's knives on her knuckles. "It's because you're watching," she'd told Crane. She had three freckles under her left eye and a crooked canine tooth, and when she put a strawberry in her mouth, she sucked on it before she bit into it. Watching that made Crane feel a bit dizzy.

Rules for impressing pretty girls:

One: Smuggle them into the most dangerous town in the zones to watch an underground fight club, and then run for your life when you get caught.

Two: No, don't do that.

Three: There are no rules.

Four: Panic?

Zenobia had made rules for Crane about how to acquire milk and how to address children; how was it she'd never said a word about impressing girls? What an appalling oversight.

The Damaskers had left their town walls and spread out, searching for the intruders who had penetrated their defences. Probably they weren't following Crane and Grace. Probably they'd go after Jasper, Ryan, and the recruit they'd stolen from the Damaskers.

Probably.

FULL bonus scene is available only to newsletter subscribers.
Sign up today at www.vrfriesen.com!

ACKNOWLEDGMENTS

I want to thank Santiago Arevalo and my sister Jen who, with incredible patience, read every single draft of this series, even as the drafts got longer and longer. You gave me thoughtful, invaluable feedback and kept me from going crazy when it felt like these books would never, ever be finished. Jen, thanks for letting me brainstorm and plot out loud and otherwise ramble interminably about my story, and for the moments of clarity you provided when my brain was going in circles. This story belongs to you as much as me.

Additional thanks to Agata Broncel for a gorgeous cover and endless appreciation to editors and readers, including Caroline Kaiser, Tessa Kostelc, and Renee Harleston, for all your helpful comments, advice and insights. All remaining mistakes are entirely mine. And thank you, Becky Mueller Callahan, for being the first to suggest that a) my gigantic "book" might actually be three books and b) that I might want to look into self-publishing. My path would've looked very different without that conversation.

Thank you to all who supported me and had utter faith in my creative journey. There are too many to mention, but a shoutout to Cora-Lee and my brother Walter who read my writing over the years and gave kind and constructive feedback. Also, thank you, Walter, for providing me a steady diet of fantasy and science fiction books in my formative years.

And for Jennifer Begin, the other Jenn in my life, my bestie since forever, between us it's never been "if" we will succeed at our dreams but "when." Your unwavering presence in my life means more than I can express.

ABOUT THE AUTHOR

V.R. Friesen has been writing stories since shortly after she learned the alphabet. She grew up on the beautiful East Coast of Canada and now lives on the equally beautiful (but in a different way) West Coast, in Vancouver, BC, with one of her many siblings and a cat. She can usually be found drinking chai lattes, cheering on her favourite basketball team, or reading voraciously in science fiction, fantasy, young adult and dystopian fiction.

Find her online at www.vrfriesen.com and on social media as @vrfriesen.writer.

facebook.com/vrfriesen.writer

instagram.com/vrfriesen.writer